OKTOBER HEAT

Doris Dumrauf

This book is a work of fiction. All of the characters, dialogue, locations, and events portrayed in this novel are either products of the author's imagination or are used fictitiously.

ISBN-13: 978-1507603451
ISBN-10: 1507603452

Cover design: Alchemy Book Covers

Acknowledgments

Oktober Heat offers a glimpse into my childhood in a West German village during the Cold War. After reading *Air Base Ramstein: Bilder, Geschichten, Erinnerungen,* I was fascinated with the early years of the military build-up and its effects on German youths. The following books were also helpful in my research: *GIs and Fräuleins* by Maria Höhn and *Die Pfalz in den Fünfzigern* by Christine Kohl-Langer.

Thank you to: Michael Geib from the Docu Center Ramstein for allowing me access to their image files; former servicemen Fred O'Keefe and Charles Martsolf; and retired police officers Jürgen Moser, Josef Baus, Alfred Preßmann, and Alfred Loserth for answering my questions.

My special thanks to the Westminster critique group and Pennwriters.

And, finally, I want to thank my husband, Don, for his love and encouragement.

1

October 1958

Walter was late again. His friend had already left by the time he arrived at Fritz's house. And all because two neighbors could not decide who owned the apples from the tree that bordered their properties. It took Walter and his police partner Schlosser two hours to settle the dispute by extending the property line vertically, which put them well into overtime.

The concert was supposed to begin at eight o'clock. Walter rode his secondhand bicycle into the parking lot of the Enlisted Club, where his dynamo-powered light reflected off the chrome bumpers of the Chevrolets and Fords of the Americans. After backpedaling to brake and locking the front to the bike rack at the far end of the club, Walter bent and removed the cycle clips from his trousers. He brushed his pant legs until he was satisfied that they were not dusty anymore. Walter wanted to look his best just in case he met a girl tonight.

He whistled "All Shook Up" as he strolled toward the brightly lit entrance of the club. He walked by a group of GIs lingering under the red canopy, smoking and laughing with their friends, and opened the double door. Inside, he drew in the chatter of the boisterous crowd as if it was fresh air.

Ah, Saturday night! The long work week was over and he could finally enjoy himself like every other youth in the village. He made his way to the bar, where he paused to scan the crowd. As he had feared, he did not detect one empty chair.

The German emcee stepped to the microphone and spread his right arm to take in the stage. "*Meine Damen und Herren*! Ladies and gentlemen! Let's welcome The Trotters, fresh from America, for their first concert at Lauterbach Air Base."

Whistles pierced the smoke-filled club, causing Walter to erupt in appreciative laughter. He lifted his hands into the air and clapped until it hurt. The master of ceremonies stepped back while the maroon velvet curtain slowly revealed the band. Walter craned his neck to view the musicians. The four male singers wore matching white jackets that glittered silvery in the dimmed light, accentuating their ebony skin.

The oldest of the three bartenders, dressed in a white shirt and a thin tie, placed a cardboard coaster in front of Walter. "Good evening, Herr Hofmann," he said. "What can I bring you?"

"I'll have a Parkbräu." Walter began to sway his upper body to the tune of "She's All Yours." After the applause faded away, he gazed across the room again, searching for acquaintances. Where might his friends be? Perhaps he would have better luck waiting for them to step up to the bar instead of trying to find them in the crowd. He put his bottle on the counter and rested his shoulders against the bar. A young German woman sat on the barstool closest to him. Her curly brown hair framed an oval face with lively, amber-colored eyes. Walter cleared his throat and stood up erect. It was now or never.

He leaned toward the young woman and said, "Good evening. It's a nice crowd tonight, isn't it?"

She gave him an indifferent look and sat flatly, "Yes, it is."

Her mouth formed a wide smile as she waved at someone behind him. He glanced over his shoulder to see a GI in civilian clothes approach her.

"Hello," the American said, taking her hands in his. She rose to dance with him and Walter plunked down on the vacant barstool. He smacked his fist on the counter. Was he never going to find a girl? Just what did this lanky fellow, with his crew cut and clean-shaven face, have that he did not? Other than dollars, a car, and all the latest rock 'n' roll records, of course.

I may not be as handsome as those fellows, but I am blond and tall like all the men in my family, Walter thought. *I have a good job. I even went to dance school before entering the police academy. What else do I have to do?*

Walter sighed and took a sip of beer. Almost all the German girls in the club were in the company of a GI. He would not find a dance partner tonight. That much was certain. It would require a miracle to even talk to a female besides the waitress.

"Good evening, Walter," said a voice by his side as a heavy hand clapped his back. Walter jerked around and smiled. The hand belonged to Fritz's father.

"How's that job of yours coming along?" Herr Müller asked.

"It's going very well, thank you. I just got off from work." Walter was surprised to see a Manhattan in Herr Müller's hand. Was this the same man who years ago had denounced any other drink than wine? Apparently, not even middle-aged Germans were immune to the craze of all things American.

3

"Are you glad to be back home?" Herr Müller interrupted his thoughts. "How long did you work in Mainz? Was it two years, or was it three?"

"It's been two years. I'm happy to be home again so I can spend time with my friends. Is Fritz here yet? No one answered the doorbell at your house." Walter did not want to spend the entire evening alone, and males outnumbered females about ten to one.

"He should be here already. Haven't you seen him yet?" Herr Müller almost shouted to be heard over the din. "My wife and I just arrived ourselves, so I haven't seen Fritz either. He probably does not want me to see him," he said with a wink. "Enjoy the show, and give my regards to your mother."

He disappeared into the throng.

Walter turned his attention to the stage again and soon his feet began to bounce to the rhythm. He had heard the summer hit dozens of times on the radio, but hearing it live was a treat he would cherish for a long time.

Walter hated to attend shows alone, but at least from his viewpoint on the barstool, he could see everyone coming and going. Half the village was here, except the people he wanted to meet.

"*Hallo, Bruderherz*," sneered a voice next to him. It was his eighteen-year-old sister Ingrid, dressed in tight red pants and a short-sleeved black sweater. Somehow, the clothes matched the sassy voice perfectly.

"What are you doing here?" Walter asked with a frown. "Does *Mama* know you're here?"

"Of course not," Ingrid hissed. "Please don't tell on me." Her eyes pleaded with him now. "She thinks I'm at the village fair in Neudorf with Anneliese."

Walter gave a short laugh. "In those pants?"

Their mother was old-fashioned, but she was not that gullible.

"I changed clothes at Anneliese's house."

Walter rubbed his chin. If he sent Ingrid home, he would have to go with her and his evening would be ruined. It was time to negotiate. "What do I get for not telling?"

"You can borrow my Elvis records for a week."

Walter pursed his lips. "All right, but be careful."

Ingrid's eyes sparkled as she began to turn away.

Walter added quickly, "Have you seen Jeff tonight?"

"No, but I just got here. Is he supposed to be here?"

Walter said, "He told me the other day he was off duty tonight and was definitely coming."

Perhaps his friend and neighbor had to work late, too, Walter added to himself. As a member of the Air Police, Jeff was stationed right here at Lauterbach Air Base. They were practically colleagues.

"Take care," he admonished his sister while she waved goodbye.

Walter watched her from behind with growing concern. Their mother would have never allowed Ingrid to leave the house in those tight-fitting, if not becoming, pants. He had little doubt where she had gotten them. Ever since she had started working at the Base Exchange, she had fallen in love with American goods: chocolate, nylons, chewing gum. But how could she afford to buy the latest records? Like Walter, she had to pay boarding wages to their mother.

He decided to take a closer look at her friends. He would never forgive himself if he didn't take care of his little sister. Never mind that she was eighteen years old. She would always be his little sister.

The band took a break and people began to throng around the bar. One of the men shouting a drink order was

Walter's schoolmate, Heinz. Walter chose not to acknowledge him. They had never been close friends. And yet, Walter almost felt as if Heinz eyed him suspiciously. He looked back in Heinz's direction. The curly-haired young man had indeed moved to the other end of the counter.

Walter glanced at his watch. Nine thirty. Time for another beer. As the mob around the counter thinned out, he turned sideways to catch the bartender's attention and a hand landed on his shoulder.

"There you are," Fritz said. "What's the long face for?"

"Nothing."

"Oh." Fritz clucked his tongue. "There aren't any single girls here tonight."

Walter nodded.

"Cheer up and join us. We saved a chair for you."

Walter paid for his drink and they wended their way around tables and chairs.

The Trotters returned to the stage and played a slow, romantic tune. How wonderful it would be if Walter could hold a girl in his arms while swaying across the dance floor. He envied the servicemen who did just that. Ever since they had arrived in town five years ago, competition for girls was fierce. And Walter feared he was losing...

After the encore ended and the curtain closed one last time, Walter and Fritz followed two other friends downstairs to the restaurant. The sturdy wooden booths and tables covered with blue and white checkered tablecloths resembled a Bavarian inn. A mural of the Alps, a lake, and a white church with a tall steeple completed the illusion.

The young men sank on carved wooden chairs and ordered *Schnitzels* from the flat-footed waitress.

"Good evening," Walter greeted her. "I didn't know you're working here now."

6

The waitress shrugged. "There aren't enough choir festivals in town to keep me busy all the time. I still work the big jobs, like the village fair."

She shuffled off. Walter glanced around, looking for Ingrid, but he saw no trace of her.

Fritz interrupted his thoughts. "I don't think we'll ever find girlfriends if we always sit together."

Walter smirked. "The thought has occurred to me. But what can we do when the girls are all taken?" Not that he had much experience with girls even though he had lived in the city for two years. Only one girl had occupied his fantasies, and that was years ago. He had admired her from afar for months, but when he asked her for a dance, she had stiffened in his arms. After that, he had not had a crush on any girl.

Across from him, Dieter smiled shyly. "I'm not ready for a serious girlfriend yet."

"You're not ready yet?" Fritz asked with a chuckle. "You're twenty-three years old. How old do you have to be to go after girls?"

"Dieter is going to be an old bachelor," Walter chimed in. "His mother is too good a cook to let him go."

Dieter's face turned pink. "That's not true."

"What? Your mother is not a good cook?" Walter teased him.

"Of course she's a very good cook," Dieter defended her. "I just don't know how to talk to a girl, that's all."

Fritz said in a more sober tone, "I know what you mean. We have some serious competition since they built all the Army installations and this base."

"They have two important things we don't have," Walter said gravely. "Cars and money. Do you think we can win girls with nothing but our charm?"

Fritz shrugged. "Perhaps we need to look further away from the base. There's a girl on the evening bus who seems to be very nice. I think I'll talk to her."

Walter grunted. For the first time, he realized a girlfriend might disrupt his clique. Who would he spend his weekends with if it weren't for his friends? He did not want to spend the rest of his life sitting on a barstool. "Let's not ruin the evening with such depressing talk. I can sleep in tomorrow and I want to enjoy myself tonight. I just have one more thing to do first." He washed down the last bite of meat with a sip of beer and excused himself to go searching for Ingrid. Big brothers were never off duty. He found her at a table with two of her girlfriends and a couple of German youth.

"How will you get home tonight?" he asked her.

"Anneliese's brother will walk us home," Ingrid said. Relieved, Walter descended the stairs to rejoin his friends. He had known the young man all his life and knew he could rely on him to escort his sister home safely.

After the manager announced the closing of the club, the friends mounted their bicycles and rode home along the edge of the moor. The fir trees moaned in the night breeze, sending a shiver through Walter's tired body. While peaceful during the day, the moor was a forbidding place after dark.

When they neared the village, Walter reproached his friends to tone down their boisterous jokes. He did not want to cause any disturbance that might bring out his colleagues from the night shift.

"Aw, you're no fun anymore since you became a policeman," Dieter complained.

The comment stung, but Walter decided to joke about it. "I could arrest you for public disturbance."

Dieter and Fritz giggled so hard that Dieter almost fell off his bicycle. They caught up with a small group of revelers. Walter sighed in relief when he recognized Ingrid's voice among them. He said goodbye to his friends and swung his leg over his saddle.

"Thanks, Theo," he said to Anneliese's brother. "I can take Ingrid home now."

If his sister was disappointed, she did not show it. Perhaps she was as tired as he was. It had been a very long day.

Walter dismounted his bicycle and pushed it by his side.

"Did you have a good time?" he asked her.

"Uh-huh." Ingrid yawned. "Did you ever find Jeff?"

Walter felt a pang of guilt. He had not thought about his GI friend for hours. "No. Maybe something came up."

"It must have been very important for him to miss the concert. He's been talking about it for weeks."

Walter grunted. What could have been so important for his friend to miss the most exciting event of the fall?

2

Walter woke up to a pounding on his door. He opened one eye halfway and glanced at his alarm clock. It was almost noon.

"Walter!" his mother cried anxiously. "Get up. There is someone here to see you."

He sniffed. "Hm, pork roast."

Walter opened his door and blinked at the sunrays streaming into the hallway skylight. His ears were still ringing from the music he had heard the night before. "What is it, *Mama*?"

His mother whispered, "Herr Schlosser is downstairs. He says he needs to see you right away."

Walter slipped into his clothes and clambered down the stairs.

"*Guten Tag*, Schlosser," he said to the stocky man in uniform. "I'm off duty today, aren't I?"

"Yes, I know, and I'm sorry that I had to disturb you." Schlosser craned his neck to make sure that Frau Hofmann wasn't listening in. "The chief ordered me to drive you on base right away. You're to report to the Air Police."

Walter rubbed his eyes. They were still stinging from smoke. "Why? What happened?"

"I don't know, but it must be important to ask you out on a Sunday."

Why would they want to see me, Walter wondered. Aloud, he asked, "Who's manning the station?"

10

"Adler. They just called me to fetch you because I was home. Where else would I be so close to lunchtime?"

"Give me a few minutes to wash up."

Schlosser stepped closer to take a whiff. "Must have been a late night, eh?"

Usually Walter enjoyed his partner's sense of humor, but not when he was still half-asleep. "I guess I do look a mess," he admitted.

"How was the concert?"

"It was a blast."

Walter started down the hall as his mother peeked out the kitchen door. "Won't you be home for lunch?"

"No. I have to leave right away."

She frowned. "But my roast is about done. When will you be back?"

He suppressed a curt response. She could never understand why something was more important than her meals. "I don't know."

Walter strode to the tiny bathroom and washed his face. The cold water invigorated him enough to reach for his comb and drive it through his blond hair. He briefly wondered what Elvis looked like in the morning. Was his hair tousled and were his eyes bloodshot? Walter hoped so.

He took the stairs two at a time and donned his green uniform before rejoining Schlosser. Heads disappeared from the windows of the neighboring houses as the two policemen climbed into the green VW Beetle and drove off.

"Good morning," the gate guard said as he approached the police car with long steps. Schlosser repeated the greeting, slowly pronouncing every syllable. The guard inspected their ID cards and waved them through.

"How did I do?" Schlosser asked while shifting into a higher gear.

"You're getting better," Walter said.

"You are so lucky that you learned English in school. It's much harder to learn it as an adult."

They passed the flight line with its idle F-84s, the Enlisted Club, and the barracks before turning into the parking lot of the Air Police. Their chief's motorbike was parked in front of the entrance. Walter climbed out of the car and Schlosser drove off.

In the outer office, an Airman Klapinsky was typing a document with two fingers.

"Go right in there," he said in the relaxed manner Walter admired in Americans, but could never emulate.

Chief Police Master Kleber sat in a chair facing the shift supervisor.

Walter greeted Tech Sergeant Brown, who he had met many times over the last year.

"There you are," the sergeant said, jumping out of his creaky chair. "I need your help. Come in and close the door behind you."

His German was slow and accented. Walter closed a door that still smelled like the lumberyard from which it had just emerged. Everything on the air base was new.

"Have a seat." The sergeant pointed at an empty chair in front of his gray metal desk. Walter followed the invitation and rested his police cap on his lap. He cast a quizzical look at his chief before facing the American. He could not understand why he, the youngest policeman and the one with the least experience at his station, had been called in.

Tech Sergeant Brown stroked his hand through his buzz-cut brown hair. "One of my men has disappeared and I need your help to find him."

Walter jerked, fully awake now.

"No one has seen the non-commissioned officer in question since yesterday afternoon," Tech Sergeant Brown said. "He walked home after work, but never arrived there."

"It seems to me that it would be a matter of the Air Police to search for him," Walter said. He was still puzzled what all this had to do with him.

The sergeant made eye contact, but Walter was unable to read his expression. A sense of dread began to grip him. Chief Kleber motioned Walter to let the sergeant speak.

"We suspect that he disappeared off base, so it is a case for the Lauterbach police," Tech Sergeant Brown continued. "I requested you because you speak some English and have friends among American soldiers. In fact, you know the missing man quite well."

Walter leaned forward. "Is it... Jeff Preston?"

The sergeant nodded. Walter shaded his eyes while he digested the news. Jeff had been renting a room with his neighbors, Rudolf and Berta Klink, for over a year now. Ever since Jeff had admired Walter's prize-winning Holländer rabbits that were caged in the yard, the two young men had become friends. Jeff had taken him to shows at the Enlisted Club after noticing that Walter loved modern music.

Oh God, please don't let anything happen to Jeff, Walter thought.

Only Airman Klapinsky's clumsy typing in the main office broke the Sunday silence.

Chief Kleber cleared his voice. "Tell us everything you know."

Tech Sergeant Brown walked around his desk and rested his lanky frame against the edge. "Sergeant Preston left our office around sixteen hundred hours yesterday. He told the desk sergeant on duty that he would walk home through the moor. We have checked the part of the path that is on base, but most of it is on German territory. I suggest you start your search there. All we know is that he did not report for duty this morning and we haven't heard a word about him."

"We'll give you two airmen to help with your search," Tech Sergeant Brown said. "They will take you to the edge of the base in one of our pickup trucks. You're to report to me every hour on the hour. That's all for now." The chief rose, but Brown motioned Kleber to remain behind.

"Since you're here, I have some other business to discuss with you."

Walter stepped into the hallway and wetted his dry mouth at a water fountain. His mother and sister would be eating lunch now and he had nothing but water to cleanse his mouth of the stale taste of last night's beer. He blinked as he followed Airman Second Class Carucci and Airman First Class Goodwell into the October sunshine. His hair still smelled of the smoke that had filled the club.

Carucci got behind the wheel of a truck and turned to Walter. "My name is Pete. Where should we start the search?"

Walter squeezed himself on the bench seat next to Goodwell and closed the door. "Jeff told me that he usually walks along Moorweg until it ends, and then he follows a field track through the moor onto the base. I believe it comes out where the new housing area is."

It did not take Walter long to find the dirt road, and the three men turned their attention to the ground. Tall fir trees swayed lightly in the breeze. In the distance, a woodpecker hammered at a tree. It was a peaceful place, particularly on Sundays when the planes were not allowed to fly. Walter could imagine why Jeff liked to walk to and from work on occasion.

The three uniformed men fanned out. They were looking for trampled grass or broken branches in the groundcover, anything that would give a hint about the whereabouts of Sergeant Preston. Walter's stomach grumbled loudly, reminding him of the missed meal, when Pete made the first radio call to the office.

"I found something." Airman Goodwell waved Walter over. "It looks like a shoe."

Both men knelt down to inspect the finding. Walter put on gloves to pick up a dirt-covered blue woman's shoe. He exchanged a puzzled look with Goodwell and rose. Nearby, a fir tree lay among the ferns. Walter walked around the trunk and started. Behind the tree, unseen from the trail, he found the crumpled, lifeless figure of a young woman.

Walter knelt down and took the woman's wrist to check for a pulse. He found none. He rose slowly, shaking his head at Goodwell. The young airman sprinted toward the truck to call his sergeant.

Walter treaded around the body without touching it further. The victim lay sprawled on her side, her right cheek touching the forest floor. Her visible, bulging eye was the color of glacier ice. There were no obvious injuries to her lifeless form.

Walter wondered whether the body had been here all night while he and his friends had bicycled home from the club. But then, they had kept to the asphalt road. He shuddered at the thought that a killer could have lurked out here in the dark while the young men were passing nearby, laughing and talking.

Within minutes from each other, Tech Sergeant Brown arrived in a truck while Chief Kleber approached from the north in a Volkswagen Beetle. He carried a camera in one hand and a small suitcase in the other.

"Have you ever taken photos of a body?" the chief asked while handing Walter the camera.

Walter shook his head. "I've watched, but I've never taken any myself."

"Now is your chance."

Walter took photos of the area surrounding the body, close-ups of her face, head, hands, and feet.

"Have you ever seen her on your rounds?" asked the chief.

Walter shook his head. "At first I thought she looked familiar, but I don't think so. I've seen plenty of girls like her, mind you. The bars are full of them."

"Yes, I know," the chief let out a sigh. "Put red lipstick on them, and they all look alike."

After the American troops arrived in the early Fifties, many women of less-than-stellar reputation had flocked from all over Germany to the villages near the county seat of Kaiserslautern to cash in on the soldiers' dollars. This young woman could be one of them.

Careful not to destroy any evidence, Walter leaned down to study her features for clues. Her face, framed by obviously bleached hair in a permanent wave, almost reached her shoulders. She looked young. Her crimson lipstick could not mask the pinched corners of her mouth. They spoke of hardships and disappointments. She was dressed in a blue blouse, a tight gray skirt, and nylons.

"I think we have enough pictures for now," the chief said at last. "If I need some more, I'll take them myself. You look around for the other shoe."

Walter was glad to get some exercise. His stomach felt queasy from the missed lunch and the presence of the young woman's body. A suspicious death was bad enough, but it was worse when it affected a young life. He circled around the tree with his eyes glued to the ground. No shoe.

"What's the matter?" asked the chief as Walter approached him. "Do you need to sit down?"

"I missed my lunch," Walter said, "and I had too much music and too much beer last night."

"Youth!" Chief Kleber shook his head. "My wife made me a liverwurst sandwich. Go to the car and fetch it. And radio Schlosser to call the *Kriminalpolizei*. This is a case for the criminal investigation department, since we are on German territory."

Walter made the necessary radio call. Then he searched the police car for another roll of film. He found it in the glove compartment, together with the sandwich. He opened the wax paper bag and chewed vigorously.

"What do you think happened?" he asked his supervisor after he returned to the crime scene.

Chief Kleber contorted his mouth to the right. "It's too early to tell. There are no obvious injuries, so we'll have to turn the body over once the Kripo gets here. My guess is it's either a head or spinal injury. There would be blood if it were a knife wound. Go on and continue your search."

He looked up and eyed Walter. "Are you all right? You look green."

"Excuse me," Walter said through clenched lips. He turned away from the officers and retched into the grass. He was grateful that the chief did not laugh at his inexperience. How could he have expected to eat without getting sick after finding a dead body? Of course, he had seen deaths during his wartime childhood and his duty in the capital city. By now, he had assumed that he was used to the sight. But seeing the corpse of a woman not much older than himself

17

in his usually quiet village was another matter. Yes, it was an entirely different matter.

Walter stepped to a nearby tree and leaned against it until he recovered. Then he grabbed the camera and stalked around the fallen tree. He took some photos of the tree's blackened crown, which had shattered when touching the ground. Apparently, a recent thunderstorm had felled it. After changing the film, Walter pulled a notebook from his pocket and stepped closer to the trunk. Two branches had broken off close to the trunk. The wounds were still fresh. He could not find the branches and concluded that someone might have collected them for firewood. Nonetheless, he jotted down his observations in the book.

More disconcerting was the fact that he could not find a purse. What kind of a young woman would go out without a handbag? His mother and sister never did. Every German national had to carry an identity card at all times. Without a purse, it would be more difficult to identify the body. He went to report his lack of findings. Chief Kleber handed him a form on a clipboard and dictated his observations to him.

When he had finished writing, Walter took a deep breath. "Chief, can I ask you something?"

"Sure, go ahead."

"Do you think..." Walter could barely utter the unthinkable words. "Do you think it's a coincidence that Jeff disappears into thin air and then we find a dead woman in the same area?"

Chief Kleber raised a bushy eyebrow. "You're the one who knows him. Do you think he's capable of killing someone?"

"No," Walter said without a second's hesitation. "But then, one never really knows what goes on in other people's minds."

18

"That's true, son."

Walter's chest swelled with pride. His chief and mentor had called him son. He was glad to have such a great supervisor and instructor.

It was evening by the time Chief Kleber dropped Walter off at home. The Kripo was now in charge of the investigation. They had requested that the Lauterbach police assist them in their work. After all, they were more familiar with the village and its residents than the city-based Kripo.

Before entering the house, Walter walked to the courtyard to visit his rabbit cages. His mother, who must have seen him from a window, joined him.

"I fed them for you," she said, her tone half-reproaching.

"*Danke*. I'm sorry you have to do this so often now, but it's important for me to keep the rabbits."

Her voice softened. "I know. You're trying to keep up your grandpa's hobby. He was very proud of them, I give him that. Almost as proud as he was of you."

Walter opened a cage and petted Max, a Dutch buck. His *Opa* had meant the world to him. When *Opa* died last year, Walter vowed that he would continue keeping *Opa's* rabbits to honor his memory.

"Why did you have to go out on your day off? Are you allowed to talk about it?" asked his mother.

Walter debated whether he should tell her anything or not. He had reached for a rabbit when she interrupted him.

"Don't pick him up now," she chided. "You'll get fur all over your uniform."

Walter acquiesced. She was right, as usual, even if she made him feel like a little boy again. After having lived away for several years, he wished she treated him like an adult. How else was he ever to gain respect in this town?

"It seems that Jeff has disappeared," he said at last. "I went out looking for him with two air policemen, but instead, we found a dead woman. I'll probably be involved in the investigation until we solve the case."

His mother raised her hand to her chin and breathed in noisily. "A dead woman? Do you know who she was?"

Walter closed the cage. "No, I couldn't find her purse. But she's not from Lauterbach, I know that much. Do you have any leftovers from lunch?"

"Yes, of course. You must be starved."

They entered the house. Walter climbed the steps to his room and changed into civilian clothes. He was lucky to have his own chamber. Many of his friends had to share a room with other relatives. But after his grandfather died last year, his mother moved into his quarters on the first floor, leaving her bedroom to Walter. He almost smacked his head on the attic's slanted ceiling, and the bed was a hand-me-down, but space was hard to come by. Many people in Lauterbach rented to Americans but so far, his mother had resisted. She would rather make ends meet on her war widow's pension and the occasional egg sales. After all, it was inappropriate for brother and sister to share a room.

He thought of Ingrid as she had appeared at the club the night before. She was growing up, for sure, but she spent entirely too much time on base. He decided to keep a closer eye on her and her friends when he had time. Time! He would not have much time in the near future until this death was solved.

"Has Ingrid been home today?" Walter asked when he entered the kitchen.

His mother turned away from the shining electric stove, her biggest source of pride. She had scrimped and saved until she could buy it last year.

"Yes, she was home earlier, but she went out again to help string the beads on the *Kerwestrauß*." She stepped to the hutch and opened one of the glass doors. "I'll be glad when the village fair is over. I hardly see her anymore and she doesn't tell me nearly often enough where she's going. Does she tell you much?"

"No," Walter said as he sat down on one of the wooden kitchen chairs. She put a plate of pork roast and potato dumplings in front of him.

"That smells very good, *Mama*. You know, I like leftovers more than freshly cooked food. I guess I got used to it after eating the cafeteria food at the police academy."

She fetched a rag to clean up a spill on the stove. "I don't know why I'm cooking for a crowd. You and Ingrid are going your own ways now and I have to keep your food warm."

Walter dunked a piece of dumpling in gravy. "Work is work. It doesn't happen too often that we find a body, thank God."

"That poor woman," lamented his mother while filling his plate again. "Do you think she was murdered?" Her eyes almost bulged out of their sockets.

"We can't rule out anything at this point. But I don't want to talk about it while I'm eating."

"Yes, of course." She pulled at a chair across from him and sat down. "How was the concert?"

Walter swallowed. "Wonderful," he said, his eyes glowing. "I saw quite a few people from Lauterbach in the audience. By the way, Herr Müller sends his greetings."

"Was he there? I thought he was so opposed to the Americans being here."

"He even had one of those new American drinks in his hand. Apparently, he realizes that he has to go with the times. There's nothing he can do about it anyway. Might as well enjoy life."

Walter put his knife and fork on his empty plate and drank a big gulp of mineral water. "You ought to go to the next concert. I can get you a ticket."

His mother smiled shyly and shook her head. "I couldn't go to such a rowdy place. It wouldn't be right."

Walter shrugged. Watching *Der Blaue Bock* was the only time she set foot in a *Gasthaus*. Even after thirteen years of widowhood, his mother worried about people's opinions. He had tried to tell her numerous times that not all the acts at the club were American bands. Quite a few German entertainers made a living touring the bases. Perhaps he could surprise his mother with a ticket when one of her favorite German singers was in town. She would be too frugal to reject a gift.

He rose from the table and put his plate into the enamel sink. It was time to listen to the hit parade on AFN. He turned on the radio and sank on the chaise longue. His mother disliked rock 'n' roll, but he couldn't get enough of it. Sure, some German singers imitated the music, but it was not the same as hearing the originals, even if he could not understand the lyrics.

Frau Hofmann took off her apron and declared that she had to see the neighbor about some eggs she had for sale. Walter hoped she wouldn't gossip about the dead woman. He had been careful not to reveal too much to her. Not that he knew much to begin with. None of the officers had seen the woman before. It was up to the coroner and the fingerprints to find out her identity and cause of death.

3

Walter stepped into the courtyard, a small basket of hay hanging on his arm. After leaving the task to his mother for two days in a row, it was time for him to feed his rabbits. He opened the cage of his favorite buck, Max. A noise behind him caused him to turn around. *Opa* Klink peeked through the picket fence that separated their property from *Mama* Hofmann's. As always, his thin gray hair was parted straight as a ruler and his narrow mustache was impeccably trimmed.

"*Guten Morgen*, Walter," he said. "I'd like to talk to you when you're done."

Walter said, "I only have a few minutes time before I have to go to work."

He began to stuff hay into a trough. After refilling the drip water bottle, he grabbed Max and carried him in his arms over to the fence.

"My, what a good-looking rabbit," Herr Klink exclaimed. "Are you going to enter him in the show this year?"

"Of course." Walter petted the fur of his black-and-white rabbit. "Did you want something?"

"Have you heard anything about Jeff? We haven't seen or heard from him since Saturday morning. It's not like him."

"No, I haven't heard a thing, and I'm worried, too. He didn't tell you he was going somewhere?"

Opa shook his head.

"You know how the military is. They send the soldiers on a mission without any notice. I'm sure he's all right," Walter said with more assurance than he felt. If Jeff had been sent on temporary duty, his supervisor would have known about it. Something was amiss here.

"I hear you found a dead woman yesterday," *Opa* said, leaning closer.

Walter sighed. The Kripo must have decided to inform the press. After all, the public could perhaps help in solving the mysterious death. More than likely, though, the local gossip machine was grinding into overtime. It was probably his own mother who had told the news to the neighborhood.

When Walter arrived at the small police station the next morning, Adler and Immler from the night shift had already taken their seats for their morning briefing. Schlosser followed right behind Walter. The meeting revealed that the night shift had been relatively quiet, except for two fights at different bars. Not bad for a Sunday night.

Chief Kleber dismissed the night shift and turned to Walter. "I took the films to *Christmann's Foto Atelier* last night. We should have the prints by noontime. Will you pick them up?"

"Yes. Any news about the woman yet?"

"No. Maybe you ought to go to the township office and write down the names of anybody who rents rooms to women?"

That's going to be a long list, Walter thought.

"What if she didn't live in Lauterbach?" Schlosser asked.

Chief Kleber raked his fingers through his receding hair. "You're right. She could have lived in any of the surrounding villages. But how did she get all the way out there? On foot?" His eyes challenged Walter to reply.

"Perhaps she took the bus to Lauterbach and walked from there," Walter said. He didn't believe this possibility himself, but feared losing valuable time by searching through endless township records.

Kleber tapped his pencil on his desk. "Perhaps it would be best if you two made the rounds of the village inns and found out who's talking. Somebody might have seen her. Nobody has reported a missing person yet, but that doesn't mean much. These women probably come and go as they please."

Walter knew exactly what Chief Kleber meant with "these women." It was a paraphrase for the women who lived with GIs without being married, something that had been unthinkable a few years ago. But the arrival of hundreds of construction workers, followed by thousands of troops, had changed everything.

"The bars won't open until evening. And I doubt that she frequented places like *Die Traube* or *Zur Post*." Chief Kleber tilted his head. "Still, I'd like you and Walter to check them out once we get the prints. People are bound to talk. Don't tell them more than they need to know. Just ask if they've ever seen the woman and if they know where she lived."

Walter sat at an empty desk and dialed Tech Sergeant Brown's number on base. The sergeant informed him that he still did not have any news about Jeff. Walter bit his lip. He still found it odd that Jeff's disappearance and the young woman's death occurred so close to each other. Tech Sergeant Brown had not mentioned any suspicions, but then, the military could be tight-lipped. If Walter harbored such thoughts, then surely it would occur to the Air Police, too.

And yet, the idea that Jeff could have committed a murder seemed entirely out of character. Walter had only known the American for about a year, but thought him to be an honest, easy-going fellow. He was embarrassed to even consider such a remote possibility.

After eating the sandwich his mother had packed for him, Walter walked two blocks from the police station to *Christmann's Foto Atelier*. He stopped to look at the shop window with its first school day and confirmation photos. Inside, he wrinkled his nose as the faint smell of photo chemicals greeted him. He studied displays of postcards, picture frames, and an odd assortment of shopping bags and purses until Herr Christmann stepped out of his studio.

"Ah, Walter, you must be here to pick up the films from last night," the photographer said somberly

He searched through a bin under his glass showcase and dropped two envelopes on the counter.

"Nice camera," he said, following Walter's gaze, which was fixated on an Agfa Silette. "Would you like to look at it?"

"How much is it?"

Christmann checked the price tag. "Sixty-nine Marks and fifty Pfennig."

Walter whistled. "No, I'd rather not. I'm saving money for a scooter. But it's a very nice camera."

Back at the station, Kleber, Schlosser, and Walter studied the photos, deciding on the least disturbing image to show around at the inns.

The landlord at the *Post* claimed that he had never seen the young woman before, but called his wife for reassurance because she manned the small post office in the same house. The postmistress, short and stocky like her husband, placed her reading glasses on the saddle of her nose. She held the image close to her eyes and then far away. At last, she shook her head. "No, I've never seen her before."

When they stepped out of the *Gasthaus,* Walter breathed a sigh of relief. "I thought we would never get out of there."

Schlosser shrugged. "Don't be so impatient. You never know what people will remember."

"I guess you're right," Walter said. "Is this your first homicide case since you came to Lauterbach?"

Schlosser paused for a few seconds. "I believe so. Of course, we've had to investigate several deaths since I moved here. Last year, for example, we found a body by the train tracks, but it turned out to be a suicide."

The *Traube* was located just a stone's throw away from the *Post.* The owner was also one of the two butchers in town and sported a well-fed belly. He studied the picture of the platinum blonde with furrowed brows.

"No," he said finally, "I've never seen her before." He lowered his voice. "Try the *Adria* or the *Mallorca.*"

Walter understood the subtle message: Women who end up dead don't patronize the *Traube.* They frequent bars.

Undeterred by the negative reply, Schlosser and Walter scrutinized the nearly empty lounge. Two men dressed in corduroy jeans and caps sat at one table, downing a bratwurst on bread while discussing Sunday's soccer games. At one of the windows sat Herr Kunze, the third- and fourth grade teacher of the village school. It was unlikely that he knew anything about the woman, but Walter decided to talk to him anyway. The teacher looked up from his *Schnitzel* and *Pommes frites* when Walter and Schlosser stepped up to him. Walter explained the reason for their inquiry and Kunze put his knife and fork down to inspect the photo.

"Is she dead?" he asked matter-of-factly.

Schlosser nodded. "Have any of the children in your class mentioned anything unusual happening at home? A new tenant maybe, or someone missing?"

"Not that I know of, but I'm not prone to listening to gossip. Let me think." He leaned back in his chair. "The Kleins, Lorsches, and Neumanns are renting rooms. Perhaps you could try your luck there."

The officers thanked him and left. It had gone as well as they could have expected. All other *Gasthäuser* were closed on Mondays, and they headed back to the station. No one had reported a missing person.

The *Mallorca* bar was quiet since it was not payday. In a corner, a gleaming Wurlitzer jukebox sobbed a blues tune. Several couples danced cheek to cheek on the glass tile dance floor. The male dancers, like the other soldiers in the room, were black and very young. Their German partners were dressed in flowered petticoats and ballerina shoes. A crystal sphere turned slowly on the ceiling, its lights twirling over the walls and the dancers' bodies.

As he entered the room with his partner, Walter wondered what induced these young people to play such mournful tunes. He himself had never cared for sentimental music, preferring instead the rousing rock 'n' roll songs of Jerry Lee Lewis or Chuck Berry. Elvis Presley wasn't bad; if only all the girls didn't go wild about him. How could a German man with average looks compete with a man as good looking as Elvis?

The landlord was standing behind the counter, his chin resting in his left hand. He looked young, in his late twenties perhaps, and gazed at the guests with bored interest. Schlosser motioned Walter to approach him.

"Everything quiet today?" Schlosser asked.

"Yes." The landlord's tone betrayed his suspicion. "What can I do for you?"

Walter showed him the photo of the dead woman. "Have you seen her in here?"

The landlord held the photo up to a lamp to study it. "Yes," he said finally, "she's been here."

Walter caught a glimpse of hope. "When did you see her last?"

"Could be several weeks ago."

"Was she alone?"

"No, never seen her alone. She always comes with a soldier."

"Did she have a steady boyfriend?" Schlosser cut in. "Was he Army or Air Force?"

"Most boys in here are Air Force."

That was all the information they could extract from the landlord. Walter and Schlosser made their nightly rounds to check the ID cards of the German women. Only this time, they also passed around a photo. It was pointless to show the image to soldiers who were accompanied by a female. The women, however, might prove useful since they would have considered every other woman as competition.

At the fourth table they approached, the policemen finally received a clue.

"I've seen her," a brunette with scarlet nails said.

"Where?" Schlosser asked. "In here?"

"No." She bit her lips. "Now I know. It was at my hairdresser."

"Here in Lauterbach?"

"No. Friseur Mattes in Reichenbach."

Walter began to jot down notes in a small spiral-bound notebook. "Are you sure it was her?"

"Yes. I remember how much I envied her hair. I thought she looked a bit like Marilyn Monroe." Her faint smile dissipated. "Guess I don't need to be jealous anymore."

"Is there anything else you remember, other than being jealous?" Schlosser asked in a clipped voice. "What did she say? Was she living with someone? A boyfriend, perhaps?"

"She mentioned that she had an American boyfriend. I'm sorry, that's all I can remember. Must have been about a month ago, at least."

The policemen thanked her and moved on. Outside, Schlosser said to Walter, "Women can be very useful to a policeman since they talk more than men. Sometimes they get off target, though, and we need to get them back on track."

Is he talking about his wife or the brunette, Walter wondered.

"Well, we've learned something tonight," Schlosser continued. "Seems like we were right to assume that the dead woman lived with a soldier. And she probably didn't live in Lauterbach since women like to use a hairdresser in their hometown."

4

Chief Kleber was pacing back and forth in his office when Walter and Schlosser entered the station. Schlosser told him about their findings from the night before.

"This isn't good. No, not good at all," Chief Kleber mumbled, scratching his high forehead.

"Why, what's the matter?" Schlosser asked.

"I just received a phone call from Mainz. The Secretary of Defense has decided to make a brief visit to the base in two weeks. And now we have a dead woman on our hands. If she was killed by an American, it could have an impact on German-American relations."

Walter looked up. He had never considered the severe consequences if the killer turned out to be an American. It was true there had been more drunken brawls and occasional fistfights since the arrival of the troops. Capital crimes, however, were rare.

Schlosser asked, "Any news about the autopsy?"

"Yes, I almost forgot," Chief Kleber replied. "The cause of death was blunt force trauma to the neck. In other words, someone or something broke the poor woman's neck."

Walter asked, "Was she killed where I found her?"

"We don't know."

"When did she die?"

"Somewhere between four o'clock and seven o'clock in the afternoon on Saturday."

Just about the time when Jeff left work, Walter thought.

Kleber sat at his desk and picked up the receiver. "Walter, I'll have to send you on base. We need to coordinate the secretary's visit with the armed forces. Tell them I want to meet with them as soon as possible. And while you're there, try to find out if they made any arrests over the weekend."

Putting his green cap on his head, Walter stepped out of the building. Although Chief Kleber had attended an English class just like all the other officers, he still felt uncomfortable dealing with the Air Police. Perhaps they made him feel inferior. Walter had no such scruples. He couldn't wait until he was able to understand song lyrics. Most of all, though, he wanted to understand what the soldiers were talking about when they walked down the streets of the village or lingered around the club.

He put the police Beetle in reverse and drove off. On Reichenbacher Straße, he had to shift into second gear because a horse-drawn wagon loaded with sacks of apples blocked him. Horse-drawn wagons and Nike missiles. No wonder people got confused.

Outside the village, Walter pulled over. Housing buildings, three or four stories high and completely identical, loomed large over the drained moor. The sound of a steamroller carried all the way to the police vehicle. It seemed as if every week, a new building sprung up on the large base. Where once, marsh warblers had raised their young, jet engines roared over the hastily built runway. Older people mourned the loss of farmland and the decline in morality, but for Walter, it was very exciting to have the base here.

His thoughts returned to March of 1945, when American soldiers had made their first foray into his hometown. The world had turned upside down twice after that.

The town mayor had ordered the villagers—mostly women and men too old to fight—to erect a tank trap at the western edge of Lauterbach. Walter's mother and grandfather were getting ready to obey the call.

"I'll come with you," Walter had said, more out of curiosity than a real ability to help. He was just eight years old.

"No," his mother said, "you stay here with your sister. And don't leave the house, no matter what happens."

Even then, he had been Ingrid's protector. Peeking through a curtain, Walter had watched the street while Ingrid played listlessly with a doll. Later, after his mother and grandfather returned, a German soldier knocked on their door. His mother answered, trembling to the core. The soldier asked for a piece of bread and some water before rushing off.

"Poor man," she said when he was gone. "I hope he'll make it across the Rhine River."

She walked to the back door. "I can't stand it anymore. I'm going over to Berta's to find out what's happening."

She was shaking her head when she returned. "No one knows anything, but *Opa* Klink went to the woods to collect firewood. He saw German soldiers fleeing left and right, leaving their gear and equipment by the side of the road. I fear the Americans are very near now. Oh God, what's going to happen tomorrow? Will we still be alive tomorrow night?"

She dropped on a chair, wiping tears from her cheeks with her apron. Walter placed his hand on her shoulder.

"I'm so glad you're too young to be drafted," his mother said between sobs. "It's hard enough not knowing whether your father is still alive or not. I could not bear losing you, too."

The next morning, Berta rushed in without knocking. "They're tearing down the tank trap because they're afraid we'll get shelled if they don't. We're staying in our basement until it's all over."

"Can we join you?" Elfriede asked. "I need some company right now."

"Of course."

Walter had resisted at first. He wanted to see what was happening, but his mother had been adamant about staying home. His grandfather, however, insisted on walking to the main road.

"Rodmann hung himself last night," he announced when he returned. No one was shocked at the news. Butcher Rodmann had been a member of the Nazi party from the beginning.

Walter had brought a book with him, but could not concentrate on it. He paced through the basement like a chicken in a cage. "I wonder what's going on out there," he said every few minutes.

"Stop pacing. You're making me nervous," his mother admonished him.

"But *Mama*, I'm bored."

"Come here." His *Opa* gave him a fresh tree branch and a knife to carve a whistle.

They spent the night fully dressed. Walter slept fitfully and woke up often. In the early morning, Elfriede Hofmann insisted on going back to their house to eat breakfast. They were walking between the two houses when they stopped in their tracks. The roar of tank chains and engines approached from the west, the direction of General Patton's army. Windows opened everywhere and the message floated from house to house, "They're here!"

Opa Klink joined the Hofmanns on the sidewalk and said to Walter, "Come on, boy. Let's go to the main road."

"Do you think that's wise?" Elfriede objected.

He shrugged. "What can they do to two old men and a boy?"

Walter's eyes pleaded with his mother until she finally relented. "All right, we'll all go."

She took Ingrid's hand in hers, trailing behind the men and Walter. The whole village had turned out to observe the arrival of the invading army. Walter joined several of his schoolmates huddling together in front of the *Gasthaus Zur Post*. One of the youth pointed at the street sign of Adolf Hitler Straße. Someone had thrown cow dung on the name. The boys speculated what the American soldiers looked like.

Walter's jaw dropped as the tanks rolled into the village. The first tank came to a halt in front of the *Gasthaus* and Walter jerked back. The soldier on top of the tank was as black as a piece of coal. He was the first Negro Walter had ever seen. Now the soldier bent down and said something into the turret. From the depths of the tank, someone handed something to the Negro. He laughed, revealing his white teeth as he threw something at the children. Walter and his friends bent down and picked up the goods. He grinned as he held two pieces of chocolate in his hand. Later, he would give one to Ingrid.

Perhaps the occupation would not be so terrible after all. He smiled shyly at the soldier, who grinned from ear to ear. Then the tank started up again and disappeared down the street.

Several officers and their entourage set up quarters in the city hall, and the rest of the army left in the direction of Reichenbach. Walter could not help feeling disappointed as the Hofmanns and Klinks returned home. He didn't know what he had expected to happen and yet, after months and weeks of anxious anticipation, it had been a quiet invasion. Later, he would chide himself as news from other Palatine towns and cities trickled in. The retreating German soldiers had taken the brunt of the attacks, being shot down like trapped animals in the narrow valleys near Neustadt. Escape was impossible there.

In the afternoon, Berta rushed into the house without knocking. "They're plundering the magazine near the railroad station. Let's go and see what we can find!"

Elfriede Hofmann gathered the children. Pulling a handcart, she led them to the magazine that the German army had deserted. The whole village had turned out to plunder. After all, the army did not need anything anymore. Elfriede tussled with a couple of women over a bale of cloth. In the meantime, Walter picked up a metal can without a label. His mother put it into the wagon without fuss. If the contents were of no use to them, they could always use it for barter.

And in 1953, the American troops had returned. This time, it looked as if they were here to stay.

At the Air Police building, Walter went over the tentative schedule of the secretary's visit with Tech Sergeant Brown.

"Have you heard from Jeff yet?" he asked at the end.

"No," Tech Sergeant Brown replied, tapping a pencil on his desk. "We searched his room yesterday with no results. He has just vanished. We have to ask for the assistance of the German police in locating him."

Walter nodded. Just one more thing to give his chief a stomach ulcer.

"I wonder if his disappearance and the dead woman are connected," he said, scratching his head.

"Right now, we have to leave all our options open and cannot exclude anything," Tech Sergeant Brown replied.

Walter asked hesitantly, "Is it possible that there could be a woman behind all this?"

"Come to think of it, he has mentioned that he met a girl," Tech Sergeant Brown acknowledged.

"Is she German?"

"Aren't they all?" the sergeant said with a chuckle.

Walter did not join in the laughter. "Has he mentioned her hair color or name?"

The sergeant shook his head so vigorously that a strand of his brown hair fell on his forehead. He quickly adjusted his hair. "No."

As he pulled out of the parking lot, Walter digested the information he had just gathered. So, Jeff had a German girlfriend. Funny he had not mentioned her to Walter, but then, Walter did not see him that often. Their work schedules were too often at odds. They were lucky if they could make the monthly ninepin meetings between the Air Police and the German police at the *Post*.

Instead of going straight back to the police station, Walter decided to stop at the place where he had found the dead woman. He stepped out of the car and approached the fallen tree. Once again, he was surprised how peaceful the place was. And yet, a young woman had lost her life here among the firs just the other day.

Walter had heard rumors that unmarried couples used the area right outside the base for their trysts during the warmer months. Perhaps she had waited for her lover here, only to get hit by his ... what? His military baton or revolver? According to the medical examiner, she had not been pregnant, so that could be ruled out as a cause for murder. Unless, of course, the girl had lied about being pregnant to force her boyfriend to marry her. However, her lie would have surfaced before the soldier received a wedding permit. It was also possible that she had more than one boyfriend. After all, the soldiers rotated so often that a woman had to keep her options open before she got too old.

Walter picked up a thin branch and began circling around the finding spot. It still irked him that the officers had not been able to find her shoe nor her purse, if she had one. With the branch, he shoved apart the ferns and grasses that covered most of the ground in the area. The coroner had decided that the dead woman had been killed where she was found.

He gripped the branch tighter. Was it a coincidence that Jeff disappeared on the same day a young woman met a violent death? Did Jeff have anything to do with the death? He shook his head. Jeff had always been friendly to his landlords and to Walter's family. It was unthinkable that he was a cold-blooded killer.

Friseur Mattes's hair salon was located on the ground floor of the house he lived in. Just a block away from grade school, Mattes held an assortment of school notebooks, pencils, fountain pens, and rulers together with men's pomade, hair spray, and facial creams for women. The barber was past retirement age. With just a ring of gray hair framing his shiny bald head, he did not appear to need his own service anymore. Walter and Schlosser had to wait a few minutes while Mattes cut an old man's sparse gray hair.

Walter cringed. It would probably be all over town in less than half a day why he was interviewing the barber.

"What can I do for you?" the barber asked, looking at Schlosser.

Walter felt a twinge of jealousy that everyone assumed his partner was the senior officer. Never mind that they were right. Some day, though, he would be the one people looked up to.

"Can we talk in private?" Schlosser asked, glancing at the customer.

"I'm about finished here," Mattes replied and removed the wrap from his client's body. The old man paid for his haircut and closed the door behind him.

Walter showed Mattes the photo. "Have you seen this woman in your salon?"

"Hm, I can't say that I have, but I only work on certain days nowadays. After all, I'm getting on in age. But my daughter would probably know. She just went upstairs." He stepped into the hallway. "Lieselotte! Come downstairs, please."

The barber's daughter took a good look at the photo. "Yes, I've given her a perm."

"Do you remember when?"

"Must have been about a month ago."

Good, Walter thought. *This corresponds with the information from the brunette at the bar.*

Schlosser asked, "Was that the first time you've seen her?"

"No, I've done her hair once or twice before."

"Did she ever mention where she lived, or with whom?"

"She kept going on and on about her American boyfriend. Said he had a big car and that he bought

39

chocolate and nylons for her. The women who waited were green with envy," Lieselotte said.

"Did she ever mention her name or where she lived?"

The beautician stretched her back. "Not that I remember. I only know that she lived in the house of a widowed mother on Grubenstraße. Papa, how many widows live in that street?"

Mattes's mind still appeared sharp. "There's Frau Schmitt, Frau Drucker, and Oma Becker. Lots of widows around here. If the war didn't kill the men, the coal mines did."

Walter busied himself writing down names. He didn't want to be reminded of his own father's death in a Siberian prison camp.

They thanked the barber and his daughter. Schlosser was already on the outside steps when Walter remembered something. "I'll meet you at the car."

Schlosser lifted a bushy eyebrow. "Getting a gift for your sweetheart, heh?"

Walter rolled his eyes and stepped to the counter. "I'd like to buy some pomade, please."

Herr Mattes smiled knowingly and picked up a tin from a shelf on the wall. "I've never sold as much pomade as in the last year," he said while Walter counted out the money. He knew why everybody bought pomade: They all wanted to emulate the rock 'n' roll singers' hairstyles.

Walter put the tin in his uniform pocket and strode to the Beetle. He sat in the driver's seat because Schlosser often let him drive.

"I've radioed the chief," Schlosser said. "We need to go back on base right away."

"What's going on? We were going to interview these widows, weren't we?"

"They'll have to wait. Something has happened on base. The chief didn't tell me what it is."

Walter turned on the siren and swerved the car around. His friends envied him for driving a car without adhering to the speed limit, but the experience was somewhat diminished by the limited horsepower of a Beetle.

Tech Sergeant Brown ushered Walter and Schlosser to one of the cells in the back of the Air Police building. Walter's jaw dropped as he recognized the man sitting on the Spartan cot. Jeff rose slowly and approached the bars. Large dark rings under Jeff's eyes betrayed a lack of sleep. A white bandage was neatly wrapped around his tussled and unwashed dark hair. Wherever he had been, it had not been a pleasure trip.

"Walter, I need your help," Jeff said, his voice pleading. "They say I killed a girl. What are they talking about?"

Walter cast a questioning look at his partner. "Isn't this a case for the OSI? Have you seen a lawyer yet?"

"The OSI was here this morning," Jeff admitted. "They weren't very helpful, though, and said it could take a while to coordinate the investigation with German authorities." He shook his head and winced in pain. "Walter, I can't wait that long and thought you might be able to help me."

Puzzled over his role in all this, Walter filled Jeff in on the few details he knew. "Where have you been all this time?"

"That's just the thing: I was kidnapped, and no one here believes me. They think I made up this whole story to escape murder charges." His words came out in a torrent.

Schlosser stepped closer to the bars. "May I say something?"

Walter was relieved that his experienced partner took over the interview.

"Please calm down," Schlosser said, "and tell us step by step what happened."

"I was walking home from work on Saturday since it was a beautiful day. Between the village and the housing area, I saw a young man who behaved very suspiciously. He carried a huge backpack on his back and kept looking over his shoulder. It seemed odd to me that he looked back in my direction, as if he had reason to be secretive. He acted as if he were afraid of being watched. I thought that was odd because he was in the middle of a moor. In the summer, I disturbed couples in that area more than once—we call it 'Lover's Lane.' But he didn't look like he was waiting for a girl. No, my policeman's instinct told me he was up to no good. I wanted to approach him and ask him what he was doing so close to the base. But he disappeared behind a tree and, before I knew it, someone hit me on the head from behind and I was knocked unconscious." Jeff gingerly touched his head.

"When I woke up, I was blindfolded and my hands were cuffed behind my back. They used my own handcuffs to do it! The room I was in was very hollow and bare. There was no furniture in it at all. I was lying on a concrete floor. Despite my pain, I would have probably tried to free myself but I realized that I wasn't alone. Someone was there to guard me at all times. Three times a day, someone gave me water and a sandwich. Today, I suddenly realized that I was alone. I soon learned why when I heard voices on the first floor. I groped around until I found my tin cup and banged it on the floor. That's how those construction workers discovered me. I think my kidnappers wanted me to be found, but that's not what the OSI says. They think that I killed that woman because I disappeared around the time she died."

Jeff dropped on the cot, which squeaked under his weight.

"But you were handcuffed and blindfolded, weren't you?"

"Yes, but they seem to think I had an accomplice who handcuffed me to make it look like a kidnapping."

"Did you see the woman before you were hit?" Schlosser asked.

Jeff shook his head and winced. "I did not see anyone except the man who hid behind the tree."

"Could you describe him?"

Jeff rubbed his chafed wrists. "I only saw him from behind. He was of average height and weight, wore a gray jacket and one of those flat caps that the old men wear around here."

Walter jotted down the description in his notebook. "How old was he?"

Jeff paused for a moment. "I'd say he was about twenty to twenty-five years old."

"So he was a German?" Americans did not wear caps like the one Jeff described.

"Yes, and the car was small, like a German car." Jeff rose and clutched the bars of his cell. "Can I speak to you alone, Walter?"

Schlosser clucked his teeth. "Well, I wanted to talk to Tech Sergeant Brown anyway."

After Schlosser closed the office door, Jeff said, "You believe me, don't you?"

Walter bit his lip. "Yes, I believe you." *I want to believe you*, he thought. "What's going to happen now?"

"They'll probably keep me here for initial questioning and then they'll transfer me to a military prison. Walter, you have to help me!"

How can I help? I'm the youngest police officer on the force, Walter thought.

"You have to find the real killer so I can get out of here." Jeff let go of the bars. "I can't believe this is happening to me."

"All right, we'll call the chief and see what he suggests. You're sure the man was German?"

"Yes."

Walter's mind raced. He could not make any promises to Jeff that he might not keep. His job was to gather facts and make arrests, not pass judgment. With more confidence than he felt, Walter assured Jeff that he would do all he could to exonerate him. If only he had more to work with than Jeff's description. It was time to study files. Perhaps the man with the backpack had been in trouble with the law before and had a record.

In the car, Schlosser radioed Chief Kleber the new development. The chief thought it best to pursue the trail of the dead woman.

Walter drove back to Reichenbach, his mind jumbled. Could he have misjudged Jeff's character so completely? He didn't think so, but then, his own co-workers had arrested him even though they knew him better than Walter did. But why would the perpetrators release Jeff unharmed while killing that woman? Or were those two crimes unrelated? Perhaps Jeff had just been at the wrong place at the wrong time.

The building of the bases had attracted many strangers to the area: construction workers from all over Germany, followed by people who hoped to find employment—legal or illegal—with the military. And what better place than the lonely moor to conduct business that was outside the law?

5

Marianne Holtz paced through the tiny kitchen, her hands clutched in fists. Even after a long day of work at the shoe store, she was too upset to sit down. Every time she approached the window, she paused to stare outside. At last, she moved a chair to the window, sank on the cushion, and twirled a strand of her permed hair over her index finger.

Her mother was standing by the coal stove; she had cooked a pot of potato soup. She filled a wooden spoon with the soup, tasted it, and nodded.

"The soup's done." She stepped away from the stove and pulled a red headscarf from her brunette hair. "Marianne, it won't do any good to stare out of the window all evening. He's not coming back. Why did you have to fall in love with one of those soldiers? Why can't you go out with a German boy like other girls?"

"Oh, *Mama*," Marianne cried, "I knew you wouldn't understand me. German boys are so boring. They walk down the street so timidly, as if they needed their mother's approval for everything. And Jeff, he's so confident, so sure of himself. He walks as if he owns the street! He makes me laugh and feel good about myself. I love him, *Mama*."

Marianne's mother wiped her hands on her blue apron. "How can you be so sure of that? You've only known him for a short time."

"Of course, two months is not a very long time, but I just know he's the right man for me. And I know he loves me too."

"So where is he? Why is he making you waiting like this?"

"I don't know." Marianne sighed. "It's not like him at all. I'm afraid something has happened to him."

"Pah," her mother countered. "He probably has another girlfriend. I wouldn't put my heart in this little affair. Come, help me set the table. Your father will be home soon."

A tear ran down Marianne's cheek. "I knew you wouldn't understand me. We're in love, and you call it a little affair. Something has happened to him, I'm sure of it."

She jumped up. In the hallway, she fetched a scarlet cardigan out of a worm-ridden wardrobe.

"Where are you going?" her mother called from the kitchen door. "It's suppertime."

"There's someone I need to see. Don't wait for me. I'll eat when I come back."

Walter parked the green Beetle on Grubenstraße. He and Schlosser exited the car to proceed on foot. Seeing a policeman come to their door was probably a frightening experience for the widows. They would have to tread carefully so they wouldn't startle anybody. Oma Becker's tiny house faced the street with its narrow side, as if it wanted to make itself even smaller. The two steps to the door encroached on the sidewalk.

Schlosser motioned to Walter to go first. Walter rang the doorbell with the facial expression he reserved for visiting friends. As expected, Oma Becker shrank back at the sight of his uniform. Walter quickly explained the purpose of their visit to relax her fears. She was indeed renting a room, but her tenant was a forty-one-year-old male refugee who worked on base.

At the second house, they learned that Frau Schmitt did not have a lodger at the moment.

A ten-year-old boy, wearing shorts and knee stockings, opened the door at the third address. He did not appear alarmed at the sight of a police officer, but instead ran his eyes up and down Walter's green uniform.

"Is that a real revolver?" he finally asked.

Walter leaned forward and suppressed a smile. "Yes. Is your mother at home?"

The tow-headed boy ran toward the kitchen and yelled for his mother. A woman stepped out of the kitchen, wiping her hands on her apron. Puzzled, Walter stared at the apron, which had the same chicken and flower pattern as his mother's. He forced himself to look at Frau Drucker's cracked, fruit-stained hands, a testimony that she was no stranger to work. Her face, while still without wrinkles, showed that she had celebrated her thirtieth birthday years ago.

She said to the boy, "Toni, go outside and play."

She stepped aside to let the officers enter the narrow hallway.

"Please come into the kitchen," she said. "The neighbors are so nosy around here."

A smirk crept across Walter's lips. Neighbors were the same everywhere.

They followed Frau Drucker into the kitchen, which seemed to be a replica of his mother's realm: a sturdy table dominated the middle of the small room while a coal stove presided over the corner, pushed aside by a gleaming electric stove. A small Bosch refrigerator stood next to a bulking kitchen cabinet.

Frau Drucker pointed at two woven chairs before sitting down. Walter pulled the photo of the dead woman from his pocket and showed it to her. A small cry escaped her thin lips. Walter and Schlosser waited.

"Yes, that's her," she murmured. The hand holding the photo trembled.

Schlosser and Walter exchanged glances. At last, they had a lead.

"What was her name?" Walter asked.

"Roswitha Gregorius." She placed the picture on the table and faced him. "Is she dead?"

"Yes."

She fished a handkerchief from the pocket of her apron dress and sobbed. "When did she die?"

"We found her body on Sunday, but she died on Saturday. Do you know how old she was?"

"Roswitha was twenty-one years old." Her voice quavered. "She was not from around here. She and her mother were refugees from Pommerania and lived in a refugee camp in Bavaria for a while. That's where her mother died of pneumonia. Roswitha came here a couple of years ago. I think she hoped to find a soldier who would marry her and take her to America with him."

"Do you know where she lived before she moved here?" Schlosser asked.

Frau Drucker shook her head.

Walter was busy taking notes. "Did she have a boyfriend?"

"Yes. The neighbors didn't approve of it, but they don't know how hard it is to survive as a widow."

Walter looked up. "I know. My mother is a war widow, in a way."

She stared at a spot on the wall behind Walter. "My husband was on a submarine for two years. When he came home from the war, I thought everything was going to be fine. But he had nightmares. After he found a job in construction, he started to drink. One day, he fell off the scaffolding and was dead on the spot."

"I'm sorry," Walter said, just to say something.

"You're probably wondering how I can afford a stove and a refrigerator. I decided to let a room so I could afford those things."

Schlosser cleared his throat. "Can you tell us more about her boyfriend or boyfriends?"

"She has had two men, boyfriends, since I've known her. Her latest boyfriend has lived here for several months now. He's a Negro. His name is Harry Green." Her eyes grew large. "Do you think he killed her?" she shrieked.

"We have to follow every lead right now," Walter said. "When was the last time you saw him?"

Frau Drucker arched her brows. "Let me think. I didn't exactly see him, but I heard him going up the stairs on Wednesday evening. Yes, it was Wednesday."

"Are you sure it was him and not some other man?" Schlosser probed.

"Yes. He always takes two steps at a time, and he whistles the same song when he comes home."

Walter nodded. Landladies were very observant and he had no reason to disbelieve her.

"Would you like to see her room?" Frau Drucker asked.

"We'll leave that to the criminal police," Schlosser said. "What color was Green's uniform?"

"It was blue, except when he wore his fatigues."

Air Force. It looked as if another visit to the base was imminent. They thanked Frau Drucker for her time. Her eyes were moist when she said goodbye. It was comforting to know that someone shed tears for a woman who had lost her homeland and family and had only wanted to better herself with an American soldier. It was too early to say whether Harry Green killed her, but Walter and Schlosser had to find out his whereabouts. They radioed their findings to the chief before returning to the base.

Tech Sergeant Brown had left for the day, but the mid-shift supervisor, Tech Sergeant Shoemaker, listened to Walter's story. Shoemaker, a six-foot-tall beanpole with a buzz cut, made some phone calls, but the military personnel office had closed for the day. He promised to call the next day as soon as he learned any news.

"Something does not quite add up," the sergeant said, steepling his fingers. "Why would Greene have a date with the girl in the moor if they were living together?"

"Do you think she went there to meet another man?" Schlosser asked.

"It's possible. I could tell you plenty of stories about goings-on around here at night and on weekends."

Schlosser chuckled. "I bet you could." He rubbed his index finger on his nose. "But perhaps they were tired of their tiny room and wanted to be outdoors."

"True. First of all, we need to find out if Green was in town when the woman was killed."

Walter picked up the spiral notebook from his lap. They had done all they could for the day. He excused himself from Schlosser for a moment. With sagging shoulders, he trudged down the hall to Jeff's cell. With a smooth chin and a straight parting of the hair, Jeff looked much better than the day before.

Walter watched Jeff intently while he related what they had learned in Reichenbach. Jeff did not appear distressed about his incarceration. Perhaps his military training had conditioned him for any type of stress. Walter told his friend that he knew the dead woman's identity now and that he was doing everything possible to find the killer.

After supper, Walter turned on the courtyard light and began feeding his rabbits. He was pushing hay down the feeding trough when a scraping noise of shoes against stone startled him. His nerves on edge over his concern for Jeff, he whirled around to face the intruder. In an instant, he relaxed.

"*Guten Abend*, Walter," Marianne said. "I'm sorry if I scared you, but I need to talk to you."

Walter exhaled slowly. He chided himself for being jumpy. Marianne was as charming as ever. She wore an azure dress with large white polka dots. Her brunette hair was full and curved upward over her ears. *How do girls do that to their hair,* he wondered. Marianne looked even more appealing than on the day she had stolen his heart.

He remembered it clearly. It was the first real dance that he had attended during the annual village fair. Marianne was a popular dancer. He had to wait over an hour to ask her for the next dance, a fox-trot. He led her over the uneven dance floor of the *Post*, his nostrils taking in the smell of her hair, a mixture of shoe leather and hair spray.

Two days later, he left town to join the police academy. From time to time, he saw her in the village and always intended to ask her out for an ice cream at the new Italian ice café, *Rialto*. But the time was never right and he had continued to admire her from afar. And now she was here,

51

in his own backyard, close enough to touch her. His heart melted away and he would have promised anything to her.

"Would you like to go inside?"

Marianne shook her head. "No, I don't want anyone to hear what I have to say. I'll just pretend that I'm looking at your rabbits."

She approached the cage. Walter found it difficult to keep his eyes off her.

"I don't know quite how to begin," Marianne stuttered. "My boyfriend has disappeared and I'm afraid something has happened to him."

Walter's legs seemed to buckle beneath him. He reached for a rabbit deep in the cage so Marianne could not see his thunderstruck face.

When he had himself under control again, he asked, "Who is he?"

"His name is Jeff Preston. He's an American soldier," she said. "I think you know him."

"Of course I know him," Walter said curtly to hide his surprise. "He lives next door to us." He bit his lip, unsure how much he should tell her. "I saw him today."

"Where?" Marianne's face looked as eager as only a young woman in love could be.

He told her the barest details of Jeff's arrest. Her face collapsed in itself. She held onto the corner of the rabbit cage for support.

"We were supposed to go to the Trotters concert on Saturday evening, but he never came by. I waited all evening, thinking that he was tied up at work. Please, Walter, you have to help him," Marianne pleaded. "I don't believe he's capable of murder."

"I don't believe it either." He picked up a rabbit and put it in Marianne's arms.

She pressed the animal against her body, stroking her trembling hand through its fur. "You have beautiful rabbits."

Walter was not in the mood to discuss rabbits with Marianne, but noticed that his pet had a calming effect on her. "Thank you. I'm taking two of them to a show in a couple of weeks. That is, if I can get the day off. We're very busy at the moment."

Her hand stopped petting the rabbit. She looked up at him with pleading eyes. "I'm sorry that I'm causing you extra work."

"I can't promise you that I'll help Jeff. I'm the youngest officer in town, and the case seems to be in the military's hands now."

Walter took the rabbit out of her hands to put it back in its cage. Touching the adored girl's warm hand sent waves of electricity through his body. He turned slightly away from her to hide his blushing face.

In a quivering voice, Marianne said, "Thank you very much anyway. Good night."

She trudged out of the courtyard like a soldier defeated in battle. When he was sure she was gone, Walter looked around for something to kick, but found nothing. Instead, he grabbed a piece of firewood and hurled it against the stone wall that separated the property from their neighbor's. The wood shattered to pieces.

He was angry with himself that he had waited too long to ask Marianne out. He had been sure to win her heart once he had a motor scooter. But he was still saving for one, and Marianne had slipped through his fingers. And why were the soldiers so popular with girls? Was it the lure of the unknown? Or was it just their money? He was disappointed that Jeff had never mentioned a girlfriend to him.

Walter himself had greatly admired the soldiers, especially when they brought the latest rock 'n' roll records from the States. Who wouldn't rather listen to the youthful, rebellious sounds of Chuck Berry or Buddy Holly instead of the stuffy German hits of the time?

But the soldiers' allure reached further. They brought the great big world into the small villages of the western Palatinate, villages that had never seen such prosperous times as the last five years. New houses sprang up everywhere. Others were renovated to accommodate bars and ice cafés. Life was certainly more thrilling than it had been before the Cold War began.

Suddenly, Walter could not bear spending the rest of the evening at home. He felt like playing a game of cards or shooting a game of billiard.

"I'm going out," Walter said as he entered the kitchen.

"I never see you anymore," his mother complained, as he expected her to do. "Have you talked to Ingrid lately?"

"I hardly see her nowadays. I can't talk to her when she and I are getting ready to go to work. You understand that, don't you?"

He didn't wait for her answer and stepped into the tiny bathroom that consisted of a toilet and sink. He applied some pomade to his hair. Then he pulled a strand downward as he had seen on Elvis Presley photos. His friend Fritz was very good at imitating the singer's hairstyle, but Walter failed miserably at it. Instead of gracing his forehead, the strand halted in midair. He moistened his fingers to bring it in line with the rest of his hair. He would never find a date if he looked like an old man. But it was no use. His hair would not cooperate.

Minutes later, he strolled down Hauptstraße, his hands in his pant pockets. So far, he had resisted buying a pair of blue jeans, the American clothing so coveted by his friends. Now he began to wonder if blue jeans were the reason why the soldiers attracted so many girls.

He had to talk to Ingrid about finding a pair. She followed the latest clothing trends and would surely help him. He wondered where he would most likely find her. Unless she was visiting friends, she would probably be at the *Café Rialto* before it closed for the winter. He picked up his pace and headed for the café, which was just two houses away from the Italian pizzeria. On one of the plastic barstools at the counter sat his sister, eagerly talking to her school friend, Edith. She took a sip of her Coca-Cola as he appeared next to her.

"Hello, sister, I need to talk to you when you have a minute," he said.

Ingrid slipped off the stool and joined him at an empty table.

Walter lowered his voice. "Do you know where I could get some blue jeans?"

Ingrid shot him a knowing look. Blue jeans were a girl magnet. "Why don't you ask Jeff?"

"Jeff is unavailable right now," Walter said. "Besides, I was hoping to find them in a legal way." He decided not to ask her where she bought her clothes. Sometimes it was better to be ignorant.

Two narrow grooves formed on her otherwise smooth forehead. "Try *Hosen Kiste* or that new store in Kaiserslautern..."

Walter sighed. He had no time to go to the city in the near future. Between the dead woman and the politician's visit, he had his hands more than full. Then there was the village fair dance next weekend. He had told his boss months ago that he wanted to attend. He decided to change the subject.

"You seem to be spending a lot of time on base lately. *Mama* is worried about you."

"Ach, *Mama*." Ingrid waved the idea away with her hand. "Sometimes I wonder if *Mama* was ever young. What's wrong with having a little fun?"

Walter paused. After the childhood they had had, how could he possibly deny her having a good time? "Be careful. That's all I can say."

She pouted. "Don't you start on me, too. You're much too young to be such a bore."

Walter sighed. There was no getting through to her anymore. He could not help thinking that she was keeping secrets from him. But the more he probed, the more she clammed up. "I guess I don't need to ask you if you're going to the village fair?"

She laughed. "Of course. Tomorrow evening, we'll finish tying some more ribbons on the blasted pole. I'm getting tired of it. And the boys are hardly helping at all. They'd much rather drink beer than do any work."

Walter chuckled. "I could have told you that beforehand." He remembered the one time he had been part of the age-old ritual. The village fair was the biggest event of the year. Young men and girls of Ingrid's age tied colorful ribbons on a limb-less tree, which they hung at the inn where the dance took place. It took weeks to finish the job.

"I've already decided I won't do it again," Ingrid said, twirling a strand of blond hair around her finger. "Isn't it exciting that Elvis has come to Germany? Do you think he will give a concert while he's here?"

"I doubt that the Army will allow him to give a concert," Walter replied.

"Yes, I guess you're right. But still, I think it's exciting. He could have been sent anywhere in the world, but he's come to Germany..."

Walter was beginning to grow tired of the conversation. He didn't like all the attention that Elvis Presley was getting. All the girls were crazy over him while ordinary guys like him could not find a date.

He rose. "Time to go and see where my friends are."

"I'll be going home in a few minutes. I have a busy week ahead of me."

Walter began walking toward the *Moorbachklause*, a small *Gasthaus* that was only frequented by Germans because it didn't have a jukebox. Halfway there, though, he changed his mind. Better to go to a bar that was popular with servicemen. Even during his leisure time, he couldn't get the murder case out of his mind. He figured a policeman was never really off duty.

A Ford Crown Victoria was parked in the courtyard of the *Luna* bar right next to the dung heap. The bar was the successful attempt of a farmer to make money off the avalanche of American soldiers that had descended on the once-sleepy village. Like most farmhouses, it combined house and barn under one roof with a barn door in the middle. Built in the last century, it had survived several wars already. It would probably survive the Cold War too, if the Cold War ever ended.

The barn's ceiling beams were stained in a warm brown tone, giving the interior a rustic ambience. A local art student had painted scenes from an Italian village on the whitewashed walls. The obligatory jukebox near the entrance played a Buddy Holly song. White soldiers in civilian clothes occupied several tables. Walter recognized the GIs everywhere because of their short haircuts. At another table, an American, dressed in khakis and a striped dress shirt, sat with three German youths. They were engaged in a lively conversation, and the language barrier did not seem to matter. Their laughter sometimes overpowered the music. Not seeing anyone he knew, Walter took a seat at an empty table. When the owner's daughter came by to take his order, he decided to pick her mind.

"Ever see any strangers around here?"

She laughed dryly. "All the time. This is a bar, you know. If you're asking if we have any regulars, yes, there are some."

"Americans or Germans?"

"A few of the Americans keep coming back. They like to talk to the young Germans. No wonder; everybody admires the soldiers and their big cars. I can't blame them for enjoying the attention."

She cast a longing look at a GI who rose to feed the jukebox.

Not you too, Walter thought. He asked, harsher than he intended, "Are there any regulars here tonight?"

She pointed at a young German man with curly brown hair. "I see him around quite often."

Walter thanked her before she returned to the counter with a tray full of empty glasses. Curly looked as if he were waiting for someone. When the jukebox stopped, Walter ambled over to the gleaming instrument to throw in a coin for "Great Balls of Fire." On his way back, he passed Curly's table. The young man was tapping his feet against the floor in a nervous manner. Walter decided to observe Curly for a while. A young girl started dancing with the striped shirt. Curly pretended to watch them, but his stoic gaze was fixed on the front door.

More couples formed. Was that how Marianne had met Jeff? Walter imagined Jeff casting glances at the brunette girl and her smiling shyly when he asked her to dance. Walter drank from his Coca-Cola and shook his head. It didn't do much good to dwell on it. He couldn't let Jeff face the electric chair, even if it meant Jeff would marry Marianne and destroy Walter's dream.

His head jerked up when the music stopped. Curly was not alone anymore. A young American, bearing a slight resemblance to actor Clark Gable, was sitting opposite him. He wore blue jeans and a white T-shirt with a pack of Lucky Strikes rolled up into the sleeve. The two men stuck their heads together and talked in an animated way. Walter strained to hear something of their conversation, but the other guests were too noisy. After several minutes, Clark Gable left and Curly hailed the waitress to pay. Walter waited until they were gone and raised his hand to call the waitress's attention. A table full of soldiers who wanted more beer held her up.

By the time Walter finally got outside, he saw no trace of the two conspirators. On his way home, he peered into gaps between houses and into alleyways without seeing a soul. If these men were up to no good, why did they pick such a public place for a meeting? Walter could not solve this question.

6

Chief Kleber was talking on the phone when Walter came to work the next morning. He waved Walter over as soon as he hung up. "That was the Kripo. They got a court order to search Fräulein Gregorius's room. I want you to go over there right away and join their search."

Walter shot his boss a puzzled look.

"It's good training for you, so I requested it," the chief said, reaching for a pencil. "Are you still going to the dance on Saturday?"

"Yes," Walter replied hesitantly.

Chief Kleber rubbed his chin. "Don't worry, I'm not going to ask you to work. But—I'd like you to keep your eyes open wherever you go, and I don't mean just on the girls. Uniforms scare people and they clam up if they see one. When you wear your civilian clothes, they'll just think you're the neighborhood boy out having a good time."

Walter told him about the suspicious-looking men at the *Luna* bar.

"That's just the thing I'm talking about," Chief Kleber said. "If I send a patrol car over there, they'll disappear and we'll learn nothing. Now go on to Reichenbach."

Detective Junker and an assistant were already at Frau Drucker's house when Walter arrived. They made good-natured jokes about showing Walter how the real police worked.

"Did the woman have any relatives we need to notify?" the detective asked the landlady.

She shook her head slowly. "No, I think she was all alone. She didn't mention any relatives and never received any mail."

Junker sighed and told her he would call her if he needed her.

"Any news about Green yet?" Walter asked after she closed the kitchen door behind her.

"I heard that Sergeant Green has been on temporary duty at Dornbach Air Base since Thursday of last week. That rules him out as a suspect," Junker said. "Let's see what we find in the victim's room."

They climbed the stairs and Junker handed Walter a pair of gloves. "Let us do the search. You just observe and learn what we're doing."

Walter looked around the small room. An old-fashioned double bed took up most of the space. It looked as if it been in the family for decades. Junker and his assistant opened the nightstands and combed through their contents. Junker held up a photo of a blond woman with a girl of about ten. "That must be her mother." He left it on top of the nightstand. The assistant asked Walter to help him lift the mattress. He used tweezers to lift a hair from one of the pillows and put it in an envelope.

"What are we looking for?" Walter asked.

"Anything that would indicate a possible motive for killing her," Junker replied.

But if Roswitha was involved in anything illegal, she didn't keep any records of it. Apart from women's personal items and a pair of rolled gold earrings, the nightstand contained nothing but lipstick, powder, hair spray, and twenty-eight Deutsch Marks.

Junker opened the wardrobe. "Green's uniforms are missing, but then, he is on temporary duty." Green's civilian clothes were carefully folded and hung neatly on the bar. Junker searched the pockets of Roswitha's jackets, yielding nothing but an old shopping list. Walter observed the detective as he searched the woman's entire belongings, even her underwear.

"What's the matter?" Junker chuckled. "Have you never seen lingerie before?"

Walter blushed.

Junker said, "You'd be surprised at what's important in a murder case. Last year, we had a case where we found a key in a pair of underwear. The key belonged to a lockbox at the train station, which was stuffed with stolen goods."

"No sign of a purse yet?" Walter asked. "Could it be that she didn't have one?"

"Every woman has a purse."

"But how come her lipstick is in the nightstand?"

"She could have had more than one lipstick," Junker said as he held up a pair of nylons. "She has three pairs of nylons. Harry kept her in good supply. Aha! What do we have here?"

He lifted a bottle of Jim Beam whiskey from the bottom of the wardrobe and held it against the light. It was two-thirds full. "We'll take this along for analysis, and the lipstick and photo. We don't have much to go on here. Some people will say that she got what she had coming to her for living in sin." He eyed the double bed. "But women like her don't give us the biggest headaches. It's the Veronikas who come here on payday and then leave when they have milked the soldiers for their money."

Walter reflected what a sad ending this girl had met after losing her home and her family. He hoped that he would never be in a situation like hers, without friends and relatives. Who could blame her for wanting material goods? It was all she had.

When Walter returned to the station, he heard a raised male voice in the chief's office. He was able to understand most of the conversation through the closed door. The voice belonged to Herr Lang, one of the biggest opponents of the American occupation and its loudest critic.

"I don't see why you have to spend much time investigating the murder of a prostitute," he ranted. "She got what was coming to her, that's all I can say. And many people share my opinion."

Junker had been right. Many townspeople were upset about loose women, yet would they resort to killing one of them? There was no shortage of suspects here.

"She was not a prostitute," Kleber replied. "And we have to treat all suspicious deaths equally, no matter who the victim is."

"You mean to tell me that the sorry life of a prostitute is worth as much as that of a law-abiding, hard-working citizen?" Lang's voice could probably be heard down the street.

Kleber seemed unfazed. "That's the law."

"It's bad enough that we're cannon fodder for the Americans and the Russians, but to put up with these tramps! It's too much," Lang yelled. "I am going to ask the town council to close all the bars."

"You do that, my good man," replied the chief calmly. "Excuse me now. I've got work to do."

Lang stormed out of the chief's office and shot Walter a dirty look before he slammed the station door with a loud bang.

Chief Kleber called Walter into his office. "Do you think he protests a bit too much?"

"You don't think that he could have anything to do with Roswitha's death, do you?"

The chief rubbed his chin. "Not directly, of course. But he's in here complaining about Americans when his son-in-law makes a nice profit building a hospital for the Army."

Walter whistled. "But being a hypocrite is not a crime, is it?"

"Be careful, son, and don't believe everything people tell you."

"Yes, I've learned that already." He was lucky to have such great teachers.

Walter told his boss how the search went.

"So the woman's purse is still missing?"

"Uh-huh, and her boyfriend is not the killer because he's been away on temporary duty since Thursday. I wonder if Green knows yet that his girlfriend is dead?"

"Call the base and find out. After that, you need to type some reports."

Tech Sergeant Brown had already notified Green and requested his immediate return for questioning. He asked Walter to come on base that afternoon to attend the interview. Junker would also be present. Walter was beginning to feel important and wondered aloud why, when his partner had to patrol the village streets on foot.

"You get along well with Americans and you speak passable English," Chief Kleber explained to him. "Schlosser is a good policeman, but he doesn't like dealing with the military. You're closer in age to most of the soldiers. I think they like that."

A few minutes later, Mayor Wagner entered the police station. He wanted to talk to both Kleber and Walter. "The fair people are going to arrive tomorrow. Can you keep an eye on them, please?"

Walter had almost forgotten about the village fair that was to set up in the open space by the town hall. In a small village like Lauterbach, there wouldn't be much more than a merry-go-round, a swing, a sweets vendor, and a shooting gallery. The workers who set up the fairground were often itinerant men from other parts of the country.

"We'll take care of it," Chief Kleber said with a sigh. "You didn't need to come all the way over here to tell me that. You could have just called me."

"I came to find out if the murder has been solved yet," Wagner confessed.

Walter suppressed a grin. If the mayor himself could not contain his curiosity about the murder, how much did the villagers gossip about it? He would have to ask his mother. He just hoped she wouldn't divulge too much herself.

Sergeant Harry Green was sitting in Tech Sergeant Brown's office when Walter arrived. Green's tall, muscular body had the color of Elfriede Hofmann's oak coffee table. He stared forlornly at his shiny black boots while Walter entered the room. Walter pulled up a chair.

I believe Harry really cared for the poor girl, he thought. He was relieved that Roswitha had found someone who cared for her.

Walter sat down and readied himself to take notes while Tech Sergeant Brown began the interview.

"When did you last see Roswitha?"

Green swallowed. "It was Thursday morning. I had to be on base by oh-six-hundred because my unit was going on a training exercise. I kissed her good-bye and said I'd be back by next Friday. She said she'd be looking forward to it. That was the last time I saw her."

"Did she see any other men besides you?"

Green's eyes grew wide. "No."

"Are you sure?"

"A man can never be a hundred percent certain of that," Harry said slowly, "but I'm pretty sure she had no other boyfriends besides me. I know there were others before me, but I didn't mind. She had to survive."

"So, you're almost sure that she didn't have another boyfriend who might have killed her?"

Green raised his eyebrows. "I thought you had made an arrest?"

"I'm the one asking questions here."

Walter was surprised about the sergeant's harsh tone. He had the impression that Green told the truth. "Did you have any intention of marrying her?" the sergeant asked.

Harry fidgeted in his seat. "I have thought about it, but I just couldn't afford it. You see, I'm sending money to my folks every month and I've heard that a soldier has to pay lots of money to get a marriage permit and ship his wife back home. I just don't have that kind of money. I liked Roswitha a lot, but…" He raised his hands, palms facing outward.

Walter scribbled to keep up. Could it be that Tech Sergeant Brown was beginning to doubt that Jeff killed Roswitha? It sounded almost as if he wanted to pin the murder on another boyfriend.

"Did you ever go to the place of the crime with Roswitha?"

"Yes, we did go there in the summer when it was stifling hot in our room. I parked the car there and we sat on a blanket to watch the stars."

"Watch the stars, eh? What do you think she could have been doing there alone? Was she alone?"

Green shrugged. "I have no idea."

Tech Sergeant Brown got up and leaned against his desk. "Tomorrow, you'll have to go and identify the body."

Green nodded. "Can I stay in my room tonight?"

Tech Sergeant Brown hesitated for a moment. "No. You'll have to sleep in the barracks until this case is solved. We want the room as untouched as possible."

He turned to Junker. "Do you agree, Detective?"

"Yes."

"Do you have any questions for him?"

Junker rubbed his thin nose. "Did Fräulein Gregorius own a handbag?"

Green's head jerked backward. "Yes," he said slowly.

"Can you describe it for me?"

"It was a red bag that she slung over her arm. It wasn't very big, just enough to carry her lipstick, powder, and handkerchief."

"What material was it made of?"

"It was imitation leather, I think. I bought it for her at the BX and she was very proud of it. Carried it everywhere."

"Very well, thank you. That'll be all for now."

Junker jotted down Green's work phone number before dismissing him. He turned to Walter, who was finishing his notes.

"A red handbag," Junker said, "that ought to be easy to find, if the killer just tossed it somewhere. We may have to retrace her steps from the house she lived in to the place where you found her."

"But that road crosses several major highways and a railroad track," Walter said. "We'd never find it."

"Probably not. But I'm still convinced that the purse will lead us to the killer somehow."

"I hope you're right, but what if the killer buried it in the moor?"

"Let's hope he was in a hurry. I'll keep in touch with Chief Kleber and suggest to him that you wear civilian clothes while you help with this investigation. People don't talk once they see a uniform."

Walter smiled wryly. "The chief suggested the same thing to me, but he only said I should be on the lookout when I'm off duty."

Junker motioned Walter to go outside with him. "I didn't want to say this in the sergeant's presence, since he speaks German. I don't believe your friend Jeff is the killer. Maybe the Air Police are just holding him to give the real killer a false sense of security."

Walter folded his arms in front of his chest. "That's what the Chief said the other day. After all, Jeff is a police officer, and he has a girlfriend. Why would he kill this woman? It just doesn't add up."

The two officers instinctively ducked as a fighter jet approached the landing strip of the nearby runway. The windows of the Air Police building shook from the deafening noise. After the plane landed and the din subsided, Junker said, "Have you talked to the girlfriend? What's her name?"

"Her name is Marianne Holtz. She came to my house on Tuesday evening asking about him. They were supposed to go out together on Saturday evening. I haven't seen her since then."

"Maybe Marianne is the key to the puzzle. Why don't you go to the girl's house tonight and talk to the family? Does she have any siblings?"

"She has two brothers. One is much younger and one is older than her."

Junker tilted his head. "Good. Wear civilian clothes and pretend that it's more of a social visit. Let me know tomorrow what you've learned."

After supper, Walter strolled to the Holtz house. Situated on Neudorfer Straße, it was one of the musicians' houses that were so common in Lauterbach and the neighboring villages. Itinerant musicians had built them in the nineteenth century from the money they had made during their travels to America or Australia. The single-story houses had two frontispieces in the slanted roof, giving them a slightly foreign appearance. Perhaps that's why Marianne was attracted to all things American, Walter mused. After all, wanderlust was in her blood.

He turned the doorbell and a dull rattle echoed in the hallway beyond the door. An eleven-year-old boy dressed in lederhosen opened the door.

"Hello, Manfred," Walter said, "Is your sister at home?"

Manfred nodded, causing his cowlick to whip up and down. "She's in the kitchen. We're eating supper."

Walter had hoped that they had finished eating by now, but he could hardly turn away now. "Can I come in, please?"

Manfred shrugged and ran ahead of him. Walter scraped his shoes on the doormat and stepped into the hallway. Manfred had left the kitchen door ajar, and Walter opened it wide. The entire family was gathered around the table that took up most of the kitchen. The parents sat with their backs to Walter, while Marianne and her older brother Benno were facing him. Marianne's eyes brightened at the sight of Walter, but Benno avoided his eyes and stared at his half-eaten blood sausage sandwich. What could be bothering him?

"Good evening," Walter said.

Still chewing, Herr Holtz looked over his shoulder.

"I've come at a bad time, I guess," Walter said, as no one offered to ask him in.

"No, no, please stay." Marianne said. "Have you seen Jeff?"

"Yes, that's why I'm here. He wants me to tell you that he's all right."

Marianne jumped from her seat.

"Finish your supper first," her mother said in a voice that discouraged argument.

"But *Mama*, he has news from Jeff," Marianne pleaded. "At least offer Walter a chair. I would do it, but I'm trapped."

Is she talking about the seating arrangements or her life, Walter thought. Mother Holtz rose with a loud sigh and pulled an old chair from a corner. Walter wedged the chair between the table and the kitchen stove. The woven seat creaked under his weight as he sat next to Marianne and glanced around the table. Benno drew his attention as the young man wolfed down his sandwich and gulped his mineral water.

"How is your mother doing?" asked Herr Holtz, apparently not wanting to talk about Jeff.

"Fine, thank you," Walter said.

Benno rose abruptly. "Can I go now?"

Frau Holtz sighed. "Yes, you can leave."

"Where are you going?" Herr Holtz inquired in a grating voice.

"Nowhere that concerns strangers," Benno hissed while banging the door shut.

Herr Holtz's face turned crimson. "If he weren't so big, I'd put him over my knee. Does anyone know who he runs around with?"

"I know he's friends with Heinz and Anton," Marianne said.

Walter made a mental note of her remark. It was peculiar how his schoolmate Heinz had avoided Walter at the concert, and now Benno left the house as soon as he arrived. Even when Walter was not in uniform, people were suspicious of his presence.

Herr Holtz turned to Walter. "Our children are growing wild. Benno never tells us where he's going anymore, Manfred chews gum all the time, and Marianne wants to go to America with a man we barely know. A man who's accused of murder." He shook his head. "In my day, we did what our parents told us to do, but the young generation doesn't care about our opinion at all."

Walter smiled wryly. His mother had the same complaint. Parents were alike everywhere. He wondered if he would be the same way, if he ever had children.

"Jeff wouldn't kill anybody," Marianne burst out. "Tell him, Walter, that Jeff is innocent!"

Walter protested. "I can't say that, but we're doing our best to solve the case."

Herr Holtz rose from the table. In the living room, he picked up a newspaper while his wife carried a pot of bubbling water from the coal stove to the corner sink.

"Do you have a message from Jeff for me?" Marianne asked.

Walter glanced at Manfred, who was engrossed in a *Fix und Foxi* comic book. "Let's go outside for a moment."

Marianne slipped on a cardigan and they stepped into the courtyard.

"It's hard to be alone in our house, isn't it?" Marianne said.

"Yes. Your parents don't seem to be enthused about Jeff."

"It's not Jeff they resent," Marianne replied. "They don't like the idea that I might go to America with him. No, they don't like it at all. *Mama* especially. She gets downright hostile when I talk about him. So I don't, unless I have to." She folded her arms in front of her chest. "When did you last see him? How did he look?"

"He looks fine, considering the circumstances. He thinks about you a lot, he says, and can't wait until he gets out of jail. Can't wait till we find the real killer…"

"Have you made any progress yet?"

Walter sighed. Finally, he was alone with Marianne, in the dark no less, and all she talked about was Jeff and the dead woman. "Do you know how many people ask me that question every day?"

She shook her head and searched in her pocket for a handkerchief. He decided to change the subject. "Do you know where Benno and his friends spend their evenings?"

"No, he never tells us where he's going since he's come of age. Why do you ask?"

Because everyone is a suspect at this point. "No reason. I just thought you might know. Does he have a job?"

"He worked at Pfaff for a while, but then he had some disagreement with his supervisor. He said he quit, but I fear that he was fired. He never stays at one job very long."

"Why do your parents let him stay at home then?"

"Perhaps they think they still have some influence over him as long as he stays at home, but you saw how much that's worth. Maybe that's why they don't like me dating Jeff. They're afraid that I'll slip through their fingers, too."

Marianne sniveled. She sank her head on Walter's shoulder, catching him by surprise. She was close enough for him to kiss her, and she was crying over another man. Life was cruel sometimes.

Why does it have to be him? He wanted to ask, but he couldn't utter a word. His arms remained at his sides. If he touched her now, he would lose his guard. And he was not the type of man who would steal another man's girl, especially if that man could not fight back.

Marianne slowly raised her head from his shoulder, her irises reflecting the streetlight.

"Why does it have to be an American?" Walter asked in a strangled voice. He had to know.

Marianne fidgeted. "Germans don't know how to court a girl," she said at last. "Jeff treats me like I'm the Queen of England, like a million Mark. A German man has never held a door open for me, but Jeff does it all the time. For the first time in my life, I feel like I am somebody special. And Jeff, he is so sure of himself. German boys are so morose. Jeff and his friends are so… so easy-going. It feels so good to be with him. I'm in love with him."

Walter remained rigid as a fence post. He did not want her to know what he felt for her, but his eyes betrayed him. Marianne let out a small cry and covered her mouth. "Oh God," she whispered. "I'm sorry. If only I had known."

Walter dug the tip of his shoe into the cobblestones of the courtyard. "It doesn't matter now, does it?"

"It matters to me," Marianne said. "It matters a lot, and if I had not met Jeff…"

"But you have met him," Walter interrupted her. He breathed in the cool evening air and decided to draw attention away from himself. "Are you sure you're not in love with his car?"

Marianne laughed. "It doesn't hurt that he has a car and takes me places I would never get to see otherwise. But don't you agree that life around here is much more exciting since they built the base? I have never felt so, so…"

"Alive?" Walter said.

"Yes." Her eyes sparkled.

Walter had to admit that she was right, even though that very base was the reason why he had to solve a woman's death right now. "Can you promise me one thing?"

"Yes, of course. I'll do anything to help get Jeff out of jail."

"If Benno ever mentions where he's going or who he's going out with, will you let me know?"

Marianne nodded. "I promise. But you don't think that he's involved in a killing?"

"I don't know. He wasn't thrilled to see me, that much is certain. I'm relying on you here."

"I promise," Marianne said again. "Are you going to the village dance?"

"Yes. Are you?"

"I don't know. It doesn't seem right while Jeff is in jail."

Jeff again. The girl had a one-track mind. Walter took his leave and walked home through the almost-empty streets. For a brief moment, he considered stopping at a *Gasthaus* to see if any of his friends were there but decided against it. He had a busy weekend ahead. First, he had to work Friday night, and then he had to rest for the big dance.

As Walter climbed the stairs at home, he noticed light shining through the slit under Ingrid's door. The strains of "Don't" sounded through the walls. He decided to knock.

"Come in," Ingrid said and he entered. She lay belly down on her bed, her feet upright in the air. A magazine with a photo of Elvis Presley lay opened on her bed. Her Elvis obsession was becoming ridiculous.

"Didn't you promise to loan me these records?" Walter said in his authoritative policeman's voice.

"I forgot. Besides, you're never home anyway."

"I could say the same thing about you. Come on, give me at least some of them. Remember, I didn't tell on you when I saw you at the club."

Ingrid rose with a sigh. "All right, but some of these records aren't mine. They belong to Anneliese, and you can't have those."

She began to rummage through her records. Walter suppressed a remark. Girls always made such a fuss about everything. In a way, he was glad he didn't have a girlfriend yet. He had enough on his mind right now without guessing a girl's thoughts all the time.

In his room, he plugged the portable record player, bought from his first wage packet, into the outlet. Slumping onto his bed, he closed his eyes and thought back over the day's events. Marianne's remarks hurt him more than he had realized at the time. It had never occurred to him that girls wanted more than a free drink from their date. He thought his attitude toward girls was just like that of all his friends. None of them opened doors for girls. Was that why they preferred Americans? Or was there more to it than that? He decided to observe the soldiers he encountered. Perhaps he could learn something from them.

7

On Thursday, Walter's shift did not begin until noon, and he took the opportunity to tend to his rabbits. He reached for a bottomless cage he had made of chicken wire and scrap wood and put it in the grassy area behind the chicken coop. Then he grasped Max and placed him under the cage. That way Max could fend for himself in the grass among the chickens without escaping into the family's vegetable garden.

Walter could not explain why he was so fond of Max. His early childhood memories included the rabbit shows he had attended at *Die Traube* with his grandfather. More than once, *Opa* took home the coveted blue ribbon, and Walter was proud when *Opa* allowed him to hold a rabbit.

Walter knelt in the grass and watched Max devour one grass stalk after the other. When he finally rose, he heard a noise similar to the scraping of a shoe on stone behind him. He swung around, but saw no one. His mother had gone to the bakery, so it couldn't have been her. Perhaps it was Berta Klink, wanting to buy some eggs. Walter stepped around the coop and peered into the yard. No one was there. Now he was even edgy in his own backyard. He breathed deeply and began to muck out the chicken coop as he had promised his mother.

When he was finished, his mother called him for an early lunch. Walter spooned the potato soup while she made a bloodwurst sandwich for him.

"Herr Lang was at the bakery," his mother said, placing the small cutting board with his sandwich in front of him. "He asked me if you're still working on the case of the murdered prostitute and I said I don't know. I didn't think it was his concern what you're doing at work. Why does he care so much about this woman? I don't like it when people call her a prostitute."

Apparently, the rumor mill was in full swing.

Walter halted his spoon in mid-air. "Herr Lang should mind his own business, from what I hear."

"Why, what do you hear?"

Walter cringed. He had to watch what he told his mother. She claimed that she never gossiped, but he suspected that that wasn't always the case. "Nothing. I just meant that he should keep his nose in his own affairs. What do people say about the case?"

His mother wiped her hands on her apron. She always did that when she felt uneasy. "You know how it is. Some people say that our town is like Sodom and Gomorrah since the base was built. They complain about the soldiers, and then they turn around and rent their own bedroom to them to make money." She shook her head. "I just wish that Ingrid wasn't so infatuated with them. I'm not worried about you. You have a head on your shoulders. But Ingrid, she seems to be so easily influenced. I worry that she may keep company with the wrong people." She sank on a chair. "*Ach*, if only your father were still alive. He would know how to keep her in check. It wasn't easy for both of you to lose your father when you were so young." She dried a tear with the edge of her apron.

Walter nodded. He had been eleven years old when the mailman brought a letter from a man in Ludwigshafen. He wrote Elfriede that he was a fellow prisoner in the Siberian prison camp and that he was with Werner Hofmann when he died. He was willing to testify to this fact in case his widow had difficulties collecting social security benefits. He went on to describe the hardships faced by the prisoners. Only one third of them survived.

Walter had only vague memories of his father. He was a mere three years old when his father was drafted, and then he only came home once on furlough. His mother had told him that he cried when she told him to shake the stranger's hand. By the time he had called the stranger "Papa," he had to leave for the Russian front again, never to return. Never to see his daughter.

"We had Grandpa. He was like a father to us. Don't worry, Mama. I'll keep an eye on Ingrid. If I have time."

"Thank you. But you have your own problems right now with this murder case. And then it is about time that you started seeing a girl…"

Walter rose abruptly. "I got to get ready, or I'll be late for work." Usually, he got along well with his mother, but she had her moments. After his encounter with Marianne the night before, he was in no mood to talk to his mother about girls. What could he do when the girl he desired was in love with another man? After years away from home, he thought he was over her. Until she had placed her head on his shoulder…

Chief Kleber was already waiting for Walter when he arrived. "I've decided to take you with me to the fairground. Sure, I could easily go alone, but I want to teach you a few things. Besides, four eyes see more than two."

Leaving Schlosser to man the station, they walked a block to the village square behind town hall.

"Do you think they'll be finished in time for Sunday?" Walter wondered aloud.

"Sure they will," the chief said.

The men who milled around the pieces of a merry-go-round and a chain-carousel appeared to know what they were doing. Several children stood at the edge of the square, quietly watching the rides taking shape. They probably envisioned themselves already riding on one of the merry-go-round's wooden ponies. The chief shooed them away, but they giggled shyly and came right back.

Walter followed Chief Kleber as he searched for the owner of the chain-carousel. The ride had been coming to Lauterbach for years, but the hired help tended to change from year to year. Those were the men Chief Kleber wanted to check out.

"What can I do for you, Chief?" a wiry man with rolled-up shirt sleeves asked. He could have been anywhere between forty and fifty years old. Walter noticed with great envy that the man's upper arms were bulging under his shirt.

"Good day, Herr Reuter. How is business going?"

Reuter scratched his head. "Not bad. The season will be winding down soon. Another couple of weeks and we're finally going home."

"Any new men in your gang this year?" Chief Kleber asked.

Reuter sneezed and blew his nose into a huge red handkerchief. "Why do you ask?"

"No particular reason."

Walter observed the square while Chief Kleber and Reuter were sparring. One of the young hands eyed the policemen with almost open hostility. What could be eating him? Only someone with a guilty conscience would stare like him. No wonder the chief kept tabs on strangers in town.

"Yes, I have two new hands this year," Reuter said. "There's Anton Molnar. He's a Hungarian refugee. And Reinhold Mielke. Came to the Palatinate to work in construction. He got laid off when work in Baumholder was finished."

Walter listened intently. Construction was still occurring all over the county to accommodate the soldiers and their recreational needs. Why then did Reinhold accept a seasonal job that probably paid less than a construction job?

Apparently, Chief Kleber had the same idea. "I'll have to check their identity cards."

The officers followed Reuter around planks of wood and seats. Reuter called the two men over.

"Can I see your identity cards?" Chief Kleber asked.

"I don't have it on me right now," Mielke said. "It's in the trailer."

"So is mine," Molnar added.

"Go get them. Or better yet, we'll go with you. That way we won't have to climb over the fairground twice."

Molnar did not appear to be upset about the request. Having lived under communism, he was probably used to frequent requests for identification. Walter found Mielke's expression harder to read. He had shoved his hands into his pockets to show his indifference to the whole process. The trailers of the fairground people were parked a block away behind the school building. The men passed a trailer with lace curtains in its windows and stopped in front of a trailer whose windows were covered with sheets. Molnar stepped in and opened a drawer before returning with his identity card. Mielke waited until Molnar came out because the trailer was too small for several people to enter at the same time. Swishing sounds suggested drawers and cabinets being opened and shut.

"What's taking you so long?" Chief Kleber asked.

"I'll be right there."

The chief raised his eyebrow at Walter, his way of indicating caution. He peered inside when Mielke showed up, his burly figure filling the doorframe.

Chief Kleber studied the identity card, slowly turning each page of the gray document. He glanced at Mielke. "I heard that you used to work in base construction. Why do you work here now?"

Mielke turned his head sideways and spat on the asphalt. "Because the damn contractor I worked for went bankrupt and skipped town. Didn't pay any of us workers, so I had to do what I could to make a living."

"All right, that'll be all for now."

Mielke snatched the document out of Chief Kleber's hands and disappeared inside the mobile trailer. Molnar remained rooted on the spot, his head bowed slightly.

"Thank you. You may go back to work now," Chief Kleber said to him.

Molnar exhaled slowly, apparently relieved that the questioning was over.

Back at the police station, the chief took off his cap and asked Walter, "Did you learn anything?"

"Yes. It appears that Mielke was hiding something, just in case we entered the trailer."

Chief Kleber rubbed his hands together. "Anything else?"

"He seems to hold a grudge against his former employer."

"Very good. I believe you'll make a fine police officer. A big part of police work is just intuition, a gut feeling that something isn't right. The bad part is that Mielke now

81

knows we're suspicious. It's unlikely that he'll do anything illegal while he's in Lauterbach. We don't have the manpower to trail him all the time. I have my hands full with the death investigation, the fair, and the upcoming visit of the Secretary of Defense. You'll probably have to work some overtime until that visit is over."

Walter tried to hide his disappointment. His forty-five hour workweek didn't leave much time for a social life under the best of circumstances.

"I'll pay you overtime," the chief continued. "Didn't you want to buy a scooter when you have saved enough money?"

Walter sighed. A scooter was his biggest wish. "All right, I'll work overtime, but..."

"Yes, I know, you want time off for the dance. You're still going to have to work on Sunday afternoon. I need you during the mock sermon."

Walter calculated. That would not leave him much time to sleep if he stayed at the dance until the end. Sometimes, he questioned his career choice. His friends who worked in factories and workshops always knew when their workday ended. Yet, the monotony of factory work had never held any appeal for him. Ever since his early youth, he had felt the need to protect and help people. In school, he had always been the one breaking up fights. When it came time to choose a profession, it was only natural that he wanted to be a police officer.

Chief Kleber and Walter began to discuss the cases on hand. There was Roswitha Gregorius, of course. An old woman had reported that one of her chickens was missing. And a fight at the *Adria* bar had necessitated the presence of the German and military police.

"On a weeknight? Usually, they only fight on weekends or payday, and payday is still two weeks away." Walter knew that because he had to work every payday since entering the police force.

Chief Kleber scratched his head. "I'm just telling you to keep an eye on the *Adria* bar when you and Schlosser go on patrol tonight."

Before typing reports, Walter reopened Roswitha's file. He thought about Jeff sitting in his jail cell and could not shake the feeling that he should be doing more to find the girl's real killer. Detective Junker had called the chief earlier to exchange notes, but had nothing new to report. The case appeared to have reached a dead end already.

What had Roswitha done in the moor, so close to the base? Did she have a date with another man? Or was she on her way to the base? All the more reason to have her purse and identity card on her. It always came back to that purse. Finally, Walter asked for permission to visit the Enlisted Club on base.

The parking lot of the club was already filling up when Walter arrived. He parked the Beetle between a Ford and a Chevrolet 210 and climbed out. Unable to control his curiosity, he sauntered around the Ford. He would have given a week's pay to get a ride in such a car. He had to force himself away from the shining chrome bumpers to enter the club.

A banner above the canopy announced the Oktoberfest with German food and a German oompah band that would play next Saturday. The bouncer recognized Walter and waved him through. Several tables were occupied with NCOs eating hamburgers or fried chicken. The jukebox played "Twilight Time" as Walter headed toward the office to speak with Manager Lothar König. Walter had to wait until König finished a phone call.

"What can I do for you, Herr Hofmann?"

"I would like to ask you a few questions, if you have time."

"Sure, I have a few minutes before the evening rush begins."

"But the club is almost packed," Walter said as he sat on the offered chair.

The manager waved his hand. "That's just normal after work traffic. Were you thinking of a career change?"

Walter shook his head. "I don't know if you've heard that a woman was killed near the base on Saturday."

König weighed his head gravely. "Yes, I heard about that."

Walter pulled the photo out of his pocket. Its white borders were beginning to look frayed.

"Have you ever seen her? Her name was Roswitha Gregorius."

König studied the photo. "Why, yes. She was in here last Saturday to talk to me."

Walter leaned forward in his chair. "This past Saturday?"

The manager eyed the wall calendar with its image of the Speyer cathedral. "Yes, I'm pretty sure it was last Saturday."

Walter leaned forward. He could not believe his luck. "Do you remember what time she was here?"

The manager pursed his lips. "It must have been between the lunch and dinner crowds, perhaps between three and four o'clock."

"Can you be more specific than that? It's really important."

König stared at the wall, which was adorned with photographs of entertainers. Walter recognized Caterina

84

Valente in one photo. "I'm sorry. I don't remember exactly when she came by. It gets very busy here on weekends."

Walter pulled out a spiral notebook and scribbled away. "What did she want to talk to you about?"

"She asked me if I had a job for her."

Walter's pencil halted in the middle of a word. "A job? What did you tell her?"

"I told her that I didn't have an opening at the moment and she should check with the personnel office on Monday."

"Why didn't she just call you first before coming all the way out here?"

The manager shrugged. "Who has a telephone?"

He was right, of course. None of Walter's friends had a phone yet. He only had one because work required it.

"Did she say why she was looking for a job?"

"She only said that she had a plan and needed some money."

Perhaps Roswitha believed that Harry would take her to America with him. Maybe she wanted to work for the passage. Or was she making plans for life after Harry?

Walter asked, "How did she get on base?"

König lit a cigarette and leaned back in his chair. "Quite a few young women wait in front of the gate until an airman comes along and signs them in. It's not difficult, especially when there is a concert the same day."

"Yes, I was at the concert myself." Walter poised his pencil again. "Did Roswitha carry a purse?"

"I don't usually pay attention to such things, but she did have a bright red handbag. I remember it because she pulled out her resume."

Walter perked up. "Did you keep the resume?" He hoped to learn something about Roswitha's past.

König tipped the ash into a metal ashtray. "No, she put it back in her purse."

"Do you remember where she lived before she moved here?"

König slowly shook his head. "No. I gave it a cursory look, but I don't have any job openings, so I didn't want to spend much time on her."

Walter rose. "Thank you very much. If you think of anything, give me a call."

"I will."

On the drive back to the police station, Walter thought about what he had learned. Whatever Roswitha's plans were, she had not shared them with her boyfriend or anyone else. Still, he would like to talk to Green again. Busy as Walter was, the interview would have to wait until the next day or week.

Walter ate the sandwich he had brought from home and the two partners began their rounds, with Schlosser at the wheel. Darkness had set in, yet the town was far from sleepy. Brightly lit taverns and bars invited locals inside, as well as the GIs with their padded wallets. Streetlights illuminated workers on their way home from their shift and groups of young people destined for a night on the town.

On Neudorfer Straße, Walter asked Schlosser to stop at Müller's house. He wanted to ask his best friend, Fritz, to reserve a seat for him at the dance. Herr Müller himself opened the door.

"*Guten Abend*, Walter," he said. "I've been thinking about you this week. How is the case of the dead woman coming along? I heard an arrest has been made."

Walter cringed. It seemed as if everyone wanted to talk to him about the murder. Usually he referred them to the newspaper, but Herr Müller was a local council member and had a right to know what was happening in town.

"The investigation continues until we have sufficient proof for an arrest," he said politely.

"I'm glad to hear that. I would be sorry to hear that your friend was a killer. But it worries me how much crime has gone up since the military arrived here. The mayor has received numerous complaints this week."

"What kind of complaints?" Walter was unaware of any.

"The usual. Drunken soldiers doing their business in people's front gardens or breaking flower pots. It seems as if everything that happens is being blamed on Americans, as if our German youth were all angels. But we know that's not true, don't we?"

Walter was unsure what to make of this remark, so he decided to ignore it. "Is Fritz at home?"

"No, he hasn't come home yet."

Walter gave his message to Herr Müller and left. What had Fritz's father meant when he said the German youth were no angels? Was he hinting that Germans committed crimes that were pinned on Americans? Or had he merely made a reference to young men who liked to dress and behave like Marlon Brando? There were a few rebellious young men in town, such as Benno, but they had not caused any problems for the police so far. He mulled over Herr Müller's comment as he climbed back into the car.

"You're very quiet today," said Schlosser as they drove on.

"I can't get the dead woman out of my head," Walter said. "Do we have any other unsolved crimes on the books lately?"

"We always have unsolved crimes. Before you joined our station, we had reports of copper theft from the base. We were never able to solve that one. What exactly are you looking for?"

"I don't know. Herr Müller said something that got me thinking. What if more than one person was involved in this case? Do you know if the chief has checked on Reinhold Mielke's criminal record?"

There was no need to check on Marianne's brother, Benno. If he had gotten into trouble with the law, it would have been all over town. And besides, the chief had worked here long enough that he would remember any discrepancies.

"I think the chief has made a call about Mielke and Molnar's records. No answer yet. And we're supposed to drive by the fairground trailers every hour, just to let them know we're thinking of them."

"Every hour? Isn't that a bit much?"

Schlosser shrugged and slowed down the car because they were approaching the *Adria* bar. "That's what he said. Here we go! Keep your eyes open."

This early in the evening, people were relatively well behaved. Schlosser turned the car around in the next street and drove slowly by the bar again. "It's quiet. Let's go to the fairground."

The carnival rides were beginning to take shape, as far as Walter could tell in the dark. A light shone from Reuter's trailer, but Mielke and Molnar's trailer was dark.

"I wonder what these fellows do at night?" Schlosser asked.

"I don't know. They're probably tired tonight. Maybe they went out for a beer and a game of cards."

On their second patrol around town, the officers entered the *Adria* bar and approached the owner. "I don't have much time for you," he said while drafting a beer. "As you can see, I'm busy."

"This won't take long," Walter said, pulling Roswitha's photo from his inner pocket. "Have you ever seen this woman here?"

The landlord blinked at the photo. "I've never seen her in here."

"Are you sure?"

"Look, I see a lot of people coming through here and while I don't remember every fellow in here, I would remember a girl like her."

He winked and handed the photo back to Walter, who snatched it out of his hand. If he had ever needed a reason to dislike the *Adria* bar, that was it. Sleazy landlords like this one gave everyone a bad name. No wonder that few locals ever frequented this bar. Schlosser and Walter worked the room, checking the identity cards of everyone who was not American. Everyone's papers were in order and no one had seen Roswitha. It seemed as if only sheer luck would solve this case.

On their way to the *Luna* bar, Schlosser asked, "Are you taking a girl to the dance?"

"No," Walter said curtly.

"Why not? Have you asked anyone?"

"I don't want to talk about it." He would rather have died than admit that he had never asked a girl out to a dance.

"All right, all right. Have it your way."

Walter stared at the people who strolled along the sidewalks. One of them might be a killer. But a killer could sometimes be better company than the annoying pity of well-meaning but happily married co-workers. Schlosser had been married for seven years now and had a little boy. He often made good-hearted fun of Walter and commented that Walter was married to his mother. As if he had any other choice when he had not been able to put aside much money yet and living space was scarce. It was much more lucrative to rent a room to an American than to a poor German, and most people had to live with their parents or in-laws.

Schlosser parked the car and got out. Walter wanted to follow, but changed his mind.

"I think I better stay in the car. I was here the other night and saw a couple of men behaving suspiciously. If I appear in uniform now, I will never be able to come here again."

"What did they look like?"

"One was an American who looked like that movie star, Clark Gable, without the mustache."

"Who?"

"Never mind." He had forgotten that Schlosser seldom went to the theater and then only watched German movies. "He had a thin mustache and pomaded dark brown hair. The other one had curly brown hair, which was lighter than the other man's, and a mole on his right cheek."

"All right, I'll look out for them."

When Schlosser returned, he said, "There was a fellow with curly hair, but he was sitting alone. We better leave now or else his accomplice, if we can call him that, will never show up."

They parked in a parallel street and walked back to a spot from which they could view the entrance. After about fifteen minutes, Schlosser said, "We better get going. We've wasted enough time here." They walked back to the Beetle and drove off.

"I can't believe that no one in town seems to have ever seen Roswitha, Walter said. "Either they're lying or we're barking up the wrong tree."

Schlosser tilted his head. "Hm. She lived in Reichenbach, right? Maybe she just didn't go out in Lauterbach since she didn't have a car. It must be at least three Kilometers from her room to the first bar in Lauterbach. The other bars are even farther away."

"She could have walked or gotten a ride."

"Did you ask her boyfriend?"

"No," Walter admitted, "but tomorrow I'll go back on base and ask him."

Schlosser yawned. "Do you ever sleep?"

Walter chuckled. "I haven't slept too much lately, and I won't get much sleep this weekend because I have to work on Sunday."

Schlosser gave him a rueful glance. "Sorry, but we're having so many guests on Sunday that I asked the chief if I could have the day off. After all, the village fair is only once a year and I don't see my brother all that often."

Schlosser's brother lived in Neustadt, their hometown, where he worked for the district government. "And then my wife's sister is coming with her husband and kids. Most of all, though, I want to be home for all the good food."

Walter laughed. Housewives put their biggest efforts into the lunch on fair Sunday, and his own mother was no exception. He would have to tell her that he wanted to eat early on Sunday. She would be disappointed that he wouldn't be home for coffee and cake, especially when Ingrid wouldn't be home either. Tradition required that she would dance the first three dances with her fair partner after the mock sermon was over. By Tuesday, Ingrid would probably be exhausted. He knew that his sister had taken Monday off, but he remembered his own fatigue back when he was one of the young men who carried the fair pole through town. It was an experience he would never repeat. His arms had ached for days.

"Do you ever get homesick?" Walter asked.

"I miss the wine fest," his partner admitted. "But then, if I lived there, I would probably have to work during the festival and wouldn't be able to enjoy it. As a policeman, I prefer a small town to a bigger one."

The rest of their shift was fairly quiet. They broke up a fight between several intoxicated airmen at the *Adria* bar. The Air Police came to their aid with a pickup truck. One of the policemen, Airman First Class Goodwell, recognized Walter.

"How is the case of the dead woman going?" he asked.

"Not too well. We know her name and who she was, but no more," Walter said, unsure how much to reveal. "I need to talk to her boyfriend again."

"All right. Just report to our office first."

Walter decided to ask the question that was most on his mind. "Is Sergeant Preston still in custody?"

"He has been moved," Goodwell said while turning away from Walter. "We ought to be going now with this rowdy bunch," he said over his left shoulder.

Walter watched as the airmen climbed on the truck bed and the police vehicle drove off. Why wouldn't Goodwell tell him whether Jeff was still in custody? Perhaps the airman did not know the answer or he had orders not to divulge information. Walter was glad that he did not give away everything he knew. His knowledge consisted mostly of suspicions anyway. Intuition and gut feeling seemed to be a large part of police work, as the chief had mentioned. Walter was glad to have a boss like Chief Kleber, who taught him the nuances of police work they did not teach at the police academy.

8

Walter had planned to sleep in on Friday morning, but his mother's new hand mixer aroused him from his slumber. She must be baking a cake for Sunday. He put a pillow over his ear. An hour later, he entered the kitchen, taking in the sweet aroma of apple cake that emanated from the electric stove. Two bowls and a rolling pin cluttered the flour-dusted table.

"I'm sorry if I woke you," his mother said while clearing a corner of the table for him. "I have so much to do today and tomorrow that I had to start early. I went to the bakery this morning because I needed bread and bought a Danish pastry for you. I know you love them."

Walter licked his lips. "Yes, I do."

"When I came home, there was a man standing by the front door. He said he wanted to talk to you. I said you were asleep and he walked away."

Walter was fully awake now. "Who was it?"

"I don't know. I've never seen him before. At first, I thought he was a traveling salesman, but he did not carry a suitcase."

"What did he look like?" Walter asked.

"He had black hair, with lots of pomade," his mother said. "He was shorter than you are. I'm sorry, that's all I remember. I didn't really pay attention to him."

"Did he ask for me by name? Do you remember his exact words?"

She paused. "Come to think of it, he asked for the man of the house."

"Are you sure his hair was black and not brown?"

"Yes, it was black as coal."

Walter chewed solemnly. The stranger could not have been the American who had talked to Curly. "I don't like it when a stranger comes to our house when you're alone."

"But you were at home."

"He didn't know that. Asking for the man of the house could have just been an excuse because you saw him."

Seeing her alarmed face, he added, "I wouldn't worry about it if I were you." *Let me do the worrying,* he thought. Now he was being watched by a stranger with pomaded hair. To distract her, he said, "I better feed my rabbits before I go to work."

"Do you have to work again?"

"I want to go on base today to talk to someone. Besides, the chief will pay me overtime, he said. I could use the money."

"You work too hard," his mother admonished him. "We don't need the money that bad."

If her hands had not been kneading yeast dough, he was sure she would have run them through his hair.

"*Mama,* there's a killer out there. I would like to do my part in catching him. Until I do, Jeff is in jail, as far as I know."

She added some more flour to her hands. "Yes, it is a shame. He seemed like such a nice man."

Walter grew tired of talking about work. "What are you making here?"

"*Kranzkuchen.*" She braided the yeast dough and put it in a rectangular baking pan. "Are you still going to the dance tomorrow with all this going on?"

94

"Of course I will. It's only once a year, after all. I have to work on Sunday afternoon, routing traffic. I need to eat lunch early."

Frau Hofmann's face drooped. "Your aunt and uncle will be disappointed if they can't meet you. After all, we don't see them that often."

Walter shrugged. "I can't help it. Tell them we'll visit when all this is over."

By "all this," he meant the village fair as much as the murder case and the visit of the Secretary of Defense.

Tech Sergeant Shoemaker was on duty when Walter arrived at the Air Police building. Walter explained that he wanted to talk to Green again.

"Can I see Jeff while I'm here?" he asked before leaving.

"I'm afraid that's not possible. Sergeant Preston has been transferred to the Mannheim jail."

Walter jerked around. "Does this mean that you still believe he killed Roswitha?"

"As long as he can't prove his whereabouts for the time of the murder until the time he was found, we have to assume that he either murdered the girl or was at least AWOL."

The sergeant resumed his duties and Walter stepped out of the building. Even to him, a police officer, the military was very tight-lipped about Jeff's arrest. He had expected to see his friend and give him some words of encouragement. Now he only hoped that he wouldn't see Marianne during the fair. She would only urge him to work harder to find the real killer. As if he weren't working day and night already.

Staff Sergeant Green worked for Civil Engineering on the other side of the base, where most of the offices were located. Walter drove past the Base Exchange where his sister worked. Nearby was the movie theater he had once visited with Jeff to watch *The Bridge on the River Kwai*. He had enjoyed it immensely and had whistled the catchy tune for days. An airman rarely needed to go off base at all. Everything was right here: the barbershop, dry cleaner, library, shopping center, and club.

Sergeant Green was out on a call when Walter entered the CE building. He passed the time by reading all the announcements tacked on a bulletin board.

Carrying a clipboard, Green greeted him solemnly.

"Let's go outside to talk," Walter suggested. He did not want any witnesses to their conversation. It was enough that the German clerks eyed him suspiciously.

Outside, Harry asked, "Do you have any news about Roswitha's murder?"

"Did you know that she was looking for a job?" Walter said.

Green's body jerked backward. "She didn't say a word about it to me. Come to think of it, though, she did complain how bored she was."

"You mentioned the other day that it was very expensive to take a wife back to America. Do you think she wanted a job to pay for her passage?"

A cloud traveled over Harry's eyes. "Do you know what it's like for a white woman to be married to a Colored man in America? They can't even sit together on a bus. I tried to tell her that, but she didn't believe me. I never made any promises to her, believe me. I tried to discourage her. 'You're better off here,' I said to her. 'You have no idea what it's like at home.' But she just laughed at me. Said she had seen movies about America. She thought everybody drove a big car over there and lived in a nice house."

Walter admitted to himself that he was equally clueless about the conditions in America. The way the soldiers were spending money in Germany, he thought they must all be rich. "Sounds as if she really wanted to marry you, doesn't it?"

"She might have thought she wanted to, but I never encouraged her. I really liked her, don't get me wrong. That's why I didn't want her to have the kind of life she would have had with me," Harry said in a hoarse voice. "But I guess it doesn't matter now."

Green really seemed to grieve his girlfriend's death. If Walter ever had any doubt that he was involved in Roswitha's killing, he was certain now that Harry could not possibly have anything to do with it.

"If you think of anything else that might be helpful to me, please let me know," Walter said and thanked Green for his time.

He sank on the driver's seat of the Beetle, feeling completely disheartened. The interview with Green had revealed nothing new, other than the dreams of a lonely young woman who had desperately wanted to find a home. Why didn't Roswitha walk along a main road? Did she have a date with another man? A man who promised her what Harry didn't? Walter could hardly interview thousands of servicemen, so he would have to rely on luck. He didn't like the odds of that.

9

On Saturday, Walter joined legions of Lauterbach men sweeping the sidewalks. The Saturday chore was even more important than usual because everybody was tidying up for the fair. *Opa* Klink carried his broom around the house after finishing off his task. His daughter-in-law, Berta, opened the front door to pour a bucket of cleaning water into the gutter.

"How is it going, Walter?" she asked.

He braced himself for the inevitable question about the dead woman. "All right."

Berta straightened up and placed her free hand on her hip. "I had to clean our staircase again, even though I just cleaned it on Wednesday. The Air Police were here yesterday and picked up something out of Jeff's room."

Walter rested his hands on the broom handle. Why had no one bothered to tell the German police about the visit? "Do you know what they took?"

Berta tucked a strand of hair under her blue headscarf. "No, I couldn't see it. They took it away in a brown paper bag. Well, I had better get back to my work. Enjoy the fair."

"Thanks, I will."

Puzzled, Walter continued sweeping. What could the Air Police have taken out of Jeff's room? Was it evidence, or was it something as simple as a razor? No, they would not have gone through the trouble for a razor, he decided. Something was going on that the military was not telling the German police. Goodwell's evasive behavior the other night confirmed that. Walter shook his head in a feeble attempt to wipe off his growing uneasiness. Even on his day off, he still thought about work.

In the evening, Walter strolled to the *Post* by himself, since Fritz lived in the opposite direction from him. The *Gasthaus* was beginning to get crowded. In the middle of the lounge stood a wood stove, its long stovepipe reaching to the chimney on the far end of the room. The smell of sauerkraut and pork chops wafted from the direction of the kitchen, mingling with cigarette smoke.

The *Stammtisch*—the regulars' table—was already fully occupied because no one wanted to miss anything. A line had formed at the bottom of the staircase that led to the dance floor upstairs. Walter got in between several giggling young girls and recognized Sonja, Fritz's sister, among them. Their petticoats brushed against his dress pants. They barely seemed old enough to be out of grade school, too young to draw his attention.

He paid the admission fee to the daughter of the house. Raking his fingers through his blond hair, he climbed the creaky steps to the second floor that generations of villagers had scaled before him. Upstairs, he scanned the room, which he knew best from the rabbit shows he had attended over the years. He crossed the uneven wooden dance floor to join Fritz, who waved at him from the opposite side of the room. Walter sank onto an empty chair and greeted his school friends Dieter, Kurt, and Michael. It had been a long time since they had all been together and there was lots of news to exchange. They had the courtesy not to ask about Roswitha, and Walter began to relax. It was good to be with his friends again.

When the band struck up *"Heit is Kerb,"* Walter turned around to watch Ingrid dance with her fair partner. She smiled at him when she passed Walter's table. Almost against his will, his eyes followed Ingrid back to her table, where she sat down next to a young man.

"Do you know the fellow next to Ingrid?" he asked Fritz.

"No, I've never seen him before," Fritz said. "Aren't you going to dance? Remember to dance with my little sister. You promised."

Walter winced. He didn't really want to dance with a young girl who would probably step on his feet, but he wanted to please his friend. At the other end of the table, near the window, he saw Marianne with several girlfriends. He inclined his head in her direction and asked Sonja to dance. The band played a fox-trot and after a few missteps, they soon fell into a rhythm together. Sonja's hand trembled slightly as he took her in his. Perhaps this was her first dance. He remembered his nervousness on the same occasion years ago and talked about village events to calm her.

As Walter returned Fritz's sister to her table, he glanced over at Marianne. She looked forlorn among the boisterous chatter of her friends. He cursed himself for doing it, but he squeezed between the chairs to ask Marianne for the next dance. She looked at him expectantly, and then whispered something to her friend.

The girl nodded so vigorously that her ponytail flapped back and forth. "Go ahead and dance. It won't do anyone any good if you just sit here and cry over your boyfriend."

Marianne rose and pushed some chairs aside. When Walter put his arm around her waist, he noticed that her eyes were red and swollen. He braced himself for the inevitable question.

"Have you seen Jeff since we talked?"

"No, I haven't seen him." At least he didn't have to lie, even though he left out the part about the Mannheim jail. How many times had he lain awake at night, dreaming of a day when he could hold Marianne in his arms, and she only talked about Jeff. How cruel life sometimes was! And yet, he felt sorry for her, alone as she was in her worry about Jeff.

"I guess I shouldn't have come," Marianne said. "I'm not a very cheerful partner tonight."

Neither am I, Walter thought. "I don't feel much like celebrating either." Suddenly, Walter could not wait for the round of three dances to end. Why had he have ever thought that holding Marianne in his arms would be a good idea? It was sheer torture.

The band struck up "Rosamunde" now.

Marianne sighed. "I'm going to miss this."

"Why, are you going away?" Walter said, pretending ignorance.

"If Jeff and I are getting married, I'll go to America with him."

"You're very sure about this, aren't you? What would you do if Jeff really killed that woman?"

Marianne shook her head. "I don't believe he did it. Do you think he did it?"

"No," Walter admitted. It would be a lot easier for him if Jeff was convicted of murder. Then Marianne would be free for him, wouldn't she?

"Then you have to help getting him acquitted."

"I'll do what I can," Walter said. "But I won't make any promises." He searched for a reason to stop talking about Jeff. "Have you asked Benno where he spends his evenings?"

"No, I haven't had a chance yet," Marianne said. "I don't want to make him suspicious."

They remained silent for the rest of the song and Walter escorted Marianne back to her table. His emotions in turmoil, he signaled Fritz to meet him downstairs. The lounge was packed and cigarette smoke hung in clouds over the crowd. The two friends had to stand at the counter while drinking their beer.

Fritz was an avid soccer player and they wiled away the time talking about their favorite club, the 1. FC Kaiserslautern. Since Germany had won the World Cup in 1954 with five players from Kaiserslautern, they had followed the club's every game.

More relaxed now, Walter gazed about the room. He froze. At a corner table, Ingrid was talking animatedly with Curly and Clark Gable. He finished his Parkbräu, excused himself to Fritz, and shoved his way through the crowd.

Sounding more confident than he felt, he said, "Hello, Ingrid. Didn't you promise me a dance tonight? Come on, let's go upstairs!"

Ingrid shot him an angry look. "I did nothing of the kind. Can't you see I'm busy right now?"

Was this the same girl who had smiled at him not long ago? Walter silently cursed his sister. He had promised his mother to keep an eye on her, but she was making it extremely difficult.

He touched her arm and said in a voice that could have cut glass, "Come on. They're playing my favorite song."

Ingrid flushed and rose reluctantly. "I'll be back," she said to the strangers.

Upstairs, she turned to Walter and hissed, "What did you do that for? You can be such a bore sometimes."

Walter placed his arm around his sister's waist and led her onto the dance floor. "Do you know who these men are? Have you met them before?"

"What business is it of yours? Did *Mama* put you up to this?"

Walter groaned. "Just answer my question: Have you seen them before?"

Ingrid hemmed and hawed. "I met them at the concert last Saturday."

"Promise me that you'll never see them again."

Ingrid stiffened in his arms. "Why?"

"Because I'm a police officer and my instinct tells me that those men are up to no good."

Ingrid glowered at him. "Ever since you joined that damn police academy, I can't have any fun anymore. You see crooks everywhere. Couldn't you be a plumber or something?"

"I'm just trying to help. What were you talking about with them?"

"That's really none of your business."

The music ended and Ingrid pried her hand from his to return to her table. At least she didn't head downstairs. Not right away. While he waited out the next dance round, two young girls took their seats at his table. He asked one of them, a mousy girl with shoulder-length hair, for the next dance, just to do something. They made small talk and he escorted her back to her chair.

The evening was not going as expected. His mind could not shut out Ingrid, Jeff, and the dead woman. Not to mention Marianne. He decided to join Fritz downstairs.

Fritz stood in a circle of his soccer pals and their girlfriends. "Come, Walter. We're going to our house for coffee and cake."

Walter agreed while the girls shrieked. He'd had enough of the dance anyway. He could not be his sister's keeper all the time and deserved to have some fun. Outside, the six young people linked arms with each other, taking up half the street and the sidewalk. They giggled and laughed as they passed along a bottle of wine. Walter felt a guilty pleasure as he laughed along with the others. After all, he did not want to get arrested by his own boss for nightly disturbances.

At Müller's house, Fritz opened the living room door with a flourish. Walter sank onto the three-seater couch, which looked more comfortable than the cocktail armchairs with their low backs. Fritz reached up to the top of the display case cabinet and carried a sugar cake with streusel topping to the kidney table. A girl with a blond ponytail offered to cut it while another girl began to boil water for the coffee.

Walter looked around the room. "I didn't know you had a television set."

Fritz grinned. "We got it last week. I'm surprised you haven't heard yet. I think my mother is telling the whole village about it. Personally, I'd rather go to a theater to see a movie."

Walter agreed. Not that his family could afford a television set anyway. The girls brought in cups of steaming coffee and Fritz admonished them to be quiet.

"Your mother will be very surprised tomorrow when she sees that her cake is gone," said the blond girl.

Fritz waved his hand through the air. "She bakes too many cakes anyway. I don't think she'll miss one."

Long after midnight, Walter looked at his watch. It was time to go home since he had to work in the afternoon.

The streets were quiet until he approached the *Post*. He could hear the band a block away, attempting a waltz. An intoxicated man tottered down the front steps of the *Gasthaus*. In a gap between two houses, a young couple exchanged fervent kisses. Walter quickened his steps. He did not want to see couples in embrace when he was alone again. When would he ever find a girl who would kiss him and go to a dance with him?

Farmer Engelmann's cows were still awake, and their moos reached Walter on his lonely walk. They sounded upset and he wondered whether one of them was calving. What an inconvenient time it would be to have a calving cow!

He did not think much of it when he heard footsteps on the sidewalk behind him. On a night like this, almost everyone in the village who wasn't a child or old person was out and about.

The steps sped up. Before Walter had time to turn around and see who caught up with him, he felt a sharp pain in his left upper arm. He winced while he clutched his arm. Blood began to trickle through the fabric of his dress coat. He pulled his hand away and gaped at the liquid.

His mind reeled, telling him to pursue his attacker. Instead, he dropped onto Lang's front steps. He remained on the spot, unable to command his legs to move. The footsteps grew distant now, crossing the street and disappearing into the dark. His boss would be furious with him for not acting faster. Walter moaned as his arm began to throb.

The thought of the chief finally calmed him down. What would his boss do if he were in this situation? Walter pulled a handkerchief from his pocket and pressed it on the wound. He decided to walk the two blocks to Dr. Theobald's house, supporting his left arm with his right hand.

Not long after Walter rang the doorbell, the hallway light came on. Either the doctor was used to nightly visitors or he was a light sleeper.

"Walter? What happened to you?" his family doctor said as he ushered him in. He opened the door to his office and walked ahead of Walter, turning on lights on the way. Walter winced as he took off his dress coat. He didn't know what hurt more, his injured arm or the fact that his best coat was ruined.

Walter had to sit on the examination table while the doctor inspected the wound. "Hm, you're lucky. The blade must have slipped off without cutting too deep. I'll clean out the wound and bandage it. You'll have to wear your arm in a sling for a couple of days." He rummaged through a medicine cabinet. "I hate the fair. Every year, I have to patch up fellows who start fighting when they had too much to drink."

"You think I was fighting with someone?" Walter burst out. "I was attacked from behind!"

Walter winced as the doctor cleaned the wound.

"I'm afraid I'll have to stitch it up," Dr. Theobald said.

"All right, but can you call Chief Kleber first?"

The doctor went to his desk to make the call. "Your boss will be over in a few minutes. Now, this will hurt a bit."

It wasn't the first time for Walter to receive stitches. Once as a boy, he and his friends had played in a war-damaged house and he had fallen through a floor. He flinched as the needle entered his skin. The doctor tied up the thread when the doorbell rang.

"What happened?" Chief Kleber asked with visible concern.

Walter told him what had occurred on his way home.

"So you didn't see your attacker at all?"

Walter shook his head. "No, by the time I got over my surprise and turned around, he had disappeared without a trace. He was probably hiding in someone's courtyard until I was out of sight."

Chief Kleber pulled a notebook out of his pocket and began to take notes.

"Do you remember when you left the *Post*?"

"Not exactly, but I think it was between midnight and one o'clock. I spent a couple of hours at a friend's house before walking home alone."

"And you have no idea who could have attacked you?"

"I did see the two blokes at the *Post* that I saw at the *Luna* bar the other night. Maybe they recognized me and decided that I was a threat to them. We need to keep an eye out for those men."

Chief Kleber wrote down the descriptions Walter gave him.

"You better get home, son," he said. "Can you stand up?"

Walter rose. "Yes."

"I'll drive you."

Walter was grateful for the ride. He had had enough excitement for one night.

"I'll patrol the village a couple of times after I drop you off," Chief Kleber said. "But I think the culprits have probably disappeared by now."

"I think so too. Thank you anyway."

Chief Kleber eyed him closely. "Are you able to work tomorrow?"

Walter stared at his boss. In all the commotion, he had forgotten that he was supposed to direct traffic during the mock sermon. "I don't know, but I think so. The doctor said I should put my arm in a sling, but my legs are all right."

"I'll check on you tomorrow before your shift begins. I'll have to write a report anyway."

A police chief was never really off duty, Walter mused as he entered the house. Just like he himself seemed to be working all the time nowadays. The handrails were on his left, so he had to use his right arm to grab them. At Ingrid's door, he listened intently but could not detect any sound. He slept fitfully because his throbbing arm woke him up. Finally, around four o'clock, he heard someone opening the front door and sneaking up the stairs. Ingrid was home at last.

10

He woke up as the eye-watering smell of horseradish assaulted his nostrils. Like all homemakers in Lauterbach, Walter's mother clung to tradition and served beef and horseradish at every village fair he could remember. The day before, she had prepared the beef broth and the bone marrow dumplings she would serve with spelt soup.

After washing up in the tiny bathroom, Walter struggled to get his arm into a checkered shirt. It was no use to wear a good shirt with his arm in a sling. It would be difficult enough to put on his uniform shirt later. He made a makeshift sling out of a towel before entering the kitchen.

His mother dipped a spoon into the horseradish. After tasting it, she glanced over her shoulder. "What happened to your arm?" she shrieked. "Did you get into a fight?"

Walter rolled his eyes. "Why would I get into a fight? I'm supposed to break up fights. No, I was attacked from behind on the way home."

He sunk on a kitchen chair and began to tell her what happened. The dull sound of the doorbell interrupted his story.

"Can you open the door?" his mother asked. "That must be Uncle Karl and Aunt Hedwig."

"Or it could be the chief."

Moments later, he returned to the kitchen with Chief Kleber in tow. "*Guten Morgen*, Frau Hofmann," he said before turning to Walter. "I patrolled the village twice but did not see anything unusual."

"That doesn't surprise me. There are so many farmyards and gaps he could have hidden in until I was gone. Did you drive by the fairground?"

"Yes, and all the lights were out. I'll write a report, of course." Chief Kleber stroked his chubby fingers through his pomaded hair. "Are you able to work today?"

"As long as I don't have to use my arm."

Chief Kleber laughed. "That's my boy. Frau Hofmann, you can be proud to have a son like him."

"Oh, I am," Elfriede Hofmann said.

"I'll be at the police station this afternoon, in case you need me," the chief said. "But first, I'm going home to have lunch."

Walter went to feed his rabbits, as best he could with one good arm. Ingrid had finally gotten up when he returned to the kitchen. Her disheveled hair smelled of smoke. She squinted at the sunlight that shone in from the window.

"Someone had a good time," he said in an edgy voice.

"Not as good a time as I could have had without you," Ingrid retorted.

"Why, what happened?" their mother chimed in.

Walter did not want to alarm her about Curly and Clark Gable, especially since he only had a hunch about them. "Nothing. Ingrid just doesn't like me being around when she goes out, that's all."

"He's your big brother and you're supposed to respect him," Mother Hofmann chided her daughter. "And now, help me set the table. Your uncle and aunt will be here any minute."

The Hofmanns had no dining room, so Ingrid put a white tablecloth on the kitchen table and began setting the good, gold-rimmed china on it. She was about to put a plate in front of Walter when she screeched, "What happened to you?"

Walter sighed. "I should have waited to tell *Mama* about it. Now I have to repeat myself."

To be out of everybody's way, Walter went to the small living room next door and pretended to read the paper. Ingrid cast defiant glances at him while she worked, and he wondered why. She was becoming more and more rebellious and he hoped that she would not get into serious trouble. After all, he was a police officer and did not want a scandal in the family. Most importantly, he didn't want her to get hurt.

Long before the parade assembled, Walter was at his post at the intersection of three roads: Hauptstraße, Neudorfer Straße, and Reichenbacher Straße. Traffic consisted of more pedestrians and bicyclists than cars. Occasionally, he redirected a bus with his uninjured arm. But now and then, an American road cruiser passed by and Walter gaped after it. He would have given a day's pay for a ride in one of those cars. Sure, Jeff had given him rides to the base, but it wasn't enough. How great it would be to go on a trip to nowhere in particular for an entire day! He could envision the stares of people in every village they passed through. Someday, he vowed. Someday. Until then, he directed traffic for Isettas and Volkswagen Beetles.

The villagers lined up along the road, wearing suits and dresses. Some of them cast furtive glances at Walter's arm sling. They all came to watch the passing of the fair pole. Blaring trombones and the dull sound of trumpets signaled that the parade was approaching. The mayor and his wife sat in the base commander's Buick Skylark convertible, followed by the mock pastor and his cupbearer in Farmer Engelmann's coach. Wearing a cutaway and top hat, the pastor for a day waved at his parishioners. For generations now, he had been part of the ritual of spoofing church authorities. An important criterion for choosing the mock pastor was his ability to hold a drink.

The horses looked festive with their red ribbons, but that did not stop them from bombarding the asphalt with droppings. The fair boys carried the fair pole with pitchforks, the girls following behind them.

Walter chuckled when he saw Ingrid step aside to avoid a pile of horse dung that laid in the middle of the road. He turned serious when he noticed her eyes scanning the audience as if she were looking for somebody. Who could she be looking for?

With bangs, chimes, and drums, the musical society rounded out the parade. The parade goers followed on their heels, walking in the middle of the street to the *Post*, which was just a block away from Walter's intersection. He could hear cheers when the tree was finally secured to clamps at the edge of the *Post*.

No matter how much he strained his ears, Walter could not comprehend the words of the mock sermon in which the mock pastor poked fun at village life during the past year in the form of rhymes. Traffic was light because almost everyone was at the *Gasthaus*. Walter was pacing around when a white Ford Taunus approached the intersection. At the steering wheel sat Curly. Walter kept a stoic face. Curly tried to turn right, in the direction of the crowd, and Walter pointed straight ahead. Shifting his head away from Walter, Curly hesitated for a moment. Without looking at Walter, he drove off in the direction Walter had shown him.

With his right arm, Walter pulled a piece of paper out of his uniform pocket and used his injured arm as a writing desk. He jotted down the license plate number before putting the paper back in his pocket. He was sorry that Curly recognized him. Now that Curly knew that Walter was a policeman, he would probably avoid him. But then again, he might stay away from Ingrid, too.

At the end of the speech, the crowd headed past Walter toward the fairground. Children pulled their parents along to be the first on the merry-go-round or at the roasted almond stall.

"Hello, Walter." Uncle Karl's voice came from Walter's side. He smiled as he whirled around. Uncle Karl had been his favorite among his three uncles because he always made jokes.

"Are you going to the fairground?" Uncle Karl asked.

"Might as well. My duties here are over," Walter said.

Uncle Karl sniffled. "I forgot my handkerchief. Can I borrow one from you?"

Walter reached into his pocket. "Here, I have an extra one."

"What happened to your arm?"

"It's a long story. I'll tell you all about it over coffee. Where is Aunt Hedwig?"

"She was cold, so she went home with your mother," Uncle Karl said. "Are you going to the dance again tonight?"

Walter shook his head. "No, I have to work tomorrow. And besides, I couldn't dance with this arm anyway."

They stood in line at the confectioneries and Uncle Karl bought a dozen *Mohrenköpfe* for his sister's family. Walter licked his lips. Although he was grown up, he always looked forward to eating these chocolate-covered whipped egg whites. Uncle Karl returned to the Hofmanns' house with his treasure while Walter wandered around the fairground. He greeted every face he recognized, and there were quite a few. Most families had company since the village fair was the most important day of the year in the Palatinate. Walter stopped near the chain carousel to talk to Dieter and his younger brother while glancing around. He saw Molnar working the command station of the carousel. Mielke was absent.

Before returning home, Walter entered the police station, where Chief Kleber presided over a pile of files.

"How was your shift today?"

"Pretty quiet. There was something I wanted to tell you, though. The man with the curly hair, he drove by in a white Ford Taunus. I wrote down the license plate number. Here it is."

He reached into his pocket and came up empty. "Oh no, it must have fallen out when I gave my uncle a handkerchief."

Chief Kleber, his pencil poised over a notepad, rolled his eyes. "Do you remember what the plate number was?"

"All I remember is that it was KL—Kaiserslautern—and C. I forgot the numbers, though." Chiding himself for his carelessness, Walter banged his right fist on the chief's desk.

"Careful; you might get hurt again," Chief Kleber said. "I'll call in the information anyway. How many cars of that description can there be in the county? It might take a little longer to get an answer, but it's not impossible."

Walter admitted that the chief was right. He filled out some paperwork before going home. His arm was throbbing by now. He was glad when he could take off his uniform and put on an old flannel shirt.

After he finished his cake, Uncle Karl and Aunt Hedwig listened spellbound to his tale.

"I must say your village fairs are much more exciting than ours," his uncle said. "But I never thought your job would affect your personal life."

"Neither did I," Elfriede Hofmann said. "Why in the world would anyone attack you?"

"It was probably some drunk," Walter said. "Don't worry about it."

I can only guess that I'm getting a bit too close to the truth, he thought. *I just wish I knew what the truth is.*

11

Chief Kleber seemed unusually thoughtful when Walter arrived for work the next morning. "Walter, I've been thinking about the attack on you, and the car you saw yesterday. Tell me everything you did on Saturday night. Don't worry. I won't tell your mother about it."

Walter told his boss about dancing with Marianne and later seeing Ingrid with Curly and Clark Gable in the lounge.

"That's very interesting," Chief Kleber said. "One of them is the same man you saw yesterday in a white car, right?"

"Yes."

"Why don't you just ask your sister who he is?"

Walter snorted. "Believe me, I've tried. But she clams up the moment I ask her who she's talking to. I don't even see much of Ingrid anymore because of my work hours."

Chief Kleber steepled his fingers. "Today is the *Stammtisch* at the *Post* and the *Traube*. It wouldn't surprise me if one of these men showed up. Let's go for a ride."

Walter gave him a quizzical look. "We're both in uniform. Don't you think we would cause a lot of attention?" After all, the traditional get-together attracted most males in the village.

"First, we both have to go home and change into civilian clothes."

Walter still hesitated.

"Come on. I'll buy you a drink."

Walter usually didn't question his boss's decisions, but this time he made an exception. "Drinking on duty?"

"Well, we can drink a Spezi or a Cola. If anyone laughs at you, you can tell them the doctor told you not to drink alcohol."

"Actually, he did tell me to avoid alcohol."

"See, there you go. I'll radio Schlosser to come back from patrol and man the station."

Chief Kleber went upstairs to his apartment and returned wearing a brown street suit. When Schlosser arrived at the station, Walter followed his boss to the police car and sat in the passenger seat.

"I didn't see Mielke yesterday when I was at the fairground," Walter said. "Molnar was at the controls of the ride, but I didn't see the other man."

"You'd think that would be his job. Perhaps he was on break," Chief Kleber said. "You're becoming a very observant police officer."

For the first time in days, Walter was proud of himself. "I was attacked. I have a personal interest in finding my attacker, and possibly Roswitha's killer."

"So you think they're all connected?" Chief Kleber asked.

"I have reason to believe so. First, I'm in the middle of a murder investigation, and then I run into the same suspicious character everywhere I go. I don't like it that he knows Ingrid."

"We'll see if there is indeed a connection," Chief Kleber said.

"Another thing that worries me is that my mother saw a stranger at our front door the other day," Walter continued.

Chief Kleber drummed his fingers on the steering wheel. "That troubles me. Your mother is alone all day unless you work mid-shift. Did she describe him?"

"She said he was shorter than I am and had black hair with lots of pomade."

"Are you sure he was not the driver of the white Ford Taunus?"

"Yes, I'm sure. The Ford driver is taller than I am."

"Have you heard anything about your American friend?"

"Nothing," Walter said in a toneless voice. "It seems to me as if the military is not telling us the truth about the accusations against Jeff. They're holding something back, I'm almost sure of it."

"Yes, it appears so."

Walter's mother was not at the house when he went inside to change. Perhaps she was out on an errand, he comforted himself. He could not worry about his mother all the time, especially when the stranger she saw the other day had not done anything suspicious.

Chief Kleber headed for the *Post*, but parked the car in a side street. After all, they didn't want to draw any attention to themselves. Boisterous laughter carried out into the street when they approached the Gasthaus. "We're going to be the only ones drinking Cola and Fanta mixed," Walter said.

Kleber laughed. "Don't worry. If anybody even notices, they'll probably think you're keeping me company."

The male crowd in the lounge was indeed well past their first drinks. Chief Kleber and Walter had to sit on barstools until a table became available. Walter did not like to be so exposed, but he did have a good view of the entire lounge. He scanned the room carefully while pretending to make small conversation with his boss.

"Do you see him?" Chief Kleber whispered.

"No."

After they sat at a vacated table, Fritz, Dieter, and Michael briefly joined them. They were about ready to pay when Walter jerked and turned his head imperceptibly toward the front door. The chief's gaze followed Curly to a corner table where Walter's classmate, Heinz Wolf, soon joined him. The two young men stuck their heads together and talked.

"That's odd," Walter said. "I haven't seen Heinz in ages and all of a sudden he shows up wherever I go. I didn't even see him come in."

"Maybe he came in through the back door."

Curly finished his drink and left through the front entrance.

Chief Kleber handed Walter a five-mark coin and said, "You pay for our drinks and I'll follow him. If he sees you, he'll get suspicious."

"What do I do now?"

"Stay here and watch Heinz. In fact, why don't you go over there and join him? You used to go to school together, didn't you?"

"Yes…"

"Well, that gives you an excuse. Come on, I have to go before I lose that man."

The chief hastened away, leaving Walter alone. He felt uneasy about his mission because he never had much contact with Heinz. Yet he realized that the chief was right. They would not learn much by simply observing. He grabbed his drink and ambled to Heinz's table.

Feigning cheerfulness he didn't feel, Walter said, "Hello, Heinz, how's it going? Mind if I sit here?"

Heinz jerked back. "Sure, why not?"

"What have you been up to since grade school?" Walter said after he sat down.

Heinz's eyes shifted about the room, averting Walter's gaze. "Oh, this and that. I was an apprentice with Baker

Jung, but I decided that I didn't want to get up at two o'clock in the morning for the rest of my life. And then I worked in construction when the base was built."

Heinz tapped his finger nervously on the table. Walter ignored the gesture.

"Excuse me, I have to go now," Heinz said and rose.

Walter cursed himself for following his boss's advice. Perhaps he could have found out more if he had simply observed whether anyone approached Heinz. Well, it couldn't be helped now. He paid with the chief's money and left because he knew he would not learn anything else at the *Gasthaus*.

Since it was not too far from the police station, he decided to walk across the fairground. Today, the fairground belonged to the children, who were off from school. Adults were easy to spot and he was not too surprised when he saw Heinz standing by the chain carousel. Walter pretended to look at the confectionary stand displays while observing Heinz out of the corner of his eye. The wave swing had reached its full speed, with little legs dangling from the chairs as the carousel's motion whirled them through the air.

Walter's former schoolmate stood among the kids and parents who waved at the lucky riders. What was he doing? Was he signaling someone that he was there or was he waiting for someone? When Heinz finally moved, Walter followed at a distance. He almost tripped over a pigtailed little girl who was balancing cotton candy in her hand.

"Watch where you're going," he scolded her and she started to cry.

Walter silently cursed because he had no time to waste. He had to find out what Heinz was up to. Was it possible that Heinz had attacked him on Saturday night?

He apologized to the girl, gave her a ten-Pfennig coin, and hastened away. Heinz had headed in the direction of the trailers, but when Walter entered Alte Gasse, he did not see Heinz anywhere. Pretending to be a passerby, Walter walked along Molnar and Mielke's trailer. He pressed his ear against the side of the trailer and listened. Indeed, he could detect two low voices inside. One belonged to Heinz and the other sounded like Mielke. Walter strained his ear, but he could not hear what they said.

He looked around for a hiding place and glimpsed a beige Goggomobil a few houses away. He strode to the small car and folded his frame to hide behind the tiny vehicle. The car was parked in front of a white house with two windows facing the street. Walter stiffened when a curtain on one of the windows moved and a woman's face appeared. He shook his head at her to signal her to move away. She paused before a look of recognition brightened her face. He breathed a sigh of relief when she followed his order.

Just when Walter thought his legs would cramp from crouching, Heinz descended out of the trailer and walked past the Goggomobil. Walter crawled along the side so Heinz wouldn't see him. When Heinz disappeared around a corner, Walter finally stood up. He followed his schoolmate when suddenly his calf spasmed. He rubbed his leg until the pain subsided and limped along. As he rounded the corner, Heinz had vanished. Walter didn't hear the grind of a car engine, so Heinz must have disappeared on foot. He cursed while he hobbled back to the Goggomobil. On a whim, he rang the doorbell of the house where the face had appeared. A woman on the verge of middle age opened the door.

"*Guten Tag*," Walter said and showed his badge. "Do you look out of your windows very often?"

The woman blushed. "Yes."

"I'd like to ask you a favor. Did you see the young man who just left the carnival trailer?"

She nodded.

"If he shows up again, could you come to the police station and let us know? Or send a kid if you can't come yourself."

"*Ja.* I will."

"Thank you. *Auf Wiedersehen.*" It was time to leave before Mielke spotted him. He chose several side streets to avoid the fairground. The chief was dressed in his uniform again when Walter arrived at the police station. Walter told him his findings and the fact that he lost Heinz again.

"I think it's time to search that trailer," Chief Kleber said with a clipped voice. He grabbed the receiver to dial the local court's number. After he hung up, Walter asked, "Did you trace the American?"

The chief shook his head. "No. When I stepped out of the *Gasthaus,* four tipsy men waited to get in. By the time I got around them, I couldn't see a trace of the American."

Now Walter understood why his boss hadn't scolded him. He had lucked out himself. How could those men vanish without a trace? It was as if the earth swallowed them up. He hoped it wouldn't take too long before they got the search warrant. He sat down and reached into his pocket. "Here is the change from this morning."

"Keep it. Consider it your fair money."

Walter smiled. Before he earned his own money, his aunts and uncles had all given him money so he could buy some sweets and ride the carousels.

"Any news on Roswitha's case?" he asked finally.

"Yes, I almost forgot. The coroner has released the body and the funeral has been scheduled in Reichenbach on Wednesday at two o'clock."

"I'd like to go," Walter heard himself say. He was not particularly fond of funerals, especially after his grandfather's burial last year. But he felt a connection to the poor woman whose body he had found in the moor.

"I want to go, too," Chief Kleber said. "I doubt that the killer would be dumb enough to show up at the funeral, but one never knows. Stranger things have happened."

"So, there are no new leads about the killing?" Walter asked.

"None whatsoever. I talked with Junker this morning and he has nothing new to report. There are no fingerprints and her purse is still missing. You've showed her picture in every bar around here and no one came forth to report anything. It seems like we're stuck."

Walter sat back in his chair, rapping his pencil on his desk.

"Stop it. You're making me nervous," the chief scolded him.

"Sorry," Walter said. "I can think better this way." The investigation of the first violent crime case he had ever worked on was not going well at all. He considered all the facts. Heinz was behaving very suspiciously. And Clark Gable showed up everywhere Walter went. Most troubling, though, was the fact that Curly and Clark Gable had talked to Ingrid. They were now aware that Walter knew her.

"I think it's time to pay a visit to Heinz's parents," Walter declared.

The chief nodded, wiping a bead of sweat from his upper lip. "Take Schlosser along."

"Are you all right?" Walter asked.

"Just a little stomach ache. I think I ate too much horseradish yesterday," Chief Kleber said. "What are you two waiting for? Go on, I'll be fine."

Walter cast a worried look at his boss and put on his coat. It was no use arguing with the chief, but he did not look well at all.

Out of earshot of their boss, Schlosser said, "I think we should take the car. That way, we can be back faster in case the chief needs us."

"Excellent idea. Can you drive?"

"Is your arm still giving you trouble?" Schlosser asked.

"It hurts less than yesterday, of course, but I would like to take it easy on it today."

Heinz lived in a one-story stone house on Neudorfer Straße near the edge of town. The entrance was on the side of the building, which gave the officers an opportunity to look around. Walter whistled softly when he saw a Ford Taunus with German plates parked in the courtyard. He jotted down the license number on a little notepad. A barn and several sheds surrounded the big courtyard. All were in a state of neglect and had not seen a broom for a while.

Walter turned the doorbell to the house with his good hand while Schlosser knocked on the wooden door.

"*Ja?*" A woman in her early fifties opened the door. She wore a dark housedress and a black apron. Now Walter remembered. Arno Wolf, her husband, had been killed during the last days of World War II while his unit was trying to destroy a Rhine bridge. Apparently, Frau Wolf had been wearing black ever since then.

"Is Heinz at home?" Walter asked.

"No." She wiped her hands on her apron. "What do you want of him?"

"Nothing. I just saw him at the *Post* this morning and forgot to tell him something." He hoped that she didn't catch the lie.

"I haven't seen him since breakfast."

Walter relaxed. His had hoped that Heinz was not at home. He pulled his badge out of his pocket and asked, "May we come in?"

Frau Wolf eyed the officers suspiciously. "Is anything wrong?"

"No. We just would like to ask you a few questions," Schlosser chimed in.

She opened the door all the way and pointed to the partially open kitchen door. A fire crackled in the coal stove and several pieces of underwear hung drying on a rack above it. The kitchen cabinet was at least fifty years old and needed a coat of paint. Walter remembered that he had visited here once as a boy. Back then, it had been tidy. Now, dishes were stacked in the enamel sink and the yellowed lace curtains in the window had not been washed for quite a while. Walter wondered whether years of widowhood had beaten down Frau Wolf. Or perhaps she did not get any help from her only son.

Walter and Schlosser sat down on shaky kitchen chairs that groaned under their weight. They motioned Frau Wolf to join them.

"Did you see Heinz on Saturday afternoon, a week ago?" Schlosser asked.

Frau Wolf asked, "What's this all about?"

"I saw Heinz on the evening of that day when I was on base to attend a concert," Walter said.

"Oh yes, the concert. He told me that he wanted to go there."

"What we would like to know is: What did he do in the afternoon before the concert?"

Frau Wolf knitted her brows. "I don't think he told me that, but he wasn't at home. He doesn't tell me much anymore these days. One would think that a grown son would be a big help for a widow, but that's not true. Most days, he doesn't even bring in firewood for me. But wait! He did bring home some firewood that day. Said he found it in the moor."

Walter pricked up his ears. "Did he say where he found it?"

She cast a defiant look at him. "I didn't ask him. It's only wood, after all. Why would I care where he found it?"

Walter decided to change the subject. "I saw a car in your courtyard. Who does it belong to?"

"That's Herr Johnson's car. He's renting a room from us upstairs."

"Does he have a first name? And what does he do for a living?" Schlosser asked.

"His first name is Frank. He told me he works as a civilian on the air base."

"What does he look like?"

Her features softened. "He's a handsome man, with brown hair and a mustache. Very handsome."

Walter had no doubt that he was the man who looked like Clark Gable. Why did he meet Heinz in Gasthauses and bars instead of in his own room? Unless they were just out getting a drink. But something about the way both Heinz and Johnson avoided the police troubled Walter. There could be only one reason why they met in public: Heinz's mother. They were taking a big risk meeting in public, but perhaps Heinz was more scared of his mother than he was of discovery.

"Where does Heinz work?" Walter asked.

A cloud traveled across his mother's face. "He finished his apprenticeship with Baker Jung, but has not had a steady job after that. He worked in construction on base for a while. But he says that he will get his big break soon, and then he'll buy me an electric stove and a refrigerator." Tears trickled down her cheek. "Where would he get the money to buy me these things? Is he in trouble?"

"We honestly don't know, Frau Wolf," Schlosser said. At least Heinz had told Walter the truth at the *Gasthaus*. The officers took their leave and asked Frau Wolf to report anything unusual.

When they returned to the police station, they found Chief Kleber doubled over on a cot in the holding cell. "What's the matter?" Schlosser and Walter cried in unison.

"I'm glad you're back," the chief moaned. "One of you better take me to the hospital right away."

Schlosser stepped closer to feel the chief's forehead. It glistened with sweat. "Can you walk to the car?"

The chief nodded meekly. "You stay here to man the station and Walter can drive me."

Apparently, the chief had forgotten about Walter's injury. Schlosser offered to change places, but Walter felt well enough to fulfill his boss' wish. Schlosser wrapped an arm around the chief's back and placed him gently on the passenger seat. With siren wailing and blue light flashing, Walter hurried to the small hospital in Reichenbach.

Walter was sitting on a braided chair and flipping through an old *Revue* magazine when a nun approached him.

"Herr Kleber has appendicitis," she said. "They're taking him into surgery right now. Good thing you brought him in time."

"Yes, I'm glad I did."

She said, "There is nothing for you to do right now. You might as well go back to work."

Walter rose. "When he wakes up, tell him I let his wife know what happened."

"I will, son. Good evening."

In the car, Walter radioed Schlosser the news before turning the key in the ignition. He was relieved that he had arrived at the hospital before the appendix might have burst. If only Schlosser and he had not believed the chief's protestations that he was fine. How dedicated he must be to his job to work through such pain. Walter wondered whether he would ever be so diligent. Only time would tell.

Much slower now, Walter drove back to the station. As he passed the *Post*, he saw several young men in various stages of intoxication standing outside the Gasthaus. The fair had not turned out as Walter had expected, but then nothing in life ever did. Perhaps he would have better luck finding a girl during the carnival season. In the near future, he had to prepare Max for the rabbit show.

"Does Frau Kleber know that her husband is in the hospital?" he asked Schlosser after briefing him on the chief's condition.

"She wasn't home when I knocked on her door," Schlosser said. "You better go upstairs and tell her."

Frau Kleber beckoned Walter to sit at the kitchen table. A small vase of asters sat on the flowery oilcloth. The furniture was so shiny, he could almost see his reflection in it. What a difference to the Wolf house! But then, Herr Kleber was a police chief and Frau Wolf a poor widow with a shiftless son.

Frau Kleber put a piece of marble cake in front of Walter and listened to his story. "I'll have to pack a bag for him," she said after she had regained her composure.

"Would you like me to drop it off at the hospital?"

She paused for a moment and shook her head. "No, I'll take it on the bus tomorrow. Visiting hours are over for today anyway. You must be tired now, what with the village fair and your injury and all."

Walter suppressed a yawn. Yes, he was tired. Since the knifer's attack, he had not had a quiet moment to himself. He rose and thanked Frau Kleber for the cake.

At the front door, she said to him, "My husband thinks highly of you. Has he ever told you that?"

"Yes," Walter said. Many of his friends worked in factories. They knew when their shift ended, but they did not have the satisfaction of making a difference that Walter's job provided.

"I called the station in Reichenbach to let them know that Chief Kleber has appendicitis and will be out sick for a while," Schlosser said. "They promised to ask around for help."

Walter dialed the Air Police number and gave them the license number of the Ford in Frau Wolf's courtyard. Better to err on the side of caution.

There was no news about Jeff. He felt a pang of guilt that he hadn't thought about his friend all day. But who could blame him for that?

"Go home, boy," Schlosser said. "The next shift arrives in a few minutes anyway."

Walter shot him a thankful look.

At home, he smacked his lips when he learned his mother had leftovers for him. During dinner, he told her what happened to Herr Kleber.

"So you and Schlosser have to work by yourselves now?" she asked.

"I hope not. We're supposed to get help from one of the other stations in the area. Between the murder case and the visit of the Secretary of Defense, there is no way that we can handle all the work alone."

"I fed your rabbits this evening, so you don't have to worry about that," Elfriede Hofmann said.

"Thanks. My arm is still throbbing a bit. I'll feed them tomorrow morning before I leave."

"You look worn out," Walter's mother said. "I think they're working you too hard at this job."

Walter gave a wry smile. "It's not just the job, it's the nightlife. I had better go to bed early tonight. The past week has been very exhausting. And dangerous." He touched his injured arm, causing his mother to wince. "Is Ingrid home yet?"

She shook her head. "No, and I'm getting a bit worried. I should have never allowed her to be a fair girl."

"How would you have stopped her? When she wants something, she won't shut up until she gets it."

"Oh, do I know it! That's why I let her go. Because otherwise, I would have never heard the end of it."

Walter put down his knife and fork. "Did you have a nice day?"

"Yes. Today is Berta's birthday and I went over to congratulate her. She invited me for coffee. They are very worried about the young man who rents a room from them. What's his name again?"

"Jeff. Yes, I'm worried, too. The military won't say why they arrested him. The longer I work on this case, the less I believe that Jeff had anything to do with the woman's death. I think there is something going on that the military isn't telling us." He rose from the table. "I'm beat. I'll check if Ingrid has a *Bravo* magazine I haven't read yet, and then I'm just going to sit down and read tonight."

Upstairs, he slowly opened Ingrid's door and looked around. She had taped a centerfold of Elvis Presley on the back of her door and an Elvis record lay on the turntable. That girl got carried away with her Elvis fascination. He hoped that it was just a phase she was going through. Walter groaned as he picked up one of the magazines on her bed. The cover showed Elvis Presley in uniform and helmet. The headline read, "Everything Revolves Around Elvis." He was about to put the magazine back when he changed his mind and took it downstairs. Who could blame the media for exploiting the arrival of the most famous rock star ever? It was a diversion from the brewing crisis over Berlin.

12

Walter rose from the breakfast table while his mother began to wash the dishes. He put on an old coat and stepped outside, whistling an Elvis tune. His arm felt much better now and he had slept soundly all night. When he approached the rabbit cages, the whistle died in his throat. Max was strung up by his hind legs from the frame of the cages. Clean cuts ran across his throat and belly. Blood had turned Max's black and white fur a crimson color. A pool of blood had collected on the ground underneath the body. Walter heard an inhuman cry that seemed to come from the center of the Earth. It took him a while to realize that he himself had let out the cry. He was shaking uncontrollably when he heard steps behind him. He raised his right hand.

"*Mama*, you better not come any closer. I don't want you to see this."

Too late. His mother had caught sight of the maimed rabbit. He touched her left shoulder to turn her away from the cage.

"Who could have done such a thing?" she let out between sobs.

Walter let go of her and clutched his good hand until the knuckles turned white. He was unable to move.

His mother pulled a handkerchief from her apron pocket and blew her nose noisily. "What do we do now?" Her head pointed at Max.

"Please, don't touch anything. There could be fingerprints somewhere. I need to go to the police station to get the camera and the fingerprint kit."

The commotion had aroused *Opa* Klink's interest. He peered over the fence that separated their properties. Walter decided to recruit his neighbor to help. The man had been a soldier in World War I and had probably slaughtered many a rabbit for a Sunday meal. He would not faint at the sight of a dead animal.

"Can you come over here? I want to make sure that no one goes near the cages until I get back from the station," Walter said.

"Why, yes," *Opa* Klink said. Walter inspected the cages without touching anything. The other three rabbits appeared to be unharmed. How had the killer known which one of his rabbits was his favorite? Only a few people in Lauterbach knew that. That could only mean one thing: Someone was watching him.

Anger and sorrow fought within Walter as he climbed the stairs to change into his police uniform. His *Opa* had been very proud of Max and had bred him especially for Walter. Now, with Max gone, it seemed as if the last link to his grandfather had been broken. By the time he was dressed, his anger over his unknown adversary had exceeded the sorrow over the loss of his pet. There would be time later, when he was alone, to mourn his pet.

He practically ran the few blocks to the police station where he found a strange officer pacing in the main office. He wore the same epaulette as Chief Kleber and held himself as erect as a broom handle. Walter disliked him from the start.

"You must be here to fill in for Chief Kleber while he is in the hospital," he said.

"Yes, I'm Chief Police Master Simmer. I'll be in charge here for a while."

Walter suppressed a cringe.

"I'm going to have to go back home," he said and explained that his pet rabbit had been killed.

"You're investigating the death of a rabbit?" Chief Simmer bellowed without hiding his contempt.

"Yes, I am," Walter said, forcing himself to sound calm even though he was trembling inside. "I believe there is a connection with the death of Roswitha Gregorius. You probably heard about that case?"

"Yes," Simmer said. "What is the status on that investigation, and why are you in charge? Aren't you a bit wet behind the ears for such a case?"

Walter's stomach contracted at the obvious bias. He breathed deeply. If the Criminal Police had asked for his assistance, this small-town officer would not have the authority to change their mind. He explained the status of the case to Chief Simmer.

"Very well, go and investigate the case of the dead rabbit," Chief Simmer said. "But don't take too long. I need you here."

Walter gathered the camera, some extra film, and a fingerprint kit. He was almost glad that he could escape the office for a while, if only the occasion had not been so close to his heart.

Opa Klink was still watching the crime scene like Walter had instructed him to do. Under different circumstances, Walter would have laughed about the shaving cream, which still enveloped his neighbor's left cheek while the right one was clean. But these were not usual circumstances.

Walter forwarded the film and took a few photos of Max from all angles, a task that took all his strength. It was useless to ask *Opa* if he had heard anything suspicious during the night. If Walter had slept through it, the diminished hearing of an old man would certainly not have detected any noises.

"Is Berta at home?" he asked the old man. It was still difficult for him to call the neighbors by their first name only, instead of adding Aunt or Uncle in front of it as all children did.

"No, she took the bus to Kaiserslautern to go shopping."

Walter sighed. For once, he could have used a nosy neighbor, and no one stepped forward. Maybe the noise he had heard the other day when he put Max on the grass was not in his imagination. It could have been Max's killer, who had scoped out the yard beforehand. The idea sent shivers down his spine. To think that the killer could have been near the house when his mother was alone at home! Or Ingrid. It occurred to him that he had not seen her for a while. He stepped into the house so that his mother didn't have to see the carcass.

"*Mama*, have you seen Ingrid this morning?"

Frau Hofmann poked her flushed face through the kitchen door. "Yes, she left for the bus when you were at the station. She looked so tired. I'm glad that the fair is finally over. I told her to come straight home from work and go to bed early tonight."

Glad that Ingrid was safe, Walter returned to the courtyard just as Schlosser rounded the corner.

"Good morning, Walter," Schlosser said out of habit. There was nothing good about this morning. "I heard what happened and came to help you."

Walter shot him a grateful look. "Have you met Simmer yet?"

"Yes," Schlosser said with a clipped voice. "A real drill sergeant, isn't he? Don't worry about him. In a few weeks, our chief will be back at the office." He approached the rabbit cages. "I'm sorry about your rabbit. I know you were looking forward to taking him to the show."

"Thank you. I know people will think it's only a rabbit, but Max was my pet." Walter's voice broke. "He was no less important to me than a dog is to his owner."

Schlosser put a hand on Walter's shoulder. "I know. I had a dog when I was a boy and it broke my heart when he died. I see you brought the fingerprint kit. Let's see what we can do."

"We probably won't get much from the cage locks," Walter cautioned. "My fingerprints are all over them. And then there are my mother's prints, of course."

"We'll take that into consideration. Did you take pictures yet?"

"Yes," Walter said. "I guess there's nothing more to do than cutting the ties and taking him into the station as evidence."

"I can do that." Schlosser inspected the other three cages. The rabbits were getting restless since they had missed their morning meal. "Too bad they can't talk. It would make our job easier today." He straightened up and looked around. "Have you spoken to any neighbors yet?"

Walter shook his head. "No. I know that Berta is not at home, and so I can't ask her until later today."

"Do you have any idea who could have done this?"

Grateful that his partner took the lead in the very personal investigation, Walter told him about Heinz's behavior and his ability to show up wherever Walter went.

Schlosser pursed his lips. "We have to ask all your neighbors if they heard anything unusual last night or this morning."

Half an hour later, they returned to the Hofmann yard without learning anything new. It appeared as if most people were either hung over from the fair or deaf. No one had heard Max's death screams. Not even Walter. Why had he chosen this night to sleep like a rock?

Walter's shoulders sagged in defeat. "I can't really blame them. I'm a policeman and I slept right through it. Of all people, you'd think that I would notice anything unusual."

"Don't blame yourself. If I had had a weekend like you had, I would have slept through it too. Between the fair, the attack on you, and the chief's appendicitis, you haven't had a quiet minute for a while."

Walter admitted that his partner was right. It was no use blaming himself, but he felt emotionally and physically drained. His opponent—if it was only one—had hurt him twice since Saturday night. It was beginning to look bad for Walter if he couldn't find the murderer soon.

In the meantime, *Opa* Klink returned from his basement with an old potato sack. He handed it to the police officers for Max's remains. They thanked him for his kindness and Schlosser placed the sack into the Beetle's trunk. Back at the police station, Walter called Detective Junker to give him a report of the events of the day before and the morning. Chief Kleber had kept in touch with the detective every day, but now that he was in the hospital, that job fell to Walter. As expected, Junker had no new information about the murder case, but mentioned that he would go to the poor woman's funeral. Walter thanked him for reminding him. He had forgotten about it.

He approached his temporary boss. "I'd like to go to a funeral this afternoon."

Chief Simmer's gaze darted from Schlosser to Walter before recognition set in. "You mean the murder victim?"

Walter nodded. "Chief Kleber thought it was a good idea and he would have gone himself, but unfortunately, he can't."

"I should go myself, but since you might see some acquaintances, go ahead and attend."

Walter walked back to his desk when he suddenly twisted around. "Have you heard from the court yet about a search warrant for a trailer?"

"No."

"In that case, you may want to get another warrant for Wiesenstraße 11."

"On what grounds?" Chief Simmer's eyes bored into Walter.

Schlosser, who was just putting a report with two carbon copies into the typewriter, paused. "I'm not as familiar with the Gregorius case as Walter is, but I agree that it's worth taking a good look at the Wolf house."

Walter related his encounters with Heinz, but the chief was unconvinced. "Suspicions are not enough reason to get a warrant. Give me more to work with."

13

Walter dropped off the film at the photo studio and made his daily round to the security guard on base. Luckily, the guard had nothing unusual to report. Walter debated whether he should stop at the Air Police building, but decided against it. He had enough to do today just staying afloat. On the way back to the station, he steered the Beetle to his mother's house. His mother always cooked for two people, just in case he had time to stop by.

They ate quietly until Walter pushed his plate away.

"I would like to go to the funeral too," his mother said.

"Why?"

"I feel so sorry for that poor woman who was all alone here and had no relatives. Someone ought to go to her funeral, don't you think?"

"Yes, you're right. There won't be many people there, other than the usual onlookers."

He floated the idea in his head. It was just like his mother to attend every funeral in the village. She had sewn herself a black skirt especially for funerals. "I'll pick you up in the police car in an hour. I can't drive directly to the graveyard, though, because I don't want anyone to see us arriving in a police car. If I want to see any suspects, I'll have to dress in civilian clothes."

"I'll lay out your suit and a shirt for you."

The charcoal suit had belonged to his uncle, who had outgrown it. The lean post-war years were over, but suits were still a big expense and passed down through the family if they did not fit anymore.

At the appointed hour, Walter returned home and put on his suit, quietly thanking Uncle Karl for being the same height. Neither he nor his mother had had time yet to take his damaged dress coat to a seamstress for repair.

Walter's mother sat upright in the car, visibly uneasy. "Are you sure it's all right for me to ride in a police car?" she asked several times.

"Yes, *Mama*, I asked for approval first. Now, remember what I told you: Keep your ears and eyes open today and tell me if you notice anything out of the ordinary."

The funeral chapel and cemetery were situated outside the village, surrounded by fields. Walter parked the car on the last side street before the cemetery.

"I'm sorry that you have to walk a bit, but I don't want any of the mourners to see the car," Walter said as he helped his mother out of the Beetle.

"That's all right, Walter. I'm used to walking."

As they walked along the cemetery wall, Walter traced his fingers over two bullet holes. The pockmarks of the war were slowly disappearing, but these attack signs of a low-flying aircraft had remained as a reminder of the past.

Mother and son entered the whitewashed chapel and took seats next to each other. It would cause fewer stares if he sat beside his mother, Walter had decided. As expected, there were few people at the service. The only person Walter recognized was Detective Junker, who had instructed Walter not to recognize him before the service began. There would be time to talk later.

Sergeant Green was not there. Perhaps he didn't know about the funeral or, if he did, he didn't want to cause a stir. A few women of the village sat on the hard chairs, women like Walter's mother who attended funerals because it was the custom to do so. Walter could barely glance at the closed coffin in a corner of the chapel. It was a reminder of his failure to find the killer. But then, the criminal investigation department had not fared better than he had. He reminded himself to be patient. Better to be slow and thorough than quick and careless.

The door opened and Frau Drucker, Roswitha's landlady, stepped inside. Walter rose and invited her to join them. She nodded and took a seat next to Walter.

"Thank you for coming," she whispered. "I know a lot of people disagreed with the way she lived, but she did not deserve to die that way."

"Not too many people do," Walter said, lowering his voice.

"Yes, of course. Harry could not get off from work to attend the funeral, but he would have felt awkward anyway. I promised to tell him where the grave is, so he can come visit it."

"That's very nice of him."

"I guess you haven't found her killer yet?"

Walter shook his head. "No. I was hoping he would come today. I guess I was wrong."

Frau Drucker placed her index finger over her mouth to silence Walter. The minister had entered the chapel. A small group of choir members, women in their fifties and sixties, began singing a hymn. After it ended, the minister gave a brief sermon about the young refugee woman who had come to the Palatinate to find a better life after war and relocation, only to be murdered in cold blood. Walter gripped the hymnbook until his knuckles turned white. He vowed to find the murderer before he could strike again. He looked around the room discreetly, wondering which one of the strangers could have killed a rabbit, let alone a human being.

Frau Drucker and Walter's mother accompanied the casket to the graveside to place a shovel of ground on the casket. Junker signaled Walter to join him right outside the cemetery wall.

"I'm glad you could come," the detective said. "Tell me again what happened since Saturday night."

Walter briefly described the attack on him, the stakeout of the trailer, and his visit at the Wolf house. His voice shook slightly when he mentioned his dead rabbit.

A breath of wind caused the men to shiver in their exposed location. Junker shook his head slowly. "Sounds like all you have right now are suspicions and intuitions. There's nothing here that would allow us to get a warrant."

Walter wished he could talk to his chief, but that was out of the question. He would be better off relying on himself to crack the case. He bid goodbye to Junker.

It was time to take his mother home. She and Frau Drucker were walking along the narrow paths that separated the rows of graves. The women were talking like old acquaintances.

"Frau Drucker has something to tell you," his mother said.

"There was a strange man at my door the other day," the landlady said.

A glimmer of hope rose in Walter. "What did he want?"

"He said he was an old friend of Fräulein Gregorius and wanted to pay her a visit. When I told him that she was dead, he looked sad. Still…" Her gaze wandered back to the fresh grave.

"Still what?"

"Well, don't you think it's strange that he showed up just a few days after she died when all this time she lived in my house, she never had a German visitor?"

Walter bit his lip in concentration. "Yes, that is very strange. Are you sure she never had any visitors besides soldiers?"

"I open the door, don't I? The soldiers who lived with her had a key, of course. But everybody else had to ring my doorbell."

Walter was becoming convinced that landladies were really detectives without pay. "What did this man look like?"

Frau Drucker furrowed her brows. "Hm, he was about thirty-five years old and had black hair."

"How tall was he?"

"He was almost as tall as you are."

"Is there anything else you remember about him?"

"He had an Eastern German accent, but it sounded different than Roswitha's. I'm sorry, that's all I can say. I told him she was dead and he left."

"That's all right, you did very well. If he shows up, or anyone else you don't know, please call our station or the criminal investigation unit. Is there a telephone in your neighborhood?"

Frau Drucker clutched her purse and nodded. "The *Gasthaus* and the post office have telephones. I better go now; I left Toni with my neighbor." She turned and stepped through the cemetery gate. Walter and his mother followed.

In the car, Walter asked, "The man who came to our door the other day, did he have an accent?"

Frau Hofmann said, "Now that Frau Drucker mentioned it, yes, he did have an accent. Of course, he only said a few words. That's why I forgot to mention it."

"Please don't tell anyone about this man."

After his mother disappeared behind their front door, he slammed his fist on the steering wheel. He had wasted an entire afternoon in the faint hope that the killer would show up. Not that attending a murder victim's funeral was a waste of time, but he had not made any headway.

The unknown visitor was a new lead, but he didn't have much to go on. The times were over when one knew all the village residents. Refugees from Eastern Europe and American soldiers were just two kinds of newcomers. The building of the base and several Army installations in the area had attracted jobseekers from other parts of West Germany as well.

Walter turned the Beetle around and drove to the police station because he still had to work a couple of hours. Simmer was on the phone when Walter closed the creaky front door, but Schlosser waved him over.

"I asked the chief's wife today how he's doing," he said. "She says he's cranky, but otherwise, he's doing fine."

Walter gave a wry smile. That sounded just like his boss.

"Did you learn anything at the funeral?" Schlosser asked.

Walter shook his head. "No. I should have known better than to think that the killer would show up at his victim's funeral."

Schlosser shrugged. "At least you tried."

Tried isn't good enough, Walter wanted to scream. He sat behind his desk and began typing the reports that had accumulated in his IN basket. He didn't even look up when the door opened.

"Walter," his mother said, gasping for air. Her navy between-seasons coat was unbuttoned. She was still wearing her apron, a sign that she had left the house in a hurry.

"*Mama*, what are you doing here?" Walter asked, fetching a chair for her.

"Ingrid has not come home from work yet, and I'm worried."

Walter's heart skipped a beat. Trying to appease his mother, he asked, "Are you sure she didn't stop somewhere, maybe at the tobacco store to buy a magazine or something? You know how much she loves magazines." He knew because he often borrowed her old magazines.

She shook her head. "No, I went in and asked Frau Albert from the tobacco store. She says she hasn't seen her at all this week."

Walter glanced around the office. Chief Simmer gave him a look that said he was not troubled about a teenage girl who did not come home on time. At least Schlosser's face showed deep concern. Walter desperately tried to think of the right questions to ask without begging for help from his colleagues. "What time does the bus get here?"

"The bus should have dropped her off half an hour ago. It would take her only five minutes or so to walk home from the bus stop."

Walter grabbed a notepad and jotted down notes. The phone rang and Schlosser answered it. He listened intently and jumped up. "There was a traffic accident on *Reichenbacher Straße*. I'll take the motorbike to investigate it. You take care of your mother."

The door closed behind his partner and Walter was on his own. Even if Chief Simmer had offered help, he doubted that he would have accepted it. He stared into space, unable to think straight. After all the excitement of the fair, he would have thought that his sister was too tired to go out. What if, indeed, something had happened to her?

"Tell me all the places she could have stopped at after getting off the bus," he said to his mother.

"Well, there is Anneliese, of course," she stammered. "And her other school friends Sonja and Karin."

"All right, I'll take the police car and talk to all these girls. You better go home now, just in case she came back. Call the station as soon as you see her."

He asked Simmer if he could use the Beetle, and his superior consented. Walter ushered his distraught mother out the door and gave her a lift to the street corner closest to their home. As he had suspected, none of the three girls had seen Ingrid. None of them gave him a second look. On another day, he would have wondered if they only considered him as Ingrid's brother or if his profession drove girls away. But right now, he could not concern himself with anything but his missing sister.

Walter sat behind the wheel of the Beetle and considered what to do next. First Jeff disappeared and now his sister. Could their fates be connected somehow? What if Ingrid's disappearance had anything to do with Roswitha's murder? Was it the killer's way of telling him to back off, just like when he killed Max? Or did Ingrid just meet with a co-worker and forget to tell her mother? He decided not to gamble on that last choice.

14

Walter put the Beetle in first gear. By now, Schlosser would be at the accident site and Chief Simmer manned the station until the mid-shift arrived. It was time to confront Heinz, even if Walter had to go alone.

Heinz's mother opened the door after Walter rapped on it.

"Is Heinz home?" he asked without bidding good evening first. There was no time to waste on pleasantries.

Frau Wolf's eyes shifted, as much as he could see in the dim light of a tiny hallway lamp. "No, I haven't seen him for hours."

Walter suspected she was lying and gently pushed her aside. At the bottom of the stairs, he yelled, "Heinz, I know you're home!" There was no answer.

"I told you he's not at home," Frau Wolf said.

Walter turned toward her, carefully hiding his disappointment. His instincts were failing him. "What about Herr Johnson? Is he there?"

"No, he's not here either."

Walter smacked the newel with his good hand and winced. Heinz had slipped through his fingers again. Dejected, he said good night to Frau Wolf and banged the door behind him with more force than he had intended. In the car, he tapped his fingertips on the steering wheel. He forced himself to think calmly. Time was of the essence. He had to find Ingrid as soon as possible.

Walter thought back to his conversation with Jeff. What had Jeff said after his captors released him? They had kept him in a hollow room with a concrete floor. Where around here could that be, except on base?

Walter radioed the station and drove on base as fast as he could. He didn't even take the time to close the car door when he came to a stop in front of the Air Police building. Tech Sergeant Brown was on duty. Walter quickly told him of his concerns about his sister.

"Do you patrol all the unfinished buildings on base?" he asked.

"We check the outside but don't deem it safe to go inside while they're under construction," the sergeant replied.

Walter scratched his chin. "So, it's possible that someone could be held captive in one of those buildings and you wouldn't know it?"

Tech Sergeant Brown raised an eyebrow. "Yes, but it's highly unlikely."

The phone rang and the sergeant answered it.

Walter stormed out of the building. He felt as if he didn't have one moment to lose. He could not wait for one of the patrol officers to return from a round to go with him.

He was vaguely familiar with the base and knew his best chance would be in the housing area. New buildings sprung up all the time to accommodate the growing number of families stationed at the base. It was also farthest away from the flight line and therefore did not undergo much scrutiny.

Walter slowly drove through the housing area, pointing a flashlight toward the buildings. Curtains on the windows told him that he was looking at an occupied apartment block. Piles of cinder blocks and a cement mixer indicated that he had reached an unfinished apartment structure. He stopped the car and got out, flashlight in hand. Already installed, the streetlights cast their glow on the asphalt. Several fir trees towered between the street and the empty building, diminishing the lights' reach. Walter had to watch his step as he approached the empty housing shell.

He cupped his mouth with his good hand. "Ingrid, Ingrid, where are you?"

A pickup truck roared up the street. It came to a sudden halt with screeching brakes. Airmen Carucci and Goodwell jumped from the police truck to meet Walter.

"Tech Sergeant Brown radioed and told us to help you in your search. He said you were really upset," Carucci said. "Is this the first building you're checking?"

"Yes," Walter said, breathing easier now. If Tech Sergeant Brown assisted him with manpower, he would find Ingrid in no time. The three-story housing unit did not have a roof yet and the railings were still missing. The policemen pointed their flashlights in every corner of the basement and the upper floors, looking for a sign of life, yet found nothing but buckets, scaffolding, and ladders.

"Did you ever find out what building Jeff was being held in?" Walter asked the airmen once they were outside.

Carucci looked skyward so Walter could not read his expression. "I don't know. I got a pass and went to Paris for a few days. No one mentioned Jeff when I came back from leave."

Walter drew in a noisy breath. The military handled Jeff's disappearance and arrest in a peculiar way. One would think that they would try to find his captors. And wouldn't his colleagues speculate about his fate? Walter had met many of them during their monthly ninepin matches and found them quite friendly. Was it possible that Carucci was lying to him?

149

Right now, Walter did not have time to probe. Ingrid was his priority.

"There is another new block around the corner," Goodwell said. They took off in the truck. The building they approached now was closest to the fence of the base.

"If I were kidnapping someone, I would hide them in this building," Carucci said.

Walter wondered whether they came to that conclusion after finding Jeff in a similar situation.

"Let's go," the airman said, "but first I want to make sure there is no one around."

The three policemen split up and agreed to meet on the other side. Walter tripped over a root and stumbled. He suppressed a curse and looked around to make sure he wasn't making too much noise.

"There's no one here," Carucci whispered when they met up. "Let's go check out the basement."

The Americans proceeded down the steps first because they had better flashlights than Walter did. Walter's hand traced along the unpainted wall. Building dust tickled his nose until he sneezed. Carucci turned around. "Shh."

Walter shrugged. It was not his fault that the place was dusty.

Both Carucci and Walter halted at the bottom of the steps. Two door openings led to opposite directions, both of which contained storage rooms for the families who would occupy the building. Carucci and Walter listened for noises, but it was eerily quiet. The men let their flashlights dance across the floor and walls while they treaded down the hallway.

Suddenly, Carucci thrust his arm across Walter's body, urging him to stop walking. Walter listened intently. A faint noise, such as a shoe scraping a floor, had reached his ears.

The policemen bolted down the hall in the direction of the noise.

In the last room on the left, Ingrid lay on the concrete floor. Her mouth was gagged with a dark blue towel. Her hands and feet were tied together with a thick rope. Next to her on the floor sat an empty plate and a tin canteen. Carucci and Goodwell scanned the entire room with their lights to make sure that no one was lurking in the dark to attack them. Then Walter rushed to his sister and knelt down beside her. He struggled to untie her gag while Carucci freed her arms.

Ingrid broke out in tears. "I thought I'd never see you again," she wailed.

"Hush," her brother said, stroking her untidy hair.

Ingrid sobbed, leaning her head against Walter's chest. He had to choke back tears himself as the tension of the past few days eased in him. He could not get the image of Roswitha's lifeless body out of his mind and thanked Heaven that his sister appeared unharmed. At least he had good news for his mother.

Meanwhile, Carucci searched the room for evidence of Ingrid's kidnappers, but they had left no traces. Goodwell returned to the truck to radio for help.

"I'd like to get her out of here as soon as possible," Walter said to Carucci.

"Yes, of course. Take her to the Air Police building. We'll wait here for reinforcements."

Walter and the American half-carried, half-supported Ingrid up the stairs and got her seated in the Beetle. The airman fetched a blanket out of the truck and wrapped the shaking girl in it. Carucci then returned to Ingrid's temporary prison while Walter drove back to the Air Police station.

He was happy that Ingrid was able to step out of the car by herself. She clung to Walter's arm as they entered the building. A young airman fetched a cup of water for Ingrid, which she drank eagerly. Tech Sergeant Brown opened the door to his office, beckoning them in. He pointed at two chairs, wheeled his chair close by, and dropped on it.

"Are you all right?"

Ingrid nodded, still unable to speak.

Tech Sergeant Brown jumped up to open the door. "Quinn, get a candy bar from the machine!"

Moments later, Airman Quinn handed a Hershey bar to Ingrid. She fumbled with the wrapper and bit into the chocolate bar as if she had not eaten all day.

"Would you like to call your family?" Brown asked Walter.

"Yes, I would like to call my mother," Walter said. Having a telephone was usually a nuisance for a policeman, but in this case, Walter was glad they were one of the few families in town to have a phone. The phone rang more than a dozen times before Frau Hofmann finally picked up the receiver.

"*Mama?*" Walter said. "Where have you been?"

"I asked the neighbors if they have seen Ingrid," she said, out of breath.

"You can stop looking, *Mama*. I found her."

He could hear her sigh through the line. "Is she all right?"

"Yes, she is unharmed." *At least on the outside,* he added silently. "Now I've got to hang up."

"Please bring her home as soon as possible."

"Yes, *Mama*."

He returned to Tech Sergeant Brown's office.

"I sent some of my men to secure that building," Brown said. "Since it doesn't have electricity yet, they won't be able to see enough to gather any fingerprints, but at least they can secure the crime scene until daybreak."

Walter agreed. He should radio the mid-shift officers at the station, but he didn't want to leave Ingrid alone. At least she seemed to be more composed after finishing the candy bar.

"Could you leave us alone for a while?" Walter asked. Tech Sergeant Brown closed the door behind him.

"Can you talk?" Walter asked softly.

"I'll try."

"What happened today?"

Ingrid sniffled. Walter fumbled in his pockets for a handkerchief. She blew her nose in it and took a deep breath. "I'm sorry I didn't listen to you. You warned me at the fair that these men were up to no good."

"What?" Walter blurted out. Ingrid winced.

"Those men you talked to at the dance?" he asked, lowering his voice.

Ingrid nodded. Curly and Frank Johnson.

Walter tensed. He could have prevented this crime if only he had prodded Ingrid more.

"What did you do after you left the house this morning?"

"I took the bus to the base as usual. But I didn't go to the BX from the bus stop. I walked to the housing area where we had agreed to meet."

"Who? The man with the curly hair and the other fellow who looks like Clark Gable?"

Ingrid wiped a tear from her cheek. "Yes."

"Do you know their real names?"

"The German said his name was Bruno Lessmeister. The American called himself Joe."

Walter clucked his tongue. "Joe. Very imaginative. His real name is Frank Johnson. At least I think that's his real name. God knows what the other man's name is. Then what happened?"

"I waited and waited. Finally, Bruno showed up. He said there had been a change of plan and we couldn't do what we had agreed on. And then someone threw a sack or something over my head and everything went dark."

Her shaky hand wiped over her dusty skirt in a futile effort to smooth the creases. "When I came to, I was lying on the floor just like you found me."

"But what was the plan?"

Ingrid looked at him without comprehension.

"You said Bruno said there was a change of plan. Why did you want to meet him in the first place?"

Ingrid seemed to shrink within herself. "Will you promise not to tell *Mama*?"

"I can't promise you that until I know what you were up to." Walter's hand cradled her shoulders. "Come on, you can tell me. I'm your brother and I'm a policeman. A crime has been committed here, and I have a right to know what happened."

Unable to look into his eyes, Ingrid said, "They said they would take me to see Elvis."

"Elvis Presley?"

Ingrid nodded.

Understanding crept over Walter's face. So that's what Ingrid had talked about with the men at the dance. He should have known just from looking at her room that the girl had a huge crush on Elvis. But could he blame her? Half of the girls in Germany seemed to be infatuated with the world's most famous soldier.

Walter suppressed a laugh. Ingrid had been through enough turmoil without his ridicule. "Why didn't you tell me you wanted to see Elvis? We could have arranged something." He had no idea how he would have accomplished that, but he wanted to calm Ingrid to ease her over her scare.

"How could you? You don't have a car," Ingrid burst out.

"I don't know," Walter admitted. "But you got yourself in a very dangerous situation here. They could have killed you just like they killed Roswitha."

Ingrid's eyes grew large. "You think they're the ones who killed that woman?"

Walter shrugged. "I can't prove it, or I would have arrested them. But I suspect they were involved in her murder, if only indirectly. Either way, I've said too much already. Just tell me this much: Do they know that I'm your brother?"

Ingrid sniffled. "I'm afraid so. I mentioned it that night after you danced with me."

Anger welled up in Walter but he tried to contain it. There would be time to scold her later. "So you went back to see those men after I told you not to? I thought you were smarter than that."

"I saw no harm in it." Ingrid blew her nose.

Walter wracked his brain for a reason why the men kidnapped Ingrid. After all, they had left her unharmed. Could it be that this kidnapping had nothing to do with Roswitha's death? Was the act committed to distract Walter from another crime?

"Please don't tell Sergeant Brown of my suspicions," Walter said once Ingrid had calmed down. "I'm not sure of anything anymore."

Ingrid did not need any convincing. "All right. Do I have to tell them what I just told you?"

"I'm afraid so. Especially since Frank Johnson is an American."

Ingrid bit her lip. "But I'm so embarrassed."

"I'll stay with you." Walter rose to call Tech Sergeant Brown back into his office. For the next half hour, he and Walter questioned Ingrid about the events of the day.

"Did they hurt you when they kidnapped you?" Walter said as they rose.

"I have a small bump on my head," Ingrid admitted. "It must have happened when they put me on the floor."

"Come on, I'll take you to Dr. Theobald."

"I don't think that's necessary," she said. "I've caused you enough trouble today."

"I can judge that better than you can."

Ingrid's shoulders sagged in defeat.

"You again?" Dr. Theobald said after Walter rang his doorbell. "Are you aware that I have regular office hours?"

"I'm not here for myself this time, but for Ingrid." Walter led his sister into the examination room. He explained to the family doctor that Ingrid had been kidnapped, but left out the part about her wish to see Elvis Presley. Even a family doctor did not need to know everything.

"I don't think there is any reason to worry," Dr. Theobald said after examining Ingrid. "Her reflexes are fine. She should take it easy for a couple of days and get some rest. Do you have any sleeping pills at home?"

Walter shook his head. The doctor rummaged in a glass cabinet and put a pill in Walter's hand. "Tell her to take this when she gets home."

Walter drove his sister home. They had barely crossed the threshold when the kitchen door flung open.

"Ingrid!" their mother wailed, her eyes swollen. "Where have you been?"

156

Ingrid stiffened. Walter hastened to say, "Let's talk about it tomorrow. We've all had a long day and she is very sleepy." His mother wanted to protest but Walter led his sister up the stairs. He waited until she had taken the sleeping pill and was safely in bed. He wished he could go to bed too, but his work was just beginning.

15

Walter should have notified Herr Simmer about the kidnapping, but realized that he had no idea where his temporary boss lived. After trying to radio Schlosser without success, he drove to the station and rang his partner's bell. Schlosser opened the door, wearing a navy and red striped robe and slippers. Under different circumstances, Walter would have laughed, seeing his partner dressed so casually.

"What happened?" Schlosser asked while ushering Walter into his kitchen.

Walter quickly recounted the events of the evening. Schlosser scratched his head and yawned. "Would you like something to drink?"

"Yes, I could use a glass of mineral water," Walter said. "I tried to radio you, but there was no answer."

Schlosser put a full glass in front of his young partner. "The accident I was called to was worse than expected. We had to close the road for a couple of hours while we waited for the ambulance and tow truck to arrive. Simmer showed up himself, just to make sure I did it right."

Walter smiled wryly. Simmer did not appear to be the kind of chief who would allow them to act on intuition alone. "So what do we do now?"

"You mean about the kidnappers? Or Roswitha's killer?"

Walter curled his lips. "They could be one and the same. Until this evening, I had thought that Heinz Wolf was in on this. Now it appears as if several men are involved." He banged his fist on the table. "I can't believe how stupid Ingrid was. I thought she had more sense than that."

Schlosser patted his hand. "She probably learned a valuable lesson today."

"I certainly hope so."

Schlosser rubbed the sleep out of his eyes and rose slowly. "I'll get dressed and then we'll go downstairs. We have to call Simmer for help. We can't do this alone."

"You want to call Simmer to help us? He hasn't been very helpful so far."

Schlosser, who was already at the door, turned around. "You're right. Maybe it's better if we call the station in Reichenbach for help."

Walter emptied his glass and gave his coworker a puzzled look. "What exactly are we doing?"

"Well, you want to catch Ingrid's kidnappers, don't you?"

"Of course."

"So we need to find out if there really is a Bruno Lessmeister."

Walter grimaced. "I don't feel like spending hours going through all the police records, and the town halls are closed right now."

"That's why we need the Reichenbach police to help us."

Understanding crept over Walter's face. "And in the meantime, we pay a visit to Frank Johnson's place, the Wolf house."

Schlosser pointed his index finger at Walter. "Exactly."

They parked the Beetle around the corner and inspected the Wolf courtyard as best as the street lamp allowed. Johnson's car was not parked in the yard. No light was visible behind the closed shutters of the house. The two officers banged on the door until a hallway light came on.

"Who is it?" asked Frau Wolf from behind the closed door.

"Police. Open up at once," Schlosser said.

"All right, all right." She had thrown a man's work jacket over her flannel nightgown when she cracked the door open.

"Yes?" She eyed the officers with a mixture of annoyance and servility.

Before Walter could say anything, Schlosser took over. "Is Herr Johnson at home?"

"No, I haven't seen him all day."

Schlosser tried to peer around Frau Wolf. "When was the last time you saw him?"

"I didn't exactly see him, but last night, I heard his heavy shoes going up the stairs."

"Are you sure it was him and not your son?"

"I know the difference." Frau Wolf seemed to have no intention of letting them in, and without a search warrant, the officers had no legal grounds to search Johnson's room. The two policemen bid a curt good night to the landlady and retreated.

"I've met some tough landladies in my time, but she's one of the toughest," Schlosser pressed through his teeth.

Walter would have chuckled if the situation had not been so serious. From the car, Walter radioed Tech Sergeant Brown that Frank Johnson's landlady had not seen or heard him today. Then Schlosser contacted the police in Reichenbach and told them to alert all guards at the German-French border.

Walter arched his eyebrows at his partner's leap of thought. "You think he escaped to France?"

Schlosser shrugged. "It's just a precaution. I don't know what to think anymore. Well, what do we do now? Go back to the police station or check the usual places?"

Walter knew what the usual places were: the bars, clubs, and boarding houses that were frequented by soldiers. "What if Johnson is hiding somewhere on base?"

"We'll let the military worry about that," Schlosser said, noticing Walter's thoughtful look. "What?"

"I wonder if we wouldn't do better keeping an eye on this house…" Walter mused.

"My guess is he's gone."

Walter fixed his gaze in the direction of the house. "Don't you think it's odd that Jeff and Ingrid were kidnapped for no apparent reason?"

Schlosser turned to face Walter. "Assuming that your friend really was kidnapped. I think his story has too many holes to be believable."

"It has occurred to me that he's lying about that," Walter admitted. "But it seems out of character for him to lie."

"Unless…" Schlosser hesitated, "unless he's been ordered to lie."

Walter admitted the possibility.

Schlosser yawned again. "Is it me, or are we doing all the work for Detective Junker?"

Walter's laugh was bitter. "Neither one of us has much to go on. I'm doing this investigation for Jeff and our Chief. I don't want to work for a boss like Simmer all the time. Do you?"

"Heavens, no."

"I hope you gave my regards to the Chief's wife today. I wish I could visit him, but I don't seem to have time anymore. Especially not during those short visiting hours at the hospital."

"Believe me, he understands."

I need him and I sure could use his advice now, Walter thought. "Yes, but I would like to ask him some questions."

"What kind of questions?" Schlosser asked. "You could ask me. I'm your partner."

Walter paused. He had not considered that he might be hurting Schlosser's feelings. "Such as, what do we do first: Keep an eye on Heinz's house, go back to the *Luna* bar and other such bars, or stake out the trailer of the fair?"

"Yes, the fair. I drove by today. They're packing up tomorrow."

Walter tapped his head with his hand. "That's right, tomorrow is Wednesday. Time to move on to the next fair. I wish we could get a warrant to search that trailer."

"On what grounds would we get a warrant?" Schlosser drove his fingers through his hair. "And we don't have the manpower to stake out the trailer."

Walter yawned. "I just want to arrest the guy who attacked me."

"You need to go to bed, son."

"How can I sleep when Ingrid's kidnapper and Roswitha's killer are still on the loose?"

"You really care about the dead girl," Schlosser said. "I hope you never lose it."

They agreed to drive by the trailer and the *Luna* bar before calling it a night. All lights were out at the fairground. They parked the car a block away and walked back. For about fifteen minutes, they staked out the trailer, yet nothing stirred. It was as if the policemen were the only humans out and about. They proceeded to the *Luna* bar. Walter did not recognize the one car parked in front of the bar. They peered into the window. Business was slow. Only one customer, probably the owner of the car, was sitting at the counter.

"Do you recognize him?" Schlosser whispered.

"No."

"No use waiting here. There's nothing going on tonight."

Schlosser turned away to leave, but Walter stood transfixed. His eyes focused on the manure pile that took up much of the courtyard. The semi-darkness muted its mundane purpose, but the lingering aroma did not.

"What are you thinking?" Schlosser inquired.

"If you had to hide a piece of evidence, where would you hide it?"

Schlosser followed Walter's gaze. "No! You can't be serious."

"Why not?"

Schlosser's face contorted in revulsion. "For one thing, that's cow dung. Stinky cow dung."

"I'm not too crazy about searching it, either. What's the other thing?"

"We have no legal grounds to search the pile. We have no warrant and no reason to obtain one, other than that you once saw Frank Johnson in the bar."

Walter's shoulders sagged. "All right, all right. I admit that it was a long shot. But when we catch a suspect, I would still like to examine that pile."

In the yellow light of the street lamp, Schlosser cast him a look that seemed to question his sanity. "Up until now, I thought you were a decent fellow. A little young perhaps, but promising."

Walter raised his palms at his partner. "I admit defeat, for now. But mark my words…"

They walked back to the Beetle.

"Right now, I just want to mark my pillow with my head," Schlosser said.

"Me, too. Let's go home."

16

In the morning, Walter cracked Ingrid's door open. Her rhythmical breathing told him that she was still asleep. His mother was already clattering cups and cutlery in the kitchen.

"I'm so glad you found Ingrid," she said when he entered the kitchen. "I knew you could do it. Was she with one of her girlfriends?"

Walter bit his lip. How much should he reveal to his mother? Finally, he decided to tell her that he found Ingrid on base, but nothing more. The investigation was still going on and he didn't know if his mother could keep her tongue tight in all the excitement.

"Please don't talk to anyone about this," he said as she placed a cup of coffee in front of him. "Tell Ingrid to stay home today and get some rest. I, on the other hand, have to go to work again."

"But Walter, you just got home. I heard you; you came in late."

"But I was so quiet when I came home. I even took my shoes off."

"I can never sleep when one of my kids is out at night."

Walter shook his head. It was a miracle that his mother got any sleep at all.

Schlosser was already sitting at his desk when Walter entered the police station. He shot Walter a quizzical look. Perhaps he was thinking about the dung pile.

"The station in Reichenbach just called. They're still searching for Bruno Lessmeister. It's probably a fake name anyway. Chief Simmer called, too. He has to go to the court in Kaiserslautern this morning and won't be in until noon or later."

Walter rubbed his hands together. "Perfect. At least he won't interfere with us this morning. Does he know about Ingrid?"

"Yes. What are you doing this morning?"

"First of all, I'm going to drive on base again to check the night reports. I'll also go to the building where I found Ingrid to see if they uncovered any evidence yet. Are you staying here?"

"Someone has to hold the fort," Schlosser said and began typing with two index fingers.

Walter stopped at the base gate as usual, but this time he parked the car on the side and went inside the guard building.

"Can I see the sign-up sheet for yesterday?" he asked the guard on duty.

"Tech Sergeant Brown has already gone over it last night, but feel free to look at it."

Walter pulled a notebook out of his pocket and scanned the sheet with his index finger. Frank Johnson's name was not on the list, but that was no surprise. He probably had an ID card. Walter wrote down the names and information of the two male Germans who had signed in. From the car, he radioed Schlosser their names even though he did not believe that they had anything to do with Ingrid's kidnapping. He had to follow every lead at this point.

166

In broad daylight, the identical apartment buildings did not make the appearance of a crime scene. Two pickup trucks were parked on the street in front of the building where Walter had found his sister. The Air Police had cordoned off the building with yellow tape. A German truck was parked in front of the next structure. Three workers were standing on a scaffolding, painting the sides. When Walter stepped out of the police car, their supervisor, wearing dirty corduroy pants and a flat cap, walked over to him.

"What's going on here?" he inquired. "We wanted to work in that building that's cordoned off. They say we can't get in there today at all. Now I have to give my other workers something else to do."

Walter apologized but had no encouraging words for him. As the agitated construction boss turned away, it dawned on Walter that Ingrid's kidnappers wanted the workers to find her. Why else would they have chosen a building that was under construction?

Walter climbed over the tape and pulled on his gloves. He followed several voices downstairs.

"Hello?" he said, his call echoing in the hollow basement. "It's me, Police Master Hofmann."

"Over here," called Tech Sergeant Shoemaker.

"Any luck?" Walter asked.

The sergeant shook his head. "No. We can't get any fingerprints from these stone surfaces. There's nothing but cinderblocks and bricks here. The kidnappers could not have found a better place to commit a crime."

"Do you think they've left the base by now?"

"What better time to sneak out than under cover of darkness? Nonetheless, I have instructed all patrols to inspect the fences very carefully today. Not that they don't do that every day anyway, but still..."

Walter's mind reeled. "What if they left the base in a car or truck?"

Sergeant Shoemaker hesitated. "That's possible, too, since we don't check vehicles when they leave the base, only when they enter. In that case, there's no way we can find the perpetrators. But we'll keep our eyes and ears open nonetheless."

Walter gritted his teeth. He hoped that the sergeant was wrong and the kidnappers had not vanished. He looked around the basement room. Nothing suggested that a crime had taken place here the day before. Only the plate and cup hinted at a human presence recently. Ingrid had had to spend an entire day tied up in here without knowing when and if help would arrive.

The Air Police seemed to be in charge of the operation, so Walter sat on the driver's seat of the police car, tapping the steering wheel. He could not help thinking that there was a connection between Ingrid's kidnapping and Roswitha's murder. He shifted the car in gear because he felt inexplicably drawn back to the murder scene. Outside the gate, he turned onto the cart road that led to the tree where he had found Roswitha. He clucked his tongue. The felled tree was still there.

A gust of wind whipped the car door as he stepped out of the Beetle. Not surprisingly, he found numerous footprints in the soft soil. People were drawn to crime scenes like yellow jackets to a plum cake. They had no idea how sickening a decomposing body smelled, and how ugly even the prettiest face turned in death.

Walter encircled the tree several times, searching for clues. At least the tree was still there. Firewood for the winter was always in high demand.

Firewood. He had heard that word recently, and not from his mother. Yes, now he remembered. Frau Wolf had mentioned that Heinz had brought home firewood on the day of the murder. Why hadn't he thought of it before? Heinz, or someone else, could have killed Roswitha with a branch from the fallen tree. And then Heinz took the wood home to his unsuspecting mother, who burned it in her kitchen stove. With the murder weapon gone, no one would ever suspect Heinz.

He sprinted back to the car and radioed Schlosser. His partner did not answer. Was he in the restroom? It was not like Schlosser to leave the station unattended.

There was no time to lose. Walter wanted to turn on the sirens, but that would have drawn too much attention to the police car. He drove a shortcut through several side streets and parked the car in front of the Wolf house. He peeked into the courtyard. Johnson's car was not there.

Walter darted to the front door and alternately rang the doorbell or banged on the door with his good arm until a piece of faded paint fell off. No one answered. Where could Frau Wolf be?

The curtains were so dense, he couldn't see anything when he peered into the windows. It was too late in the year for gardening, but Walter decided to check the garden anyway. After glancing around the vegetable patches, he headed toward the barns. He opened the creaky door to the former cow barn and stepped inside. He pulled his gun out of its holster and checked his blind spots. Without cows and people to milk them, the barn was as forlorn as a cemetery. Yet it would be the perfect place to hide something.

Walter took a cursory look around and closed the barn door behind him. He returned to the car to radio Schlosser. This time, his partner answered.

"Walter, you better get back to the station right away," Schlosser said.

"Unless it's a life and death emergency, I'm busy."

"There's a young woman here who wants to see you. She says it's urgent."

Walter could visualize his partner's sneer. "A woman? What woman?"

"Her name is Marianne and she has something to tell you."

Walter hesitated for a second. "I'll be right there."

No matter what Schlosser thought, Walter knew that Marianne had not come because she longed to see him. Perhaps she had some information about Jeff or her brother that she wanted to share. When Walter arrived at the station, Schlosser could hardly keep himself from staring at her. He winked at Walter, but Walter shot him looks that should have burned his skin.

Marianne paced in the waiting area. Walter offered her the chair in front of his desk.

"Benno is gone," she blurted out while sitting down.

"What do you mean, gone?" Walter asked. He had purposely placed a desk between him and the girl he had adored for years. That way, she could not lean on his shoulder and he wouldn't lose the composure he had carefully developed over the past few days. "Let's start at the beginning."

"I told you the other day that he comes and goes whenever he likes. When *Mama* went into his room this morning, she saw that he had not slept in his bed. Then she opened his wardrobe and half of his clothes were gone."

Walter's pencil danced over his notepad. "Didn't you say the other day that he was friends with Heinz?"

"Yes," she said, her ponytail bobbing up and down. "He spends a lot of time with Heinz and Anton. At least, that's what we hear from people who see them together."

Walter raised his eyebrow ever so slightly. Heinz again. Whatever his classmate was involved in, Walter vowed to get to the bottom of it. "Where have they been seen lately?"

Marianne fidgeted. "I have not heard anything, but they have been seen going into bars."

"Yes, I've seen Heinz a few times recently." *Just not today, when I was looking for him,* he thought.

"Do you have any idea where Benno could have gone?"

"*Mama* thinks he wants to join the French Foreign Legion," Marianne said. "He always goes on and on what an exciting life they lead while he's stuck in this boring old village."

"Exciting?" Walter mused how thrilling the life of a mercenary soldier could possibly be.

"Yes. He always talks about how they get to go to Africa and even Indochina. He wants to get out of this sleepy town and see the world."

Walter rubbed his chin. "Did your mother send you to me?"

"No, she doesn't know I'm here." Marianne glanced at Schlosser, who pretended to be busy filing reports. She leaned forward in her chair and lowered her voice. "Between you and me, I say good riddance. Even *Mama* doesn't seem to be too shook up about it. Benno has been such a nuisance the past few years that it'll be good if we can have a normal family life again. But I'm afraid Benno might have done something wrong or else he wouldn't have disappeared so suddenly. I always thought he was just a big mouth. Always talking about the places he wants to see some day and such. All the while he didn't even pay for the food he ate."

Walter did not want to know every detail of her family life and steered the conversation back to facts. "So you noticed this morning that Benno was gone? When was the last time your parents saw him?"

"*Mama* says he ate breakfast yesterday morning and said he had to go downtown looking for a job." The words tumbled out of her mouth now. "I'll be damned if he went looking for a job."

Walter had never heard a curse from her lips and regarded Marianne in a new way. Perhaps dating Jeff had been her happiest time in years.

He tapped his pencil against his lips while leaning back in his chair. Benno's disappearance coincided nicely with Ingrid's kidnapping and Heinz's vanishing. But he didn't want to tell Marianne about Ingrid. It was an ongoing police investigation and his sister would not want her misfortune gossiped about in the village. Not that he suspected Marianne of gossiping, but one could not be too careful. After all, she worked in a shoe store.

He had escorted Marianne to the door when she looked over her shoulder. "Have you heard any news about Jeff?"

Walter almost bumped into her and stepped back to put a distance between them. He shook his head. After she said goodbye, he breathed a sigh of relief. It did not hurt as much as the first time she asked him to find Jeff, he told himself. He even felt a pang of guilt that he had not thought of Jeff all day. Yet the Air Police had behaved so evasively about the subject that he had given up asking about him.

His first duty was to find Roswitha's killer. With Jeff's honor intact, he could then marry Marianne. No, Walter forbade himself to think that far ahead.

"Did you hear that?" Walter asked his partner after closing the door.

"Every word," Schlosser said, barely suppressing a grin.

"What's so funny?" Walter asked gruffly.

"Nothing."

Walter decided to change the subject. "I can't find Heinz anywhere. The Air Police can't find a trace of the kidnappers and there was no one at the Wolf house, not even his mother. Remember when we checked the murder scene? It looked as if one of the branches broke off the tree, but we couldn't find the branch?"

Schlosser nodded, his eyes glued on Walter.

"Frau Wolf mentioned that Heinz brought her some firewood the very same day. She burned it, of course. And even if she didn't, how would we find the piece that killed Roswitha?"

Schlosser shrugged. "She didn't bleed, so there would be no blood on the wood. You're right. That gives us nothing to work on."

Walter plopped on his chair and clasped his hands behind his head. The long hours he had worked lately were taking their toll on him. More to the point, the futility of all his efforts wore him down. "Should we alert the French border guards?"

"It can't hurt," Schlosser said, "but do you really think Benno crossed the border legally if he did something wrong?"

Walter's good hand smacked the armrest. "Probably not. It isn't very difficult to cross the border anyway. Back in school, we went on a hiking trip near Dahn. We crisscrossed the border from one castle to the other and no one ever bothered us."

Benno did not strike Walter as an avid hiker, but if he hitched a ride to a town near the border, he could have easily crossed it in the wooded hills to the south.

"True," Schlosser said, "but I'll make the calls anyway. I'm sure you're busy with other problems."

Walter's mind raced. The more time passed, the more likely it was that Heinz and Benno, not to mention Frank Johnson, had vanished. Where could they all have disappeared to? Could they have left the country? The firewood seemed to be the only connection between Heinz and Roswitha. It was a stretch to try to pin the murder on Heinz. Even harder to understand was Ingrid's kidnapping, unless the perpetrators wanted to tell Walter to back off. Perhaps it was time to revisit any unsolved cases on the books. There had to be a solution somewhere in the files. At the moment, though, he was too restless for office work.

Walter put on his overcoat.

"Where are you going?" Schlosser asked.

"To the fair."

Schlosser pursed his lips. "Hmm, I never trusted those two workers completely. They behaved a bit suspicious, if you ask me. I'm going with you."

"What about Simmer?"

"He just called and said he would be delayed in court. Something about a witness being late. Besides, we won't be long."

They walked the two blocks to the fairground and stopped in their tracks. It was deserted. Nothing but a puddle of oil remained of the trailer.

"We need to find out where they're going next," Walter said.

"The town hall should have records about that. It's lunchtime now, but it's worth a try."

They proceeded to the town hall. Hall was too strong a word for the square, two-story structure with its green shutters and weather vane on top of the tiled roof. Its stone staircase, leading from both sides to the heavy front door, was its most impressive attribute.

Schlosser knocked on the door of the registration office, but no one answered. He pushed down the handle and found the door locked.

"I'll just go home to eat lunch," Schlosser said. "There's nothing we can do until he comes back."

They parted in the hallway of the station and Schlosser climbed the steps to his apartment. Walter paced through the station, unable to sit still. Suddenly, it occurred to him that he did not need to ask the clerk where the fair people had gone. This late in the year, only two fairs would take place the coming weekend. One of them was in such a small village that it probably could not support a chain carousel. That left Haimbach. Walter rubbed his hands together. Haimbach was just ten Kilometers to the west, the direction of the French border.

He took two steps at a time and banged on Schlosser's door. His partner opened, still chewing.

"Sorry for interrupting your lunch. I need to go on an errand," Walter lied. "Can you man the station?"

Schlosser grumbled and asked his wife to fill a plate for him. He would finish his meal at his desk. Walter felt a twitch of guilt over his deception. He would have felt much safer with his partner, but someone had to remain at the station.

He got into the Beetle and drove off. There was no time to waste if he wanted to catch any suspects before they crossed the border.

Outside of town, a wagon loaded with potato sacks delayed his progress. The road was narrow and curvy with limited visibility. He had to wait for his chance to pass the farmer when he could see a stretch of open road ahead. As he neared Haimbach, his stomach began to grumble. Perhaps he should have followed his partner's example and gone home to eat. Now he didn't know when he would get his next meal.

He had not been to Haimbach in ages, but traditionally, the fairgrounds were in a schoolyard or near the mayor's office. Haimbach was no different. The village had developed along the straight main street. The whitewashed Catholic church, visible from afar, presided on a slight elevation over its parish.

As Walter turned into the schoolyard, he nodded with satisfaction. The wagon train that had recently arrived looked like Herr Reuter's carnival ride. Walter turned the car around to park on the street. He jumped out of the Beetle and strode toward the carnival workers' trailer. He tried in vain to catch a glimpse of the interior through the drawn curtains. He banged on the door but received no answer. Perhaps they were already setting up or had gone to Reuter's trailer for lunch. Walter followed the aroma of onions and potatoes to the other side of the school, where the owner's trailer was parked. He opened the door that was ajar.

"Smells like stew in here," he said, smacking his lips. His stomach did a somersault.

Frau Reuter was setting the table. "Yes, officer. You must be from Lauterbach. I saw you there the other day, talking to my husband."

"Yes, I'm Police Master Hofmann."

"Would you like some stew?"

"I sure would, but I don't have time right now. Is your husband around?"

"He went to the town hall to register us. He should be back soon."

"I'm actually looking for his workers, Molnar and Mielke."

"Did you check their trailer? Perhaps they're changing for lunch."

Walter shook his head. "I knocked, but there was no answer. I didn't see them on the way over here, or else I wouldn't bother you."

"No bother," she said with a smile. "I'm used to being interrupted."

Walter admired her gentle disposition. He wondered how his mother would cope with cooking for several hungry men every day. One could probably get used to everything.

"I'll be back in a few minutes. Tell your husband I'm looking for him."

"If you see Mielke and Molnar, please tell them lunch is ready."

Walter nodded and returned to the trailer. Now he had an excuse to take a peek. He knocked on the door and it gave way. It had been unlocked all this time.

"Well, well, what have we here?" he said to himself. The inside of the trailer looked as if a strong gale had whipped through it. Drawers were left partially open and piles of socks, underwear, and corduroy jeans lay strewn all over the floor. The closet doors stood ajar. Trousers and shirts, while neatly draped over hangers, were shoved to one side, revealing a cleared area in the wardrobe.

"Looks like somebody left in a hurry," Walter mumbled.

"What are you doing?" said a voice behind him. Walter's hand touched his gun holster as he spun around. He was relieved to see Molnar by the door and not his coworker.

"I knocked, but no one answered," Walter said. "You've got quite a mess in here. Going somewhere?"

Molnar climbed into the trailer, keeping his distance from Walter. Years of oppression apparently had taught the Hungarian to be on guard at all times. Walter searched Molnar's face for signs of guilt, but found surprise instead. Whatever had occurred in here, Molnar seemed to be just as surprised as Walter was.

"No, I'm not going anywhere. I just got here."

"Where have you been?" Walter asked.

"I was at the tobacco shop buying a pack of cigarettes." Molnar pulled a pack of Reval out of his shirt pocket.

"Where is Mielke?" Walter asked.

"We arrived here together, but then he said he had to make a phone call. There is a booth by the intersection. I went to the tobacco shop and came back to find you here."

Walter remembered seeing the phone booth on the way, but that didn't mean that Mielke had actually made a call. Neither Heinz nor Benno had a phone. "What was Mielke's mood this morning?"

Molnar blinked. "Mood?"

"Yes. Did he seem nervous or calm?"

"He acted a bit strange this morning, come to think of it," Molnar said. "He kept asking what time it was, like I wear a watch at work."

"Do you have any idea what was in that wardrobe?"

"No. I have my own wardrobe over there." Molnar pointed to a small closet at the back end of the trailer.

"Did you ever see the contents of Mielke's wardrobe? Did he ever open it when you were around so you could look in?"

"No. He was real funny about that. He never opened it when I was in here and if he did, he usually stood so that I could not see anything."

Walter wished he and Schlosser could have gotten a warrant while the carnival was in Lauterbach. Chief Kleber had been right to be suspicious.

"Don't you think that's rather peculiar? And did you never get curious and look inside when he was not around?"

Molnar lifted his hands with palms outward. "I learned under Communism never to ask questions. I just want to stay out of trouble." His voice pleaded with Walter. "You have to believe me."

"All right, all right. No one is accusing you of anything." Walter stared at the wardrobe. "When did you get paid?"

"This morning. Herr Reuter paid us before we left Lauterbach."

So Mielke had some money in his pocket. But how could he have taken his clothes and the contents of his wardrobe without any vehicle?

"Did you go anywhere last night?"

"Yes, I went to a *Gasthaus* and drank a couple of beers."

"What was the name of the *Gasthaus*?"

Molnar scratched his head. "I can't remember."

"Must have been more than a couple of beers, eh?"

"No, I only had two beers," Molnar said.

Walter had no doubt he was telling the truth. "Where was it?"

"There was a post office in the same house."

"That's the *Post*. Did you go alone?"

"Yes, I went by myself. I joined some local men who sat at the regulars' table."

"Did Mielke tell you what he was up to last night?" Walter asked.

Molnar breathed out slowly. Perhaps he was glad that the conversation steered away from him. "No. Look, Mielke and I weren't friends. We had to work together, but that was it."

"If you think of anything, please tell Herr Reuter."

"Yes, I will."

Walter said goodbye and returned to Reuter's trailer. Reuter sat at the table and sawed his knife through a piece of meat. "Please sit down and have a plate of stew with us."

Walter debated. It was not proper to accept food from a possible informant, but he was famished.

Frau Reuter did not wait for his answer and ladled a heap of vegetables and meat on a plate. "I'll be really upset if you don't taste my stew."

Walter gave an embarrassed laugh. "All right, I'll try it." He placed a forkful in his mouth. "Hm, this is delicious." He faced Herr Reuter. "Did you see Mielke last night?"

"Last night? No, I was in here doing paperwork, and my wife was mending clothes. Did you see him, Elise?"

His wife shook her head.

Walter faced her. "Did you ever enter the trailer he slept in, like to tidy up?"

She cackled. "Of course not. I'm not their maid. I have enough work to do as it is."

Walter groaned. Once again, no one had seen anything. "Do you know that he has disappeared?"

"What?" Reuter looked up from his plate, his bushy eyebrows forming arches on his forehead.

"Yes. Some of his clothes are gone and the contents of his wardrobe are missing. Molnar says he was real secretive about his wardrobe."

Reuter banged his fist on the table. "That does it! After everything I've done for him, hiring him when no one else would. What am I going to do now? I can't set up the carousel with Molnar alone."

His wife put a hand on his shoulder. "Shht, you could maybe find someone in the village to help."

"Putting together a carousel isn't child's play, you know." Reuter rubbed his forehead with his hand. "Had I known this, I wouldn't have paid him this morning."

Walter sympathized with the carousel owner, whose season might end early. But he had bigger problems than losing money. "Do you have any idea where he could have gone? Does he have any relatives around here he could stay with?"

"He didn't talk much about himself. I don't think he had any family around here," Reuter said. "Come to think of it, he was very tight-lipped. I always thought he was an odd fellow."

"Seems as if you were right." Walter rose and thanked Frau Reuter for the lunch. He trudged back to the car and sank on the driver seat. Where could Mielke have gone? How could a man disappear in broad daylight, especially when he didn't even own a bicycle?

He opened the glove compartment and pulled out a map of the Palatinate. His index finger traced the route from Lauterbach to Haimbach and then to the French border. Not long ago, the French border had been right behind the last houses of the village. Now, the Saarland was officially part of the Federal Republic again and the border had moved westward. What if Mielke was still in the Palatinate? And where was Heinz? Walter's finger came to a stop over the name Bensdorf. He smiled as he remembered the summer camp for orphaned children he had attended there when he was twelve years old. It had been heaven to romp through the woods and roast bratwursts over a campfire. The camp was located in a former hunting lodge and would be deserted in late fall. And then it occurred to him where Heinz might be.

17

Walter radioed the station.

"Where are you?" Schlosser asked. He whispered, "Simmer is in a real snit because you took off alone."

Walter hastened to bring his partner up to date. Schlosser whistled, but over the air, it sounded like a storm was forming. "I think I know where Heinz is hiding, but I can't be sure. I'm going after him." *Let's hope I'm right,* he added silently.

"Be careful, and ask the local police for back-up. Do you hear me?"

"Why don't you take care of that for me? I have to go." Walter released the radio handle and turned the ignition key. Within minutes, he was driving on the federal road toward Schönau, the last town before Bensdorf and seat of many schools. He had to stop at a pedestrian crossing to let a group of children cross the street with school satchels on their backs. A block further, a little girl twirled a hula hoop around her spindly legs. Walter's mouth twitched. On days like today, he envied these children their carefree existence. They did not have to experience the deprivations of war and post-war that his generation had faced.

Outside of Bensdorf, it began to drizzle and Walter had to turn on the windshield wiper. Gray clouds pushed away the autumn sun that had illuminated his westward drive before lunch. A farmer lumbered behind his horses and plow, turning over the earth before winter arrived.

A sign on the road pointed left to the camp and Walter turned onto a narrow road. It was barely more than a cart way. Walter leaped from his seat when the car bounced through a pothole. He stopped at a fork in the road, unsure where to turn. To his left, the track turned around a corner and disappeared behind poplar trees. To the right, the dirt road ascended and then vanished at the crest of a hill. Walter turned right and climbed up an elevation. The road showed ruts and hoofprints before it abruptly ended at a chain that stretched across the road. This appeared to be a privately owned forest.

Walter cursed and backed the car up to turn around. He inched the Beetle back and forth to avoid being stuck in a ditch. Finally, he had the car at a point where he could return to the junction. He crawled around the corner. The track narrowed and crossed a creek over a plank bridge.

Recognition was beginning to set in. Now he knew his way because he and the other boys had waded in this creek to cool off on hot summer afternoons. Heinz had been their ringleader and had received several reprimands during those two weeks. Apparently, he had not changed.

Walter smiled as he remembered the carefree days of his stay at the camp, the only vacation in his life. The two-story red sandstone building had once belonged to a duke who had entertained his noble friends here, especially during the annual hunt. With its high ceilings, massive wooden doors, and thick-walled cellars, the lodge had seemed as large as a palace to Walter. He had never tired of exploring the barns.

Walter's smile faded as he neared the former lodge. It looked much smaller than it had seemed to his younger self. He could not believe that twenty boys, several chaperones, and a cook had once slept inside. Russet ivy crawled over the stone wall that surrounded the property and the gutters hung crookedly on the side.

Walter remembered a farm a little further down the road. It was around a bend, out of sight of the mansion. He brought the car to a halt in front of the farmhouse, grabbed his stick, and got out. A calico cat jumped off a wall and rubbed Walter's legs. He petted her before she returned to her post. Walter smiled. He had a way with animals. They seemed much less complicated than humans.

He sighed as he strode toward the mansion. Putting on his gloves, he approached the iron gate. A chain lay on the ground, a broken padlock on top of it. Walter suppressed a cry of joy. Whoever had broken the lock could not be the rightful owner or tenant because he would have had a key. Walter cringed when the gate creaked as he opened it. He wanted to go undetected.

Weeds had taken over where once potatoes, carrots, and beans had thrived in the fertile ground. Walter knelt down to inspect some tire tracks in the dirt driveway. Someone had been here recently with a car, judging from the distance of the tracks. He rose and followed the tracks around the house where they ended by a back door. He hesitated. Should he hide behind one of the apple trees nearby and wait until someone came out? But what if Schlosser had not called the police in Schönau and the stranger cleared out before help arrived? No, he decided. He would not let Heinz slip away again.

The thought of Ingrid made him hesitate, and caution descended on him. His mother could not take any more excitement this week, and he certainly did not want to meet Jeff and Ingrid's fate. He slunk along the house and approached the former stable that formed an L shape with the main house. He slowly opened the half door, careful not to make a noise. If there was more than one intruder, then it was quite possible that one of them was in the stable. His footsteps seemed to thunder on the stone floor. He entered the tack room and whistled under his breath. It was stuffed to the ceiling with cardboard boxes of Chesterfields, liquor, and construction material. Copper pipes and electrical wires were scattered all over the floor. Perhaps this was the answer to the copper thefts on base Schlosser had mentioned.

Footsteps crunched on the stones of the walk. Walter headed for the first box, where he crouched in a corner. He had to know how many men he was dealing with before showing himself. Besides, he hoped they would talk, thus revealing their guilt and a possible motive for their presence.

Walter discerned two voices in the courtyard. They sounded as if they were arguing. Good. The more disagreements they had, the better. It would be easier for one criminal to tell on the other. Perhaps they might reveal each other's guilt in their anger.

One voice belonged to Heinz, but Walter could not quite make out the other one. He crawled to the window and took off his cap before inching his eyes above the windowsill. Heinz stood in the courtyard talking to another man who had his back turned toward the stable. It was Mielke. If they were waiting for other members of their gang, then Walter was seriously outnumbered. A more experienced officer could probably apprehend more than two suspects, but he could not take such a risk with his injured arm.

Mielke's voice grew shriller by the second. Did he have cold feet now? Walter wondered how those two men came all the way out here without a car. Screeching car brakes on the dirt road answered his question. Heinz sprinted to the gate and opened it. A car approached on the driveway, sending Walter's mind reeling. How could he check the make of car without being seen, himself? When coming into the stable, he had counted four boxes on each side. In a crouching walk, Walter moved to the last box that faced the courtyard. He put his cap on the floor and inched his head toward the window. His calculation had been correct. He could see the license plate from his position. The car was a white Ford Taunus, the same make of car he had seen when he directed traffic at the fair.

He pulled a notepad out of his pocket to jot down the license plate number. This time, he would not lose the note, he swore to himself. He repeated the letters and numbers over and over until he knew them by heart. A man climbed out from the driver's side. Walter recognized him as Frank Johnson. The American opened the trunk and the three men walked toward the stable.

Walter's head shot down and he crouched behind the partition. Judging from the clinking sound of bottles, the three accomplices were in the tack room now. They were carrying box after box of liquor outside to load into the car. It was probably not the first shipment Johnson had transported in the Ford. But where did he take them?

Walter peered over the box partition again. He suppressed a whistle when he noticed that Mielke wore a cap. Hadn't Jeff mentioned that the stranger in the moor had worn a cap?

Finally, the trunk slammed shut. The car must be loaded now. The Ford's tires crunched as the driver turned it around in the courtyard. Heinz and Mielke remained in the yard talking. Walter pressed his ear as close to the window as he dared.

"I want to get my share right now," he heard Mielke saying. "Things are getting too hot for me. That young cop has been sniffing around too often."

"You mean Walter? Don't worry about him; I know him from school. I can trick him any day. He has no idea what we're doing."

Really? You must think I'm dimwitted, Walter thought.

A short pause followed. "I want out," Mielke said firmly.

"All right, all right. But you're missing a great opportunity to get rich."

"Get rich? You haven't paid me in weeks! Get rich." He spat on the ground. "I want my money now. After all, you have used me long enough. I'm the one who risked being detected when I hid the cigarettes in my wardrobe all this time."

Walter listened attentively. So that's how they had transported the stolen goods.

"I was getting tired of the fairgrounds anyway," Mielke continued. "But now winter is coming and I don't have a job."

"A job? You don't need a job if you listen to me."

"I'm tired of listening to you. I want out," Mielke said, raising his voice.

Heinz shrugged. "All right. Let's go in the house. I wanted to wait till Frank comes back, but I guess you don't want to wait."

"No, I don't."

The men walked toward the main house and disappeared behind the back door. Walter crawled to the other side of the stable and stretched. His legs were beginning to tingle from crouching. He hurried to the tack room and looked around. He wanted to take something that had fingerprints on it and settled on a carton of Lucky Strikes. With great difficulty, he stuffed it into an inside pocket of his jacket and returned to his old position.

A few minutes later, the two men stepped out of the house. Without looking back, Mielke strode through the gate and disappeared. Heinz stared after him, rubbing his neck. Finally, Heinz was alone. It was now or never. Heinz returned to the tack room and Walter rose slowly. He debated whether to pull his gun out of its holster or carry the stick he had brought from the car. He snapped off the holster cover and bent to the floor to pick up the stick where he had left it. Better to have two choices than none.

Where were the police from Schönau? They should have been here now, unless they were held up. Walter regretted now that he had not waited until he could take Schlosser along. How could he have been so stupid to think he could arrest a killer all by himself? Chief Simmer would be seething. The thought of Simmer's scorn jolted Walter to action.

He barely breathed while he inched his way to the tack room. Heinz was standing in the middle of the room staring at the contraband. Perhaps he calculated how much more money he would now make since he only had to share with Johnson.

Walter grabbed his stick tighter and said, "Finally I've found you."

18

Heinz spun around, for once at a loss for words. After a few seconds, he said, "Well, you're much smarter than I thought."

"That's a compliment I cannot return," Walter said.

Heinz had apparently regained his composure. He said with a smirk, "Would you like some coffee for your mother? Don't wait too long to answer, because Frank will be back at any moment."

"Did you kill the girl?" Walter blurted out while blocking the doorway.

Heinz did not even make an effort to deny it. "She deserved to die," he said through clenched teeth. "I bet she was one of those sluts who slept with any soldier that comes along with pockets full of money. I know her kind." Spittle formed on Heinz's lips as he took a step closer to Walter.

"Really? Isn't that what you're after, money?"

The right hook came out of nowhere, sending Walter staggering. In his effort to steady himself, Walter had stepped halfway from the threshold. Heinz took the opportunity to hurry through it. Instead of running outside, however, he dashed along the center aisle of the stable. Walter regained his foothold and sped after him. If Heinz wanted a fight, he would get one. He debated whether to unclasp his handcuffs but decided against it. Heinz was rummaging through an old workbench.

Walter checked his corners and decided to give himself room on all sides. Finally, Heinz had found what he was looking for. He whirled around and flung himself at Walter. The knife blade glinted even in the semi-darkness of the stable. Walter leaped out of the way and spun around, careful not to turn his back on Heinz. He immediately regretted having put the cigarette carton into his pocket. It impeded his agility quite a bit.

Walter began to move sideways in a semi-circling motion. Keeping just out of arm's length, Heinz followed suit. If he wanted a boxing match, Walter was clearly at a disadvantage.

"So, you would really risk injuring an officer?" Walter taunted. "Haven't you committed enough crimes already?"

Heinz's face was red with anger. "What crimes?"

"For starters, you just as much as admitted that you killed Roswitha," Walter said in an icy voice.

"I did nothing of the sort. I just said that she deserved to die, but she could have been killed by one of her boyfriends," Heinz said, twisting the knife in his right hand.

"Boyfriends? She had more than one?"

Heinz breathed hard now. "Girls like her use men wherever they can find them."

Walter fixated his eyes on the knife. "What's the matter? Did she reject you?"

A cloud seemed to pass over Heinz's eyes. He firmed his grip on the knife, moving it just inches away from Walter's cheek.

Walter tried a different approach. "What about your mother? Doesn't she deserve better than having a son in jail for murder? Who's going to look after her?"

The hand that held the knife dropped just a fraction. "But it's for her that I've been smuggling. I want her to have a refrigerator and an electric stove. Now I'm almost at a point where I could buy those things, and you have to ruin everything."

"I think you did it to yourself," Walter said in the calmest voice he could muster. He had to try to defuse Heinz's anger. Anger at being caught.

From the corner of his eye, Walter had watched Heinz's hand. Heinz had talked himself into a rage, slightly easing the tension on his arm. It was now or never. Walter's right fist hit Heinz's arm from underneath, throwing Heinz off guard. The knife flew up in the air, barely missing Walter's nose. Walter unhooked his handcuffs from his belt and grabbed Heinz's wrist. He pivoted the suspect around and struggled to place the other wrist into the handcuff. Finally, Roswitha's killer was arrested. With his good fist, he gave Heinz a shove in his lower back to point him toward the exit.

"Hey, what was that for?" demanded Heinz.

"That was for kidnapping my sister," Walter said.

"I had nothing to do with that," Heinz protested.

Walter gave him another shove, with lesser strength. "Who did?"

"Bruno and Johnson."

So Bruno had given Ingrid his real name. Very dumb of him.

"Tell me one thing: What were they planning to do with Ingrid?"

"I had nothing to do with it." Heinz said. "We kept running into you so often lately, it was time to divert your attention. They thought you would be so busy looking for your sister that you wouldn't have time to snoop around."

Walter gritted his teeth. "You haven't answered my question yet: What were they planning to do with Ingrid?"

"Nothing. They figured that the construction workers would find her the next morning, giving them enough time to move the loot to a safe house."

Walter motioned Heinz to keep going.

"Aren't you going to take the cigarettes with you?" Heinz asked.

"No, I've got enough evidence to throw you in jail," Walter said. "I'll let customs deal with your loot."

"How long have you been in the stable?" Heinz couldn't seem to stop talking.

"Long enough to see Mielke, Johnson, and you loading the car."

Heinz's shoulders sagged. At last, it seemed to dawn on him that he had reached the end of the road.

Nonetheless, Walter decided not to take any chances. He hooked his good arm under Heinz's and escorted him to the road. The drizzle had now evolved into a steady rain. By the time they reached the police car, Heinz's hair glistened with moisture. Walter opened the passenger door and pulled the seat back forward.

"Get in there."

Heinz still didn't move. Walter grasped a shock of Heinz's hair and pulled it downward.

"Ouch," Heinz said.

"I told you to get your ass in there. Do you need a special invitation?"

Heinz grunted and bent over to clamber onto the back seat of the Beetle. Walter wiped his handkerchief over his wet face and sat in the driver's seat. He would drive to the police station in Schönau to ask for assistance transporting his prisoner to Lauterbach. He locked the passenger door and turned the car around in the farmer's driveway.

The windshield wipers squeaked across the windshield, providing the only noise inside the car. Walter sat rigidly behind the steering wheel. He would not relax until Heinz was under lock and key. The car skidded on wet leaves as he turned onto the country road that led to Schönau. Rain fell in big drops from the poplar trees lining the road. The farmer was still behind his plow, hunched against the rain and wind. The few shoppers clutched their bags under their drab umbrellas.

Walter pulled up at the small police station and blew the horn several times. A few seconds later, a red-haired police master stepped out of the building. Walter explained who the prisoner was and together they led him into the station.

Walter hung his wet cap on a coat rack and hurried to a desk. "Watch him while I'm making a phone call." He grabbed the receiver without waiting for a reply.

Schlosser answered the phone at the first ring. "Where are you?"

"I'm at the police station in Schönau. And I arrested Heinz Wolf."

"Thank God," Schlosser said, letting out an audible sigh. "Are you all right?"

Not really. Walter regretted that he had gone to the old summer camp alone, but he would never admit that to his partner. "It was a close call. He tried to stab me."

Schlosser let out a cry. "Are you hurt?"

"No," Walter said. "I need you to make some phone calls right away. First of all, here is Johnson's license plate number. This time, I got it." He spelled the letters and numbers slowly so Schlosser could jot them down. "Next, there really is a Bruno Lessmeister. And third…"

"Hold on, give me time to write. All right, go ahead."

"Mielke, the fairground worker, was also involved. Just like we suspected. Hang on a second."

He strode to the chair where Heinz sat slumped over. "Where did Mielke go?"

"I don't know."

"Do you want to think about that again?"

"I'm telling you, I don't know." Heinz sounded desperate now. Perhaps he was telling the truth after all.

Walter waved him aside and returned to the phone. "Heinz doesn't seem to know where Mielke went. Go ahead and notify customs and the border control."

"I'll do it right away. What did they all do?"

Walter breathed in deeply. "I'm not sure yet, but I found a whole booty of cigarettes, liquor, and construction material."

Schlosser whistled over the air. "What are you going to do with Heinz?"

"I don't know. What do you suggest?"

"Wait, I'll ask Chief Simmer. He's back now." Schlosser returned less than a minute later. "He wants you to bring the prisoner here to our station. We can put him in the holding cell in the basement."

Walter scratched his head. "I guess he wants to interrogate him. As if he had anything to do with catching him."

"I suppose so. See you soon."

Walter placed the receiver back and asked the station chief, "Can I borrow your officer to take the suspect back to Lauterbach?"

The chief nodded. Walter explained to him where he could find the booty that he had had to leave behind. Walter hoped that Johnson had not returned in the meantime to pick up the remaining evidence.

Five minutes later, Walter was driving back to Lauterbach with Police Master Biehl and Heinz. Heinz appeared resigned to his fate. If Walter didn't know any better, he would have never assumed that this weak man had threatened his life.

Schlosser shot Walter a warning look as they entered the station. It meant *be careful*. Chief Simmer was drumming his fingers on his desk. Walter's temporary boss appeared agitated.

"Young man, where have you been all afternoon?" he demanded, ignoring the fact that he had not been there this morning to tell Walter what to do.

"I was out arresting a smuggler," Walter said with all the calmness he could muster. After all, he had been doing all the legwork while the chief had spent most of his time in court.

"Smuggling? Do you have any proof of it?" Chief Simmer asked as he rose from his chair.

Walter pulled the pack of cigarettes out of his inner pocket. Heinz's face drooped at the sight of it. "There should be fingerprints on it. I've told the chief in Schönau where the loot is. He promised to call later with a report."

A slight smile traveled across Chief Simmer's face. Perhaps he gathered that this was an opportunity to earn laurels from his superiors for his temporary duty in Lauterbach. Walter almost expected him to click his heels together.

Schlosser and Biehl led the prisoner to a conference room in the back of the building. Walter grabbed a notepad and pencil and followed behind the chief. He did not want to miss this interrogation. After all, he had risked life and limb to catch the suspect. Chief Simmer dismissed Biehl and sent

Schlosser back to the office with orders to bring Roswitha's file.

"You can take notes for me," Chief Simmer said, glancing at Walter's notepad. If his temporary boss wanted to pull rank, so be it.

"Name?" Chief Simmer asked in a grating voice.

"Heinz Wolf." All the cockiness seemed to have left Heinz and his voice was barely louder than a whisper. Schlosser came in with the file and shot a look at Walter that said *don't let him bother you.*

Walter lowered his eyelids to signal that he understood. He jotted down notes as the interview progressed.

"Where were you on the afternoon of Saturday, October fourth?" the chief asked.

"I was out with friends."

"Where?"

"I don't know." Heinz said. "We were just taking a walk."

Chief Simmer's eyebrows arched. "A walk? Where did you walk to?"

Heinz fidgeted. "Nowhere in particular. We just walked."

Simmer shot up from his chair. "Young man, you were caught with smuggled goods and you're telling me you just went for a walk." His voice sounded dangerously calm. "And I'm told that we have evidence that you have killed a young woman. What do you have to say to that?"

Heinz's face turned ashen. "What evidence?"

Walter cleared his throat. Since he had performed the investigation, he felt a need to have a say in it. "Your mother told me the other day that you brought home firewood for her. Judging from the place where I found the body, we have reason to believe that she was killed with a branch from the fallen tree that lay next to her."

Heinz's mouth contorted into a savage grin. "That's all you got? That's not evidence, that's just the babbling of an old woman. I've brought home firewood before. Everybody does that ever since we lost our forest to the building of the base."

Walter secretly admitted that Heinz spoke the truth. Even Walter had collected firewood in the moor before joining the police academy. Fear settled in on him. Fear that the evidence he had gathered was dangerously thin. Could it be that Roswitha's killer would slip through their fingers?

Walter said, "We have an eyewitness who saw Mielke hiding behind a tree and then someone knocked the witness unconscious. Since you're best friends with Mielke, I can only assume it was you." Walter regretted the word as soon as he had spoken it.

"Assume?" Heinz spat the word. "You have no evidence at all, do you?"

Chief Simmer leafed through the file. "This report says that the woman's purse and one shoe are missing. What did you do with them?"

The veins on Heinz's temples popped out. "How should I know? I'm telling you, I didn't kill her."

Walter decided to speak up, no matter the consequences. "It was a white purse made of fabric."

"No, it wasn't. It was a red purse..." Heinz's voice trailed off as soon as he had spoken the words.

19

"Aha," Chief Simmer was as close to a smile as Walter had ever seen him. "Now we're getting somewhere. What did you do with the purse?"

Heinz folded his arms in front of his chest without speaking. Simmer interrogated Heinz for another fifteen minutes without any admission from him. Finally, he asked Schlosser to take the prisoner to the holding cell.

When they were out of earshot, Walter said to the chief, "I have an idea where the purse could be, but I admit it's just a hunch." He told his temporary boss of the bar where he had seen Curly and Johnson and that there was a pile of manure in the courtyard.

Chief Simmer pursed his lips. "There are lots of dung piles in this village. Don't his parents have one?"

"His father is dead and his mother gave up farming after that. So Heinz couldn't have gotten rid of the purse at home. I believe that the gang used the *Luna* Bar as a headquarters to plan their next crime."

"If he isn't talking by tomorrow morning, you and Schlosser may search the dung pile for the purse," Simmer said without moving a muscle in his face.

Walter winced when he realized that he would have to dig through a pile of manure. What would his friends do when they heard about this? Someday his hunches would get him into big trouble.

His mother and Ingrid were waiting in the kitchen when he arrived at home. Ingrid's usually rosy cheeks were still pale.

"How are you doing?" he asked her as he dropped into his chair. His mother put a plate of potato salad and minced meatloaf in front of him. "Hmm, that smells good. I'm starved." He ate a few forks full of food while Ingrid picked at her sandwich. "How are you?" he asked again.

"I'm fine," she said, but her shifty eyes betrayed her.

He decided to talk to her alone after dinner. She would probably be more at ease when their mother was not listening in on them. At the end of the meal, Walter pushed his plate away and rose to browse through the newspaper. He studied the local news and was relieved that there was no mention of Roswitha's death investigation. His mother washed the dishes while Ingrid dried them. The siblings heaved a sigh of relief when Frau Hofmann declared that she would visit their neighbor Berta.

"Sit down," Walter said to Ingrid as soon as their mother closed the door behind her. "I've got some news for you and didn't want *Mama* to hear it."

He related most of the events of the day after urging her not to tell anyone for now. He left out the part about the missing purse. After all, the investigation had only just begun.

"So, you think that Heinz killed that woman?" Ingrid asked.

Walter shrugged, unsure how much to reveal to her. He was not allowed to talk about open cases. "I don't know what to think anymore, but I'm hoping to find some evidence soon that might implicate Heinz in the crime. I can't believe Johnson would be stupid enough to commit murder in a foreign country. And I really want to know who killed Max."

"How can I help?" Ingrid asked.

"Tell me step for step what happened yesterday morning. Was there anything peculiar about the man who threw a sack over your head? What did he smell like? How tall was he? Anything."

Ingrid knitted her brows. "He smelled like he was a smoker," she said slowly.

"Cigars or cigarettes?"

"Definitely cigarettes."

"All right, that's better than nothing." Walter stepped to the kitchen cabinet and pulled out a drawer halfway. He rummaged through it until he found a piece of scratch paper and a pencil. Back at the table, he began to jot down notes.

"How tall was he?"

"About your height, maybe a bit shorter."

"Did he say anything at all?"

Ingrid shook her head. "Everything went so fast, I didn't pay much attention whether he said anything or not. But I don't think so." She began to sniffle. He looked up from his notes and patted her hand.

"Oh, Walter," she wailed, "you have no idea how scared I was. I scolded myself for being so stupid. I kept thinking: What will they do to me if they come back?" Her eyes grew large. "Do you think I'm still in danger?"

Walter rested his chin on his thumb and index finger. "I don't think so. According to Heinz, they wanted to divert my attention by kidnapping you. They thought I would be so busy looking for you that I wouldn't have time to go after them. Until we arrest the killer, though, I don't want you to go out alone after dark. And don't talk to strangers."

201

Ingrid wiped off tears with her left hand. "I've learned my lesson now."

"So, you don't know whether he was German or American?"

"I'm pretty sure he was German."

"Why?"

Ingrid's lips twisted into a slight smile. "Have you ever seen an American with a potato sack? Where would they get one from?"

Walter rubbed his chin. "Did the sack smell like potatoes?"

"No."

There were probably hundreds of sacks in the village, so Walter decided to try a different approach. "Did they say who would drive you to see Elvis?"

"They said the American would drive, of course. He was the only one who had a car."

Despite his exhaustion, Walter could not sit still anymore. He dropped his pencil on the table and jumped up. His chair fell backward, causing Ingrid to flinch. He picked up the chair and put it down with a thud. Stalking through the kitchen, he said, "I can't believe you wanted to go on a ride with complete strangers! Don't you have any common sense? And all this just after that young woman was killed. I really expected more sense from you."

Ingrid sobbed while rummaging through her pocket for a handkerchief. "I'm sorry. I wasn't thinking about that. You are always so uptight about everything, so I was afraid to ask you to take me to Bad Nauheim."

Walter stopped pacing and grabbed the back of his chair with both hands. "Promise me that you'll never do anything like that again. This could have ended badly for you." He sank back on his chair. "How much does *Mama* know?"

Ingrid blew her nose. "She knows that I've been kidnapped, but she doesn't know why." Her eyes pleaded with Walter. "Please don't tell her."

Walter drove his fingers through his hair. Even when he was not wearing his hat, he could feel an impression in it. "All right, we'll tell her that some of the fair boys played a prank on you. But there is no guarantee that gossip won't carry the real story to her sooner or later. Are you sure no one witnessed your kidnapping?"

"I saw no one around, and the building was not finished yet."

Walter decided to leave the subject alone. He was too exhausted to think about the consequences of her actions tonight. In a few days, he would talk to her again.

He rose. "I'm really tired now. I just want to listen to some music and go to bed early." He turned on the radio and rotated the dial until he found AFN. Soon, the Platters' "Twilight Time" filled the airwaves. He sank on the chaise longue and closed his eyes. On days like this, he wondered why he had chosen to be a police officer. His friends never had to work overtime. But then, they did not have the satisfaction of helping people like he did. Still, he did not look forward to searching a stinking dung pile the next day, even though it had been his own idea.

20

Many eyes followed Schlosser and Walter as they walked from the police station to the *Luna* bar. The bar was closed, of course, since it was only mid-morning. Schlosser rang the bell on the house door and a young woman answered after a few seconds. She was the same woman Walter had talked to on that evening when he had first seen Curly.

"Good morning, Hilde," Schlosser said, "Is your father at home?"

Hilde wiped her hands on her apron. "He's changing clothes right now. He just finished milking the cows."

"You still have cows? Isn't business good enough at the bar?" Schlosser remarked.

Hilde fidgeted a bit. Apparently, she was not sure what to make of this visit. "Yes, business is good, but Papa wants to keep our three cows until they stop giving milk. He's old-fashioned that way."

"Understandable. One doesn't want to sell a good milk cow," Schlosser said jovially. "Do you know how long he will be?"

"Not very long. Would you like to come in? I'm fixing lunch now, but you could sit in our living room," Hilde said and stepped aside from the door.

"If it's all right with your father, we would rather have a look at the bar instead," Schlosser said, winking at Walter.

"I guess he wouldn't mind," Hilde said. She reached for a key that hung from a hook on the wall. "I've already cleaned it this morning." She unlocked the door from the hallway and stepped aside to let the officers pass.

Walter followed Schlosser inside. Their heavy steps echoed in the empty bar. The stale smell of cigarette smoke hung in the cold room. No detergent in the world could get rid of it, as it crept into the drapes and woodwork. All chairs were turned upside down on the tables to make the cleaning easier. Was this the same room that had teemed with lively dancers when Walter visited just a few days ago?

Hilde turned to leave, but Schlosser motioned her to stay. "Could we ask you a few questions, please?"

"Me?" She stopped in her tracks. "What can I do for you?"

"Do you remember a German fellow with curly hair who met an American man in here?"

Hilde rubbed her chin. "Yes, I think I know who you're talking about. Comes in here quite often."

"Really? When was the last time you saw him?"

"Hm, I can't remember. But I don't think he comes in here when it's slow. I've only seen him when it was really crowded."

"Thank you, you may go now."

Relief spread over Hilde's face as she turned toward the door. When she was out of earshot, Walter whispered to his co-worker, "See why I can't find a date? Everybody clams up when a policeman is around."

Schlosser chuckled. "Yes, I'm beginning to see your problem. And now she, too, knows that you're a cop." He nudged Walter's shoulder. "Relax. Some girls like uniforms. My wife did."

Walter perked up. "Does she have a sister?"

"Two, but they're both married." Schlosser turned around when the landlord entered the taproom. The faint smell of cows lingered around him, reminding Walter of what lay ahead. "Good morning, Herr Biehl. We have a couple of questions for you, if you don't mind."

Biehl's gaze darted back and forth between Schlosser and Walter before it came to rest on the old gloves sticking out of Walter's pockets. "Why don't you sit down, gentlemen?" He lifted three chairs off a table and put them on the floor. The three men took their seats.

Schlosser asked, "Have you ever bought any liquor under the table?"

Biehl looked so thunderstruck that Walter was convinced of his innocence. "No, I haven't. I swear."

"All right, don't get upset. I have to ask these questions," Schlosser appeased him. "The main reason we're here is a different one. We were wondering if we could examine your dung heap out front."

Biehl's lips turned upward in a faint smile. "You want to look at my dung heap? Whatever in the world for?"

"We're looking for some evidence in a crime," Schlosser said.

Biehl shrugged. "Be my guest. As long as you put everything back as it was. I'll even give you a pitchfork."

"Do you have two? It would go faster if we both had one," Walter said. He knew who would do the work if they only had one fork, and it would not be Schlosser.

"Sure," Biehl said as he rose.

Walter and Schlosser returned to the farmyard to wait for Biehl. As Walter slipped into his old gloves, Schlosser shook his head. "You think of everything. I forgot to look for something old. Now I'll have to wear my police gloves and get them stinky."

Biehl returned, wearing a work jacket and carrying two pitchforks. Apparently, he did not want to miss the spectacle that would surely follow.

"Well, let's get started," Schlosser said, rubbing his hands. He and Walter began to pick up piles of muck and put them in the dirt next to the dung heap.

Schlosser turned his head away from his work. "Ack! Why did I ever listen to you? You owe me a beer if we don't find anything in here."

Walter chuckled. "I think we need a beer either way."

Biehl stood in front of his house, his arms folded in front of him. Soon his daughter joined him. A little girl with pigtails strolled by on the sidewalk, holding the handle of a small basket in her arm. When she saw the uniformed police officers digging through the muck pile with pitchforks, she stood still and stuck a thumb in her mouth.

Schlosser put on a grim face and said, "Boo."

The girl pulled the thumb out of her mouth and began running. When she was at a safe distance, she stopped again and stared at the officers. Windows began to open in the nearby houses. Homemakers and old men leaned outside to see what was happening.

"I'm glad the older kids are in school or else we would have to charge admission," Schlosser whispered to Walter.

Ignoring the onlookers, the officers stubbornly worked, piling one heap after the other in the dirt while turning their heads sideways. Once on the ground, they spread the muck to make sure they did not miss any foreign objects. Finally, Walter cried out, "I think I found something."

His manure fork had hit a hard object. Carefully, he lifted a fork full of muck and brought it to their eye level. "Look, there is a sling!"

He pointed at a loop that penetrated through the dung. Schlosser placed a prong through the handle while Walter dug around the object with his gloved hands to free it. With a triumphant smile, Schlosser held up the pitchfork. "Well, I'll be. That looks like it could be a bag. It's hard to tell at this point. Grab the handle and try to shake off as much dung as possible without damaging it."

Walter did as he was told, holding the item at arm's length so he would not be bombarded with muck. Schlosser stuck his pitchfork into the pile and came over to inspect the bag. "Do you think that's the woman's bag? What did it look like?"

"Green said it was a red bag with an arm sling. I do believe this is it!"

Walter suppressed the urge to shout with glee. Police officers didn't do that. After all, their investigation was about a violent death, not a case for celebration.

Schlosser fished a paper bag out of his pocket and unfolded it. Walter placed the purse inside and put it on the ground. He was tempted to open the purse to see if Roswitha's ID card was inside, but he feared a reproach from his temporary boss.

"What do we do now?" Walter asked.

"Shall we look for her shoe, too?" Schlosser suggested.

Walter shrugged and picked up the pitchfork again. They already smelled like stable boys. A few minutes more would not make much difference.

"My wife won't let me into the apartment tonight," Schlosser complained.

"Simmer might not even let us into the station," Walter said with a chuckle.

They continued working carefully, because the shoe would be at about the same height where they found the purse.

"I don't think it's here," Schlosser said. "Perhaps the shoe was not taken by the same person who took the bag."

The men jabbed their forks into the pile and walked toward the bar entrance. In safe distance from the dung, Walter breathed in deeply. The little girl had left. In her stead, two little boys peered through the wire fence of the neighbor's garden. He said, "We still have to put everything back. I'm sorry for putting you through this."

Schlosser shrugged. "Don't be sorry. At least we found what we were looking for. I would never have thought of looking here. Chief Kleber will be very proud of you, you can be sure of that."

Walter's face brightened. "I believe he will." He felt guilty because he had not thought about his chief in days. How could he, with so much going on?

Biehl approached the officers. "I would offer you something to drink, but since you're on duty..."

"I'll take a Coca-Cola when we're done," Walter hastened to say. He had to get the foul taste and smell out of his throat.

"Me too," Schlosser chimed in. They returned to the dung heap and began forking the muck back on the heap. When they were finished, they walked toward Biehl's front door, where his daughter waited with two open bottles of Coca-Cola. She couldn't keep her eyes off Walter.

Schlosser winked at him when she left. "Looks like you're making quite an impression on her."

"Pfft, she probably laughs about me behind my back," Walter said, taking a big gulp.

Schlosser sipped on his drink. "Why are you so negative about girls? Just because you couldn't find a girl at the fair doesn't mean that no one likes you. Do you know that I envy you sometimes?"

Walter jerked back. "You envy me?"

"Yes. You're young and carefree. You can go out and not come home until it's time to go back to work. Sometimes I wish I had waited a bit longer to get married. Go out and enjoy yourself before you get tied to one girl."

Walter contemplated his bottle. "I never looked at it that way. Of course, I don't want to get married yet. I just want to take a girl out once in a while and feel that she likes me."

Schlosser put his empty bottle on the windowsill. "I know what you mean. Don't worry. You will find a girl, and probably when you least expect it. I have one piece of advice for you, though. When you like a girl, don't wait too long to tell her how you feel. There's plenty of competition around nowadays."

He knew. Walter had tried hard to conceal his crush on Marianne from his friends, to no avail. It must have been written on his face. He tilted his head back to empty his Cola. "Let's get back to the office."

He picked up the paper bag and they returned to the police station.

"Did you have any luck?" Simmer asked. He waved his hand in front of his face to disperse the smell that announced his two officers.

"Yes," Walter said with a faint smile. He refrained from grinning because a police officer was not supposed to do that. He was about to place the bag on Simmer's desk, but his supervisor coughed in disgust. "Can't you put this thing somewhere else?"

Walter withdrew his arm and went into the hallway, followed by Schlosser and Simmer. Schlosser cleared some room on a little table and Walter gingerly pulled the purse out of the bag.

"Let me see," Simmer said, drawing closer. Walter turned the purse around, causing Simmer to flinch. "I guess you were right. This thing smells like it has been in a dung heap for a while."

"Do you want to open it?" Walter asked.

"No, you do it. You're the one wearing gloves. I don't want to get my fingerprints on it," Simmer said.

Careful not to damage any possible prints, Walter struggled with the clasp. The three officers sighed deeply when Walter opened the bag. Besides a small wallet and a lipstick, they saw a gray ID card peeking out of the back compartment. Walter whooped for joy while Schlosser fetched two pencils to open the cover of the identity card.

"Is that her?" Schlosser asked when he opened the page that contained a photo. Walter took one look at it and nodded. Roswitha had been a brunette when the photo was taken. She probably thought that she would find a boyfriend faster as a blonde. Instead, it had ended her life at an early age.

Walter shuddered when he thought of his petty complaints about not finding a girl. After all, Roswitha had been almost his age when she died.

Simmer studied the personal data. "Walter, you're going to have to take this purse to the station in Reichenbach. They'll check it for fingerprints or send it somewhere else. Let's hope that we find the killer that way."

Walter swallowed at the word *we*. As if Simmer had anything to do with solving this case!

Chief Simmer addressed Schlosser. "You might as well go with him, and take the prisoner along. We simply don't have the manpower to watch him here."

On his way home from work, Walter stopped at the tobacco shop.

"Good evening, Walter," said the shop owner, Frau Albert. "I heard you've had quite some excitement today. And you smell like it, too."

Walter raised his eyebrow. Word got around fast in a small town. He walked to the magazine display and halted when he spotted three beer steins on a shelf. Crests adorned one side and hunting scenes the other. He turned to Frau Albert.

"Are you selling souvenirs now?"

She smiled shyly and shrugged. "A few weeks ago an American asked me for a stein. So I thought it might be a good idea to carry some."

Walter pulled a *Bravo* magazine out of the rack. He walked to the counter, where he picked a pack of chewing gum out of a rack.

"Have you solved that murder case yet?" Frau Albert asked as she took his coins.

Walter made a blank face. "I can't comment on it yet."

Frau Albert rang up his purchase. "Ah, that means that you're getting close, right?"

Damn, he had to watch every word he said.

Leaning closer, the shop owner probed, "Did you find any evidence in that dung heap?"

"Good evening, Frau Albert," Walter said while he made for the door.

At home, he walked in through the back door, grabbed an old pair of pants from a coat rack, and hung his cap on a hook. He descended the steps down to the cellar, where he took off his uniform. He hung the clothes on a clothesline and changed into the clothes he wore when he mucked his rabbits. Hopefully, his mother had fed them today.

Ingrid and his mother were talking in the kitchen when he walked in.

"How are you today?" he asked his sister, eyeing her carefully. Her face still had a pallid appearance. "Here, this will cheer you up." He put the magazine next to her plate.

Ingrid whooped. "Thank you. I didn't have time this week to get it myself."

She started to leaf through *Bravo*, but her mother interrupted. "We're eating supper now, so put that thing away until we're finished."

Ingrid groaned and put the magazine on the chaise longue. Frau Hofmann ladled three sizzling potato pancakes onto a plate. She breathed in noisily as she set the plate in front of Walter. "Phew, where have you been today?"

Walter, who was just leading a spoonful of applesauce toward his mouth, stopped in midair. "You two must be the only people in the village who don't know that. Frau Albert at the tobacco shop knew it, and she probably told everyone she saw today."

He recollected the dung heap tale and his mother wrinkled her nose. "I hope you left your clothes downstairs."

"Yes, *Mama*. I am going to have to wear them tomorrow, so if you could brush them a bit, I'd be grateful."

Ingrid had other concerns. "Does this mean you might be close to arresting the men who kidnapped me?"

Walter swallowed a piece of pancake. "I can't make any promises yet, but maybe we can get a useable fingerprint from the purse. I hope we will, so we can put this nightmare behind us."

"I think we can all agree on that," his mother said and sank heavily on a chair. She grabbed a slice of bread from the breadbasket and spread butter and applesauce on it.

"Aren't you going to eat pancakes?" Walter asked between bites.

She shook her head so vehemently that her headscarf slipped onto her forehead. "No, I had some for lunch. You know I don't like to eat a warm supper." She pulled her scarf off. "You look tired, my boy. I think you need some rest. You won't go out tonight, will you?"

Walter looked up from his plate. "No, *Mama*. I've had enough excitement for one week, and it's not even over yet."

Walter went into the living room to pick up the newspaper. He was exhausted. He looked forward to Saturday evening when Fritz celebrated his birthday. All their friends would be there. He needed something to look forward to this week and hoped nothing would prevent him from attending.

Walter settled into reading the paper. He wished that Jeff were here so he could drink a beer with him while listening to some music. Jeff. Where was he now? He had not thought about his friend in days, but figured that the fastest way to free the young American was to work this case as long as it took.

21

The phone call came at mid-afternoon. "We have a match on the fingerprint we lifted off the purse," the chief of the Reichenbach police said to Walter.

Walter sat up straight. "May I ask who the match is?"

Chief Zimmermann said, "I'd rather tell you that in person."

Walter covered the receiver with his hand and asked Chief Simmer, "Can I go to Reichenbach? They made a match on the fingerprint."

Chief Simmer nodded.

"I'll be over in a few minutes," Walter said into the phone and hung up.

Walter could barely contain his excitement on the way to Reichenbach. The desk sergeant on duty led him to the chief's private office.

"Come in, Herr Hofmann," Zimmermann said. "How is Chief Kleber doing?"

Walter said, "I don't know. The last I heard from my partner was that he was doing fine and was anxious to get home."

"That sounds just like him. He probably can't wait to get back to work. And he missed this big case. What a shame."

Walter flinched. He did not possess the detachment of a more experienced officer yet. "Who were the fingerprints from?"

The chief opened a thin file. "The fingerprints were from your prisoner, Heinz Wolf."

Walter took a deep breath. "I'm glad I arrested the right person, then. But you could have told me that on the phone."

"Sure, sure, but I wanted you to be present during the interrogation. Hopefully, he confesses. If not, then seeing you might speed things along a bit. After all, I hear you had quite a personal involvement in this case."

Walter ran his fingers through his hair. He was pleased that he could witness an interrogation, but felt uneasy about Ingrid's involvement in the case. "I'd like to leave my sister out of it, if that's possible."

"Sure," the chief said soberly. "Let's go now." They entered the interrogation room when another officer brought in the handcuffed prisoner. Heinz hesitated when he saw Walter. The officer led Heinz to a chair opposite Zimmermann and Walter and told him to sit down. The officer then placed a notepad and pencil on the table before taking a seat.

"Where were you on the afternoon of October fourth?" Zimmermann probed. Heinz glared at him.

Zimmermann nodded slightly at Walter, taking him by surprise. Walter had only expected to witness the questioning, not take part in it.

"Since I caught you with a room full of smuggled goods, I must assume that the dead woman, Roswitha Gregorius, surprised you during one of your smuggling runs," Walter said. "Am I right?"

Heinz remained silent. Walter found the quietude more unnerving than an outburst of anger.

"And then you knocked an off-duty military police officer over the head and kidnapped him, together with your accomplices," Walter continued.

Heinz broke the silence. "You have no proof that that was me."

"We don't need proof," Zimmermann interrupted. "We found the dead woman's purse, and your fingerprint was on it."

Heinz's jawbones twitched. Good, Walter thought. He's getting angry. Maybe he will confess now.

"You seem surprised that we found the purse, since you hid it so well," Walter continued. "It wasn't easy, but you see, the purse was hidden in a dung heap in front of your headquarters. That's where I saw your accomplices several times, and so it was an easy conclusion that you might have hidden some evidence there."

"There must have been a hundred fingerprints on that purse," Heinz blurted out. "A girl like that, she must have had a dozen boyfriends..."

"You don't know much about women, do you?" Walter said, not feeling so sure about his knowledge of women himself. After all, he only had intimate knowledge about the women in his household: his mother and Ingrid. "Girls don't let anyone touch their purses, not even their girlfriends. And least of all their boyfriends."

Heinz looked as if he were ready to spit. "I saw her during the warmer months with a Negro in the woods. They're a disgrace, all of them. She deserved to die, I'm telling you."

"Is that why you killed her, because she went out with a Negro?" Zimmermann asked. "Or did you want her for yourself?"

Heinz's face was scarlet red now. "They killed my father. They all deserve to die!"

"Who killed your father?" Walter and Zimmermann blurted out simultaneously.

Heinz's voice sounded like a squeaking door now. "Don't act like you don't know. The Americans killed my father when he was ordered to blow up a Rhine bridge in the spring of 1945."

Now Walter remembered. Heinz's father had died during the last days of the war while retreating over the Rhine River with his company. Somehow, Heinz seemed to believe that the American troops stationed here now were responsible for his father's death.

"And you, how can you be friends with them after losing your father in the war?" Heinz now attacked Walter.

Why did so many people remind Walter of his father's death lately? He tried to calm his voice before replying. "My father died in Siberia. The Americans had nothing to do with it. The soldiers that are here now were boys then, just like we were during the war."

Zimmermann interrupted the sparring classmates. "Let's get back to the dead woman. Did you kill her because she witnessed your smuggling operation?"

Heinz's eyes were fixed on a scratch on the table. "I didn't kill her," he murmured.

The room turned so quiet that Walter could hear the officer's pencil writing on the pad.

"What?" Zimmermann and Walter exclaimed.

"I didn't kill her," Heinz repeated, sounding more confident.

Walter sat up straighter in his chair. He did not know what to do next. They didn't teach you these things at police school.

The chief cradled his chin with his left hand. Obviously, he was trying to buy time. At last, he asked, "Why didn't you say so before?"

Heinz' mouth curved upward into a smirk. "Because no one asked me. You were all so sure that I killed the woman that no one bothered to ask me if I killed her or not."

Walter cleared his throat. "If I remember right, you didn't answer any of our questions. And after you had a lot of time to think about it, you're telling us that you're not a killer. Why should we believe you now?"

Heinz jumped up. The chief and Walter both jerked, ready to tackle him if necessary. "Because it's the truth. I didn't kill that woman!" he screamed. "And I don't want to go to jail for a murder I didn't commit."

Zimmermann spread out his arms, palms down. "Sit down and calm your voice."

Walter expected another outburst, but Heinz complied.

"Let's talk about the crime you admit to committing: smuggling," the chief said, resting his palms on the polished table. "Who are your accomplices?"

Heinz leaned back in his chair, folding his arms in front of his chest.

Zimmermann raised his voice. "Come on, we already know that the carnival worker and an American named ..." Zimmermann looked questioningly at the note-taking officer. "An American named Frank Johnson were involved in your smuggling ring. Was there someone else?"

"Maybe, maybe not," Heinz replied defiantly.

"Who was the leader?"

Heinz remained silent.

"All right," Zimmermann said, banging his fist on the table. "I'm calling the Air Police now. They've arrested Johnson this morning. Maybe he will tell us who his partners were. But remember, if you confess now, you might get a shorter sentence than otherwise. It's your choice."

Heinz's face changed from defiance to resignation. "I was the ring leader," he murmured.

"Come again?"

"I was the ringleader," Heinz's voice, though louder now, betrayed his fear.

The chief nodded his approval. "How long have you been smuggling?"

"About three months."

"How many men were involved?"

Heinz stared at the ceiling for a few moments, apparently debating whether to betray his accomplices or not. Finally he said, "We were four men."

Zimmermann counted on his fingers. "You, Johnson, and Mielke. Who was the fourth one?"

"I don't know his real name. He called himself Müller." His laugh was bitter. "A real original name, wasn't it? But we all knew it wasn't his real name."

Walter sat up straight. "Did Müller have curly hair?"

"Yes."

"Do you know his whereabouts?"

Heinz shook his head. "I never asked him where he lived. He seemed to come out of nowhere whenever we had a delivery to make."

Zimmermann checked whether the officer had caught up with his notes of the investigation. "Why did you start smuggling?"

"I needed money," Heinz said with a shrug. "And the Americans owed me something for killing my father."

"You smuggled to seek revenge for your father's death?" Zimmermann probed further.

"Yes."

Walter searched Heinz's face. The war had been over for more than thirteen years, but Heinz still had not gotten over it. He felt a pang of sorrow for his misguided adversary, but chided himself for it. His job was to catch and interrogate criminals, not to feel sorry for them.

"Who stole the contraband, and where?"

Heinz shifted in his seat, remaining silent.

"Come on," Zimmermann probed. "It will all come out anyway. If you don't tell us, I'm sure your friends will."

Heinz stared at the table in front of him. "Johnson worked in the liquor store on base. It was really easy for him to make some cases disappear, he said."

"And the cigarettes?"

"He didn't say where he got them, and I didn't ask."

"You didn't ask? And you're the ringleader?" Zimmermann asked incredulously. "Who did you sell your stolen goods to?"

Heinz glared at the chief. "There are enough bar owners around here who don't mind buying stuff under the table."

Zimmermann rested his chin in his hand. "You didn't happen to smuggle the stuff into the *Saarland*, did you?"

The *Saarland* had reunited with the Federal Republic the year before, but the economic transition was not complete yet.

"Perhaps."

Any empathy that Walter had felt for his schoolmate was vanishing now. He was anxious to urge the interrogation along, but decided to watch the chief instead. After all, he was here to learn from a more experienced police officer while his boss was on sick leave.

"And what did you do with the money?" Zimmermann asked.

Heinz's head tilted toward the ceiling. "I hid it in our attic," he said at last.

"You didn't spend any of it?"

Heinz's jawbones seemed to be ready to crack his skin. "Damn it, all I wanted to do was buy a refrigerator and an electric stove for my mother."

"You could have gotten a job and saved the money," Zimmermann said.

"That takes too long. I wanted her to have these things now and not in three or five years. She works so hard. I wanted her life to be a little easier."

"Well, you now have made her life much harder," Zimmermann said, his voice softening. "How will she feel now, having a son in jail for murder?"

The veins on Heinz's temples seemed to pop out of his head. "I told you, I didn't kill her!"

Zimmermann shrugged. "Why don't you tell us what happened on the afternoon of October fourth? Did you make a smuggling run that day?"

Heinz' eyes were fixated on the writing officer's hand. His jaws clenched and unclenched in quick succession. "Yes, we had arranged a delivery that day. I was supposed to wait for Johnson near the fence. He was to pick up the goods on base and pick me up outside the fence. We would then meet up with Mielke and Müller, who were scattered in the moor, pretending to look for berries or firewood."

"But something went wrong?" Zimmermann asked.

"I was held up at home by my mother. She wanted me to repair the front door, which was dragging on the floor when she opened and closed it. It took me much longer than I thought it would. I hurried through the village as fast as I could without looking suspicious, but I was about half an hour late when I got to our rendezvous point."

Walter leaned forward, listening intently. He would soon learn what had happened in the moor before he and the Air Policemen searched for Jeff.

"Was Johnson there?"

Heinz shook his head. "No, he wasn't. I paced along the fence for at least another half an hour, but he never showed up. I grew angrier and angrier by the minute, feeling that he had betrayed me. He must have taken the booze to the bar owner himself, cutting me out of my share, I thought."

"Where were Mielke and the other man?"

"They weren't there either. By then, I was furious and cursed their hides from here to Ludwigshafen."

Zimmermann asked, "What did you do then?"

"Finally, I decided to go to the *Luna* Bar for a drink to calm down. Something had gone wrong, and I figured that perhaps one or all of them would meet at the bar and regroup." Heinz cleared his throat. "Can I have something to drink?"

Zimmermann nodded to the note-taking officer, who closed the door behind him. A few seconds later, he returned with a glass of water.

Heinz took a sip. "I didn't walk very far when I came to a tree that had been felled recently."

Walter leaned forward in his chair. He did not want to miss any of Heinz's words.

"I wanted to go on, but something caught my eye."

"What was it?" the chief asked.

"It was a woman's shoe."

Walter's hands became moist. *Now it comes,* he thought. *Now I'll finally hear what happened.*

"I stopped to look closer at the shoe when I saw a woman lying behind the log. I figured she was sleeping and thought it was rather odd that she had taken off one shoe first. I was a bit scared and wanted to run away first. But then I became curious. I walked up to her and saw that she was not breathing or moving. Now I was really afraid. I've seen women in the moor before, usually waiting for their boyfriends. I looked around if anybody had seen me. When I decided that the coast was clear, I took off. I walked all the way to the *Luna* Bar without stopping."

Zimmermann waited until the officer had finished writing. "The woman's name was Roswitha Gregorius. Did you take her purse?"

Heinz grimaced as if caught in the act itself. "Yes, I did."

"Why?"

"I don't know anymore. I guess I thought I could sell that, too. It didn't take me long to realize my mistake. But I was afraid to go back because I feared that someone might see me near the body. So I was stuck with it. I hid it in my backpack. Later, when I left the bar and it was dark, I threw it on the dung heap. Then I fetched the farmer's fork and piled some dung on top of it. I thought no one would ever find it there until much later." He cast an admiring look at Walter.

Walter gave a wry smile. He had been very proud of himself for finding the purse. And now it turned out that it was unnecessary. Schlosser would never forgive him for that. He could imagine the ribbing he would get from his partner. "Is that all you took, the purse?"

Heinz fidgeted in his chair. "No. I saw a branch lying near the dead girl and picked it up."

"Why?" the chief asked again.

"I thought if I brought my mother some firewood, no one who saw me would get suspicious and ask me why I was in the moor."

"What did you do with the branch after you got home?"

"I threw it on our pile of firewood behind our house."

Zimmermann rolled his eyes. "I wish you had left the murder scene alone. Then perhaps Walter and his chief might have been able to collect evidence and catch the killer already."

Heinz's eyes grew large. "Am I going to get charged with that?"

"Yes," Zimmermann said gravely.

Walter listened intently. Fate had given him another mentor and he wanted to learn as much as he could from him. His colleagues, all fairly new on the job themselves, had never worked on a murder case and were of no help to him.

"Is there anything else you took and forgot to tell us?" Zimmermann asked with a hint of sarcasm in his tone.

Heinz shook his head. "No, I swear, that's all."

Zimmermann sighed. "Do you have any idea where your accomplices might be by now?"

Heinz stared at his fingers. "With the exception of me," he said with a dry laugh, "none of us had what you call a permanent address. They could be anywhere by now."

Zimmermann rose. "If you think of anything, let me know. We'll catch your buddies eventually. Right now, we are most interested in finding a killer."

The note-taking officer finishing writing and put the handcuffs back on Heinz's hands behind his back. Walter stared after his schoolmate, who now looked like a boy caught stealing candy at the grocery store.

As the door closed behind them, Zimmermann said to Walter, "Lies have short legs. Remember that, young man."

Walter chuckled. "My mother used to say that to me when I was a kid. She was right, of course. And now I have to start all over again looking for Roswitha's killer…"

22

Walter was alone at the station when the phone rang.

"Good morning," said a familiar voice, "this is Tech Sergeant Shoemaker. Could you come on base this morning?"

"Sure," Walter said, "as soon as my colleague comes back from patrol."

"All right."

An hour later, Walter headed to the base on the station's motorbike. He preferred the bike to the car, at least during the warmer months. It gave him a feeling of independence, even though he only used it for work. And until he could buy a scooter, it was his only means to impress girls. Not that there were any girls in the streets at this time of day.

Although the gate guard recognized Walter, he quickly glanced at Walter's ID card before waving him through.

Walter turned into the parking lot of the Air Police and silenced the engine. Several Air Policemen milled about the outer office, smoking cigarettes and drinking coffee. Walter wondered why they interrupted their conversation when he entered. Could they be talking about his inability to find the girl's killer? Wonderful. Was he the laughing stock of the base now?

He did not have time to finish the thought because Tech Sergeant Shoemaker ushered him into his office.

"There is someone here who would like to see you," he said, opening his door wide.

Puzzled, Walter stepped inside. A uniformed man sat on the chair in front of Shoemaker's desk with his back to the door. Walter wondered where he had seen such a head of black hair before when the man turned around.

"Hello, Walter."

"Jeff," Walter exclaimed. He stepped forward and stretched his hand out to his grinning friend. "You look good for someone who's been..." He searched for the right words because he did not want to embarrass his friend. Jeff was wearing his uniform. Could it be that the military had dropped the charges against him?

Jeff's grin waned. "Sit down." He jumped up and pulled a chair from the far side of the wall. Tech Sergeant Shoemaker took a seat behind his desk and lit a cigarette. He offered one to Walter, who shook his head.

"I don't quite know how to begin," Jeff said, looking at his shoes in obvious embarrassment.

"Why don't you begin at the beginning?" Walter suggested.

"You see, I wasn't in jail at all," Jeff said and sipped from his coffee, "except for the little scene I played for you in our holding cell out back."

Walter gaped at Jeff and then looked at Tech Sergeant Shoemaker for confirmation. Tech Sergeant Shoemaker nodded. "Yes, he's telling the truth."

Walter clapped his hand on his upper leg. "But then why all this deception?" he asked at last. "Where were you all this time? Marianne is worried sick over you. And I've been working day and night to...to..." He searched for the right word in English and came up empty. Middle school had not supplied him with a legal vocabulary.

"To exonerate me?" Jeff offered.

"Yes." In truth, Walter had no idea what the word meant.

"I can't tell you where I was because I was working on an ongoing investigation. I didn't tell Marianne about it because I wasn't allowed to do so." Jeff's mouth turned upward. "Believe me, it was very hard for me to deceive all of you. But I hope you'll forgive me when you learn the details."

Walter still struggled to digest the news. He doubted that he would ever understand the way the military operated. "Then you were never kidnapped at all?"

"Now, that part is actually true," Jeff said. "But I wasn't held for a day, just an hour or so. Then my kidnappers got cold feet and left me blindfolded and handcuffed in an almost-finished building in the housing area. I waited a while, and when they didn't come back, I got up and freed myself from the blind by rubbing my head against the rough wall. I was walking along the road when a patrol picked me up."

"I still don't understand," Walter stammered. "You could have just told me what happened, especially after I—we— found the dead woman."

"I just told you, I'm working on an investigation."

"It had nothing to do with your kidnappers?"

"No."

"Does it have anything to do with the smugglers?" Walter asked, getting exasperated.

The Americans exchanged glances.

"I think it's time to put all our cards on the table and tell each other what we know," Tech Sergeant Shoemaker said.

"I would appreciate that," Walter said, "Should we call in Chief Simmer?"

His temporary boss would probably be upset if he were not the first to know everything. Walter was not sure what exactly he would learn, but he had taken enough chances lately.

"He already knows what he needs to know," Tech Sergeant Shoemaker said. "He thought it would be best to inform you what's going on, at least the part that isn't classified."

Classified? This was getting more mysterious all the time. What in the world were the Air Policemen talking about? And why were they talking to him?

Tech Sergeant Shoemaker extinguished his cigarette in an ashtray. "What Jeff has been trying to tell you is this: We have reason to believe that there is a criminal act occurring on base that we can't solve by ourselves."

"You mean smuggling?" Walter interrupted. "I know about that. The head of the smuggling ring confessed yesterday. We're still looking for his accomplices. Or were you talking about the woman's murder?"

Tech Sergeant Shoemaker leaned forward in his chair. "Tell us all about the smuggling."

Walter told him what he knew and how he had followed Heinz to the old country estate.

When he had finished, Tech Sergeant Shoemaker scratched his head. "We have not heard about missing liquor or cigarettes. Perhaps the store wanted to solve the problem internally. We wanted to discuss another incident with you."

"Another incident?" Walter's gaze traveled from one to the other, but he couldn't read their expressions. "What are you talking about?"

"Let me tell him," Jeff said. "Pete and I were patrolling Building 210 when we came upon a German man who was searching through a trash can. I asked him in German what he was doing. He said gruffly that he was a janitor and emptied the trash cans every night. We couldn't verify this information and had to let him go. Walter, he was not emptying the cans, just rummaging through them. Later, I learned that German janitors usually work during the day and not at night. We never asked the man's name, and so we couldn't ask the Personnel Office about his identity. We did learn, however, that the janitor of that building is a woman."

Walter felt like he was supposed to ask something. "Can you tell me what this man looked like?"

Jeff rose and paced through the office. "All I remember is that he had black hair and smelled of pomade." He stopped walking and looked thoughtfully at Walter. "He spoke German, but it sounded different than your accent."

Walter's head jerked up. What had Frau Drucker said after Roswitha's funeral? There was a man at her door who had an East German accent. "How tall was he?"

"I think he reached my shoulder."

Walter nodded. Jeff was several centimeters taller than he was.

"The dead woman's landlady told me there was a man at her door recently who fit this description," Walter said to the Americans. "She had never seen him before."

Tech Sergeant Shoemaker rose, reached for his coffee cup, and went into the outer office. He returned with a full cup. "Thank you for telling us your observations. We have to work together to solve this crime, if indeed a crime has been committed."

"But it isn't a crime to search through trash cans, is it?" Walter asked.

"It is if he kept what he found," Shoemaker replied.

They still did not make sense to Walter. "What could he have been looking for? Office supplies?"

Shoemaker shrugged. "We don't know," he admitted. "We can't exclude the possibility that he was looking for documents. Classified documents."

"They threw secret documents into the trash?" Walter blurted out.

"All office buildings are equipped with safes, and all Top Secret documents are placed in there. However, the janitor might not know that and that's why Jeff found him searching through a trash can," Tech Sergeant Shoemaker said. "We talked with the building chief the next day and he promised to investigate the matter. The documents in that office are all accounted for."

"I still don't understand what Jeff's *arrest* has to do with anything," Walter mused. The military's ways were still a mystery to him.

Shoemaker took in a deep breath. "The arrest was a ruse. We wanted to give the German authorities the impression that we took an active role in this investigation and to show our goodwill by making a quick arrest. And we wanted the real killer to feel so confident that he would make a mistake and reveal himself."

Walter contemplated the answer. He faced Jeff. "So, if you weren't in jail, where were you all this time?"

"I'm afraid he can't tell you that," Tech Sergeant Shoemaker answered before Jeff could. "After he discovered the stranger, we sent Jeff on an undercover assignment. After all, he is our best German speaker."

Jeff's mouth turned into a grin. "Thanks to my grandmother who only spoke German with me and my brother. But I loved her German food even more than her stories."

The three officers broke into laughter. After they calmed down, Shoemaker continued, "It turned out that our suspicions were correct. He traced our man to a café in West Berlin. I don't suppose I need to tell you what that means?"

Berlin! Tension about the divided city was growing every day. The Soviet Union grew increasingly restless about the steady stream of skilled professionals who defected from East Germany via West Berlin daily.

Walter fidgeted in his seat. "What did you need me for?"

Shoemaker sipped from his coffee. "We need you and your partner because we want to set a trap for our suspect."

Walter contemplated his options. He had enough to do already for sure. Chief Simmer piled more and more work on him while he himself spent half his time in court. But a possible spy in his little village! How could he turn down an opportunity like this?

"Tell me what you have in mind," he said.

After supper and a nap, Walter dressed in civilian clothes and walked to the station. Schlosser, also out of uniform, was waiting for him. They mounted the motorbike with the sidecar. That way, they would look like a couple of friends going out for a ride. On base, Schlosser dropped Walter off at Building 210 and drove off. Only one staff car was parked in the parking lot. Walter walked toward the entrance to find the door unlocked. Satisfied, he nodded. At least he would be able to enter the building, if need be, without having to wait for Jeff and his master key.

Careful not to make noise, he closed the door and turned toward the road. An Air Police pickup truck drove by slowly and came to a halt in front of the next facility. The street lamp shone on Jeff and another Air Policeman. They exchanged greetings after catching up with Walter. Walter stared at his friend until Jeff chuckled in a low voice.

"You're making me nervous. Yes, I'm back and everything will be as usual."

Not everything, Walter thought. Before Jeff went away, Walter had at least held some hope of dating Marianne some day. Some day... He chided himself for hesitating too long. With so many GIs around, could he blame a girl when she fell in love with one? But why did it have to be Jeff?

He hoped to rekindle his friendship with Jeff, despite his feelings for Marianne. At least it didn't hurt as much as it did last week.

"You know what to do?" Jeff asked one last time, yanking Walter out of his thoughts.

"Yes," Walter said.

"Okay, go ahead. We'll watch the entrance."

Walter opened the door of the office building and stepped inside. He scaled three steps to the first floor hallway. He was supposed to act like an office worker who knew his way around the many doors. Most doors were closed, revealing no lights underneath them. Walter walked, more confidently than he felt, toward the exit on his left. All was quiet here and he turned toward the other exit. One lonely light shone underneath the last door. Walter hesitated for a moment, but could only discern the turning of paper. He took a deep breath before opening the door.

"Who are you, and what are you doing here?" a uniformed man said, looking up from a thick file. From the stripes on his uniform, Walter concluded that he was a non-commissioned officer. Walter said quickly, "I'm a police officer in Lauterbach."

"Nice uniform," the NCO chuckled.

Walter smiled, embarrassed. "I can show you my badge."

"Please do."

Walter slowly pulled his badge out of his trouser pocket and flashed it at the NCO. The American asked, "What are you doing here?"

"I don't have time to explain now, but have you been here long?"

The NCO sighed. "Since oh-seven-hundred-thirty this morning."

"Have you seen a janitor in here tonight?"

The American tipped his pencil against his chin. "No. Our janitor comes in around nine o'clock in the morning."

"Man or woman?"

"Woman, and she's old enough to be my mother."

Walter shrugged. "I'm looking for a man."

"Sorry, I haven't seen anybody." The NCO jerked his head. "I did step out for an hour or so to eat dinner."

"Well, thank you. I think I'll have a look around the rest of the building anyway."

Walter searched the second floor without success. Perhaps the suspect had grown more careful after Jeff and his partner discovered him. Or he had simply tried his luck in another office.

"No luck," he said to Jeff as he approached the Americans. "Perhaps we have to check every facility."

Jeff's partner hurried to the truck. "The sergeant in charge says we should search the office buildings," he said after returning.

For the next hour, they drove around the base, stopping at every facility that still had lights on. Walter's mission was to pretend that he was an employee who had gone back to retrieve something he had forgotten at work. He was relieved that he never had reason to use the lie. Deception was not his strong suit. He much preferred to confront a suspect without resorting to trickery.

"Now what?" Jeff said at last, looking from Walter to his partner. "There is no reason to go to the clubs or the BX. Those buildings wouldn't have any documents a spy would be interested in."

"Not unless they threw away the recipe for their goulash," Walter quipped.

Jeff laughed his infectious laugh, and Walter knew that the old bond was as strong as ever. He turned serious. "Why don't they just check everybody who leaves the base?"

"Good question, but most German employees take the bus or bicycle to work."

Walter yawned. Lack of sleep was beginning to wear him out. He had never felt so tired in his entire life. "How long do we have to do this?"

"As long as it takes," Jeff replied, suppressing a yawn himself.

Walter's fingers played piano on his upper lip. "Where does the trash go after the janitors collect it in each building?"

The airmen looked at each other and shrugged. Jeff called his supervisor and learned that the trash sometimes was burned at the heating plant. "Let's go," Jeff said. "But that's the last place we'll check tonight. Tomorrow is another day."

The heating plant was a one-story building close to the flight line. A faint light shone from a small, rectangular window. Other than that, the unit was windowless. The parking lot was empty except for a motor scooter with German plates.

Jeff whistled through his teeth. "Perhaps I should go in first since there is no reason for you to be here, Walter. Stay within earshot, though, just in case I need you."

Walter twitched his mouth. He didn't like the idea of being left out. "I don't know. I think I should go with you. If the person inside has nothing to hide, then he won't mind me being there and if he does, you might need an extra pair of hands and ears."

Jeff tilted his head. "No, we patrol this building every day. Our man might become suspicious if we suddenly show up with a German. Don't worry. You'll get your chance to shine if it comes to that."

Walter waited in the truck while the air policemen disappeared in the plant. Jeff was wrong if he thought Walter wanted to earn accolades for catching a criminal. Just arresting a suspect and restoring order was enough for him.

They returned less than five minutes later. Jeff grinned while he scooted next to Walter onto the seat.

Walter turned his head. "Well?"

"The plant operator does have black hair," Jeff said, "and he is about the height you described. What I can't figure out is why would this man show up at the dead woman's house and yours?"

Walter had no reply to that. Not a day went by that he didn't wish Chief Kleber was back. He could ask him, but he would rather bite off his tongue than asking Chief Simmer the same thing.

"Maybe we have the wrong idea," he said. "Maybe it's just a coincidence and he has nothing to do with Roswitha at all. There must be many black-haired men around here."

"I don't believe in coincidences," Jeff said and radioed the station about their observation. "Perhaps we're going at it from the wrong angle? Anyway, we're not getting anything accomplished tonight. Go home and get some sleep. You look like something the cat dragged in."

Walter agreed. Jeff radioed the station again to summon Schlosser. The airmen dropped Walter off at the station and continued their rounds. When Schlosser appeared with the motorbike, Walter climbed wearily into the sidecar.

"Any luck?" Schlosser asked.

"Yes and no," Walter replied and related the adventures of the night to his partner. "What do you think? I'm too tired to make any decisions tonight."

"Then don't. Tomorrow is another day."

Walter smiled. That was exactly what Jeff had said. Schlosser dropped him off at home and drove off. After the excitement of the day and the exhausting search at night, Walter had a hard time falling asleep. He was relieved that Jeff's arrest had been a ruse. Nothing would stand between Jeff and Marianne now. Marianne. It was best not to think of her anymore. Better to contemplate the identity of the dark-haired stranger. First he showed up at Roswitha's lodgings, then at Walter's house, and now on base. What could possibly connect all these locations?

Walter rose at the usual hour and ate three marmalade sandwiches for breakfast. While his mother fixed his coffee, he absentmindedly scanned the newspaper headlines. He breathed a sigh of relief when he did not find any reference to the discovery of a smuggling ring. Nonetheless, it would not take long before people would start talking about Heinz's arrest.

"I heard you come home last night," Frau Hofmann said. "Do you have to work so much?"

Walter shrugged. "Herr Simmer is piling more and more work on me, that's for certain. He seems to have it in for me, though I can't for the life of me figure out why. Is it because I'm the youngest officer at the station?"

"Well, whatever his reasons, I'll be glad when Chief Kleber comes back to work," his mother said while she set the table for herself and Ingrid.

"You and me both," Walter said, putting his cup on the saucer with a clank. "I never knew how good I had it until the chief got sick. But it's no use. I've got to go to work now."

"Already? You just came home!"

He passed Ingrid in the hallway, her eyes cast downward. Her cheeks looked less pale than yesterday. Walter hoped that no one had witnessed her unfortunate encounter in the housing area. If anyone had, word would soon leak out and she might become the laughingstock of the town. Worse yet, the police would have to deal with a public outcry for their safety. When it came to Heinz and his consorts, Walter did not believe they had the personalities of cold-blooded criminals. Chiefs Zimmermann and Simmer had not thought so, either.

23

After the daily morning meeting with the night shift ended, Chief Simmer called Walter into his office. He wanted a full report about the searches from the night before.

"Well, what will you do now?" Chief Simmer tapped his hands on his armrests and looked Walter right in the eye.

He's testing me, Walter thought. "I think I'll call the base personnel office to find out who works at the heating plant."

Simmer nodded his approval. "Very good. I see you're very thoughtful and promising. You'll probably have to go on base to look at the files, but you may call first to give them time to pull the files for you."

Walter's mouth formed a slight smile. A compliment from Chief Simmer weighed much more than Chief Kleber's kind words. "Can Schlosser come with me?"

"Sure."

Walter was about to go to his desk when a thought occurred to him. "Any news on the smugglers who disappeared?"

"No, not yet. I'll let you know as soon as I hear anything."

Walter and Schlosser headed back on base with the motorbike. The civilian personnel office was a one-story, prefabricated building across from the enlisted men's barracks. A spider plant in one of the casement windows made a feeble attempt at a homey feeling. The manager,

Herr Christmann, waved the policemen into his office. His wooden IN and OUT baskets were overflowing.

"Please excuse the mess," he said in a hurried tone. "The base is growing so fast, we can't find enough qualified people to work here. There are plenty of people looking for work, but most of them don't speak English or can't type…" He wrung his hands in frustration.

"My sister works at the BX," Walter said.

"Really? Does she like it?"

"Yes, she does. Sometimes I think she likes it a bit too much." Walter smiled wryly. "And she makes more money than at a German store."

"How true," Christmann said. "And yet, we are still lagging behind the wages they pay in other German states, which is why I can't find personnel. They can make more money elsewhere. Anyway, what can I do for you?"

Schlosser began explaining and let Walter finish. Walter appreciated it that his partner included him in the conversation.

"The heating plant? Yes, my secretary has just brought in those files." Christmann reached for three files and handed them to Schlosser. Apparently, he was a stickler for seniority. Schlosser kept one file and gave the other two to Walter.

"Would you like to sit in a quiet place to look through them?" the personnel chief offered.

"That would be excellent," Schlosser answered.

Christmann led them to an unoccupied classroom. "This is where we hold our English tests. We don't have one scheduled today, so take as long as you like."

The partners sat down in the last row. Walter chuckled when he read the blackboard. "I am injured," read the white chalk outline. It was not that long ago that he and Schlosser had to take the mandatory English class. Of course, Walter had outshined everybody because he had learned English in middle school while Schlosser and the others still struggled with the English language.

Walter opened a file and studied the photo of the heating plant employee. It soon became apparent that he was not the man they were looking for. The photo showed a young man from Kaiserslautern, about Walter's age, with reddish hair. He closed the file and looked sideways at his partner. "This one is out, I think. What about yours?"

Schlosser's finger traveled along the first page. "I'm not sure. Take the other one."

Walter opened the last file and froze. An about forty-year-old man stared back at him from the passport photo. His hair looked raven and slick, just like Jeff had described him.

He pointed at the photo and said, "You can stop looking. This is our man."

Walter put the file between them and they both studied the man's resume. "Name: Lothar Falk. Let's see where he's born," Walter said.

"Grimmenhalde, Sachsen," Schlosser read.

Walter banged his fist on the table. "Yes! Frau Drucker said he had an East German accent. Roswitha also came from the East."

"Perhaps they knew each other?" Schlosser offered.

Walter stroked his chin with his thumb and forefinger, lost in thought. "Could she be his relative or former girlfriend? Or do you think that Roswitha spied for him?"

"Let's not get ahead of ourselves," Schlosser cautioned. "Right now, he is nothing but a heating plant employee. Whoever put that flea in your ear that he's a spy, I do not know. Let's just write down where he lives."

Walter obeyed. He took out his notepad and wrote down the man's address and his supervisor's name. He also copied the man's schooling and work history before he started working on base. Then they returned the files to Herr Christmann's office and climbed on their bike. Schlosser drove straight to the heating plant. It was time to talk to Falk's supervisor.

A waft of liverwurst mingled with coal dust greeted them as the police officers opened the door to the plant. A stocky man sat at a wooden table, biting into a sandwich. His rolled-up sleeves revealed taut muscles, muscles he had doubtlessly developed during years of shoveling coal into the furnace. He stopped chewing when Walter and Schlosser closed the door behind them.

"Time for a second breakfast," Schlosser said.

The man nodded and gulped down his food. "What can I do for you?"

"We're looking for Lothar Falk. Is he here today?" Schlosser asked.

"No, he works nights this week."

Schlosser's mouth turned upward. "That's too bad because we really want to talk to him. Perhaps you can help us."

"I would offer you chairs, but as you can see, we're not equipped for company," the boiler man said, pointing at a folding chair in the corner.

Schlosser waved his hand. "Never mind that. What's your name and position here?"

"Arthur Bachstein, and I'm the supervisor of this building. Not that there is much to it, but it's a job."

Schlosser asked, "How long have you known Lothar Falk?"

Bachstein scratched his temple. "I started working here three years ago, and he came about a year after me. That would make it two years or so."

Walter pulled a notebook and pencil out of his pocket. "Would you consider him a good worker?"

Bachstein shrugged. "He does his job, no more, no less. Sometimes he grumbles that his back hurts, but that is part of the job."

Schlosser asked, "What exactly are his duties?"

Bachstein pointed to the heating room. "We have to make sure that these furnaces never go empty."

"Does his job require emptying trash cans in other buildings?"

Bachstein gaped at Schlosser as if he had asked him to eat a piece of coal. "Why would he do that?"

"That's what we're trying to find out."

"No, that's not part of his duties."

"Thank you. Has he ever left his work station without asking for permission?" Schlosser asked. "I mean, besides lunch breaks and such."

Bachstein's forehead formed two parallel lines. "I sometimes come to work early, and once I found the plant deserted. When Falk came in about fifteen minutes later, I asked him where he was. He said he had to go to the club to make a phone call. I said that we had a phone right here, but he said that it was a private call and he didn't want to use a government phone for that."

Walter's pencil danced over his notepad. "Do you remember when this happened?"

Bachstein slowly shook his head. "No, I can't remember when that was. Perhaps two, three weeks ago."

"Anything else?" Walter asked. "Is he married?"

"No."

"Where does he live?"

"He's renting a room in Herrenhausen."

"How does he get on base?" Schlosser asked.

"He has a motor scooter because the buses don't run at night when he needs to work."

Walter fought hard to remain stoic while his insides screamed with joy. A scooter would enable Falk to come on base any time he wanted. "Does his ID card allow him to come on base on weekends?"

The boilerman nodded vigorously. "Yes, of course. We take turns working weekends."

Schlosser's head jerked slightly. "May we see your work schedule for October?"

Bachstein rummaged through a metal file tray. "Here it is. I knew it was here somewhere."

He handed the paper to Schlosser, and Walter stepped close to his partner to peek at it. His face drooped when he saw that Falk had not worked on the day of the murder.

Schlosser apparently noticed the same thing. "Was Falk off on the day of October fourth?"

Bachstein said, "Let me see." Schlosser handed him the schedule. "Yes, he was off that weekend."

"Did he mention what he did that Saturday?" Walter asked. Was he getting closer to solving Roswitha's murder? Or was it another cold trail?

Bachstein paused, then shook his head. "No, not that I remember. He never talks much. He's very reserved." He looked from one officer to the other. "Why are you asking all these questions? Did he do something wrong?"

"Sorry, I can't answer that," Schlosser replied.

Bachstein's eyes pleaded with Walter now, but he was unmoved. Keeping secrets from family and friends had been difficult during his first years on the job, Walter admitted to himself. Nowadays, he had gotten used to it. After all, the people he talked to often had secrets of their own.

Bachstein walked to the furnace room to check if the furnaces needed more fuel. "Are we almost done here?" he asked when he returned. "I need to throw some coal on the fire. Make yourself comfortable if you have some more questions for me."

Schlosser raised his palms. "No, I don't think that's necessary. For the moment, we've asked everything we need to know. Or do you have anything to add, Walter?"

Walter was pleased that his partner included him in the interview, even let him take the lead. He studied his notes since he did not want to overlook any detail. "Did Falk miss a day when he was supposed to work this month?"

Bachstein scratched his head. "I don't think so, but I can't be sure without looking at the time cards." He opened a file on his desk. "No, he did not have a sick day. Wait a minute..." He fetched the work schedule from another file and compared the two papers. "It looks like he did switch a shift with his coworker once."

Walter's eyebrow twitched. He complimented himself on probing further. "What day was that?"

"That was on October sixth, a Monday. He was supposed to work the day shift, but worked the night shift from Monday to Tuesday instead."

Schlosser asked, "What about the rest of the week? He couldn't have worked two shifts in a row."

Bachstein skimmed the schedule. "You're right. He worked the swing shift on Tuesday and then worked his regular day shift the rest of the week."

"Thank you," Schlosser said. "You've been very helpful."

The officers turned around and exited the building. Outside, Schlosser asked, "Are you thinking what I'm thinking?"

Walter suppressed a grin. It was too early for that. "Seems like our friend comes and goes whenever he feels like it. First he makes a phone call, then he checks trash cans, and then he switches a couple of shifts. He could have had a meeting with someone."

"Or maybe he has a girlfriend? Anything is possible."

Walter tilted his head. "I don't think so. The trash cans don't fit in with that theory."

Schlosser grinned. "Good. I was just testing you."

Walter was getting exasperated at being tested. "Now that we are in agreement, what do we do next? Wait for Falk and catch him in the act?"

His partner shrugged. "Why don't we radio Chief Simmer and let him earn his keep?"

Simmer was indeed interested in their news, but also had some of his own. "I'm going to have to ask you two to come back to the station. We need to talk about the visit of the Secretary of Defense."

"Does this mean we should abort our interviews for today?" Schlosser asked, sounding disappointed.

"Not just for today, but for the next few days."

Walter felt defeated as the two officers climbed on the bike. Being pulled away from a case when they were so close to its conclusion—or so he hoped—was almost more than he could take. Had the long hours he had put in lately all been for naught?

Yet, as the junior officer on the force, he was hardly in a position to argue with a superior. Until the visit of the politician was over, he would not have any time to spare for

Falk's case, if indeed it was a case. Nonetheless, he would call Junker to exchange notes.

Chief Simmer paced in front of a blackboard. "This is where we are standing so far." He paused, rubbing his hands together. "The Secretary of Defense will arrive on October twenty-sixth by car. The German police will escort him from the Autobahn exit to the base. We'll get assistance from the stations in Reichenbach and Holzhausen. Also, Kaiserslautern and Neustadt will send officers to help us. Any questions?"

Schlosser raised his hand. "How long will the secretary's visit last?"

Chief Simmer consulted his paperwork. "Only about two hours. He is supposed to arrive around two o'clock in the afternoon and leave before four o'clock."

Walter sighed. At least the visit would be brief. "Where will we be stationed?"

"You two will be posted on the flight line when the secretary arrives there. He is supposed to inspect the new hangar and some of the American troops before he has a meeting with the base commander. I want my men to make a good impression. That means haircuts, if necessary. I will personally inspect both of you."

"I just got a haircut before the fair," Walter protested.

Schlosser chuckled while Chief Simmer ignored the comment. They went over the timetable for the visit, discussing all the details. The Beetle and the motorbikes needed to be washed and polished to make a good impression, and their uniforms would have to be in shipshape.

Walter made a mental note to check for any missing buttons. Finally, the briefing came to a close.

"Let's go over your findings from today," Simmer said. "Or better yet, I want your reports before the end of the day."

Walter feigned enthusiasm. Reports were not his favorite part of police work. While he could type faster than most of his fellow officers, he considered them the most boring part of his duties. He would have rather continued searching for Falk on base. An hour later, he put his report on Simmer's desk. His temporary chief studied the paper and nodded.

"Hm, looks like our friend Falk has secrets. What do you think our next step should be?"

Walter hesitated. He couldn't believe Chief Simmer really wanted his opinion. It was probably another test. "We don't have any authority to search his room in Herrenhausen, but perhaps we could talk to his landlady?"

Chief Simmer paced the room, folding his hands behind his back. "You're right. We don't have the manpower to watch Falk day and night. So far, our suspicions are too thin to put in that much time. But a little chat with his landlady can't hurt. Tomorrow morning, you two will go to Herrenhausen and ask around. Find out where he gets his hair cut, what *Gasthaus* he frequents, that sort of thing."

"Yes, sir."

When his shift ended, Walter stepped out of the building, placing his hat on his head. He strolled to the tobacco store to pick up some chewing gum before heading home for supper.

He and his fellow officers sure had their hands full right now. Besides Roswitha's unsolved death, they had to deal with a politician's visit, a smuggling ring that was still at large, and a man who snooped through trash cans in buildings where he didn't belong.

Politics took a front seat right now. Until that visit was over, Walter could do nothing more than keep his eyes and ears open. He or Chief Simmer called Detective Junker almost every day to check on the progress in the murder case. The answer was always no. Walter clenched his fist. He vowed to search for the woman's killer, even if it took years.

Walter had walked a block when he felt as if someone followed him. He tensed up, remembering the knife attack after the fair. Yet who would attack him at this hour? He looked over his shoulder and relaxed. A boy was skipping along the sidewalk, apparently trying to catch up with him. His thick carroty hair framed a freckled face. He looked to be no more than six years old.

"Mr. Policeman," the boy said, his voice squeaky.

"Yes," Walter said with a smile. He bent down to the boy.

"I have a confession to make," the child said, his voice not much more than a whisper.

"Go on."

"Last week, I stole an apple from our neighbor's tree. They looked so good that I just had to have one. The man saw me and said I had to tell a policeman what I did. Are you going to put me in jail now?"

Walter suppressed a laugh. "What's your name?"

"Jürgen."

"Jürgen, tell your neighbor that you told a police officer what you did and that he accepted your confession. Can you remember that?"

Jürgen nodded, his big eyes fastened on Walter. Walter reached into his pocket and brought out the chewing gum. "Would you like a piece of gum?"

Jürgen broke into a big smile. "Uh huh."

Walter gave him a piece and the boy said, *"Danke!"* before running off with the gum.

Walter straightened up and continued his walk, whistling "Jailhouse Rock." All tension had evaporated from him when he arrived at home. His mother baked apple pancakes for him. She poured a second batch of dough into the pan when the phone rang.

"Can't they even let you eat anymore?" his mother complained.

Walter jumped up. "I'll get it." He had left work less than fifteen minutes ago, so what could be that important?

"I hope I'm not disturbing your supper," Simmer said as Walter answered.

"As a matter of fact, I was eating," Walter replied.

"I just heard from Junker. He got the fingerprint report from the purse. Your friend Heinz is in the clear on that crime at least. They were able to pick up half a print from the purse. Now, all we need is a suspect who matches it."

Yes, that's all we need, Walter thought as he hung up.

24

Schlosser and Walter parked the Beetle a few houses away from Falk's residence and walked back. The house was a one-and-a-half-story stone structure, just like Walter's family home. Hanging boxes full of asters in all four front windows smiled at the visitors.

Schlosser signaled Walter to look around for signs of Falk's scooter. If he was home, he had probably parked it in the courtyard or a barn. They climbed the three steps to the front door and turned the ancient doorbell. A few moments later, a young boy opened the door, which dragged on the linoleum floor. At the sight of the police officers, he hesitated for a second before asking, "Yes?"

Schlosser hastened to say, "*Guten Tag.* Is your mother or father at home?"

"My father works mid-shift today, but my mother is at home," the boy offered.

"Can we talk to her?"

"Of course." The boy ran down the hall and opened a door a with frosted glass window.

"*Mama,* the police are here. They want to talk to you."

Walter heard a disapproving reply from the Hausfrau. "Tell them to come on in, will you."

The two officers wiped their feet on the sisal doormat and followed the voices to the kitchen. A men's shirt lay on an old blanket covering the entire kitchen table. The landlady put an iron back on the stove and wiped her hands on her apron.

"I'm sorry for the mess," she said as she pulled two chairs away from the table for the officers.

"You're probably wondering why we're here," Schlosser said while he and Walter took their seats.

"Yes."

"Is your tenant, Herr Falk, at home?"

Frau Reichert exhaled. She looked visibly relieved that the officers were not concerned with her family. "No, he's not. In fact, I haven't seen him at all today. He keeps odd hours."

"Do you know when he'll be back? Has he said anything to you the last time you saw him?"

Frau Reichert shook her head.

"Tell us a bit about him. He must share his kitchen and bathroom with you, so you should know a lot about his habits."

"I don't know if it's a lot. Of course, he shares the bathroom with us and I fix his breakfast most days. He eats lunch or dinner at the *Glocke,* usually."

Walter made a note on his notepad.

"Has he ever mentioned to you where he's from originally?" Schlosser asked.

Frau Reichert cupped her chin with her hand. "Not really. He just said that he was from Saxony and lost his whole family in the war. I think he lived in Bavaria for a while. I'm sorry, that's all I know."

Walter wrote down the sparse information. If their suspicions about Falk were true, he had good reason to keep secrets from his landlady. They would probably not learn much from this interview.

"Does he ever have any visitors?" Schlosser continued.

Frau Reichert shook her head. "I have never seen anyone visit him."

"How about mail? He must get mail from somebody."

"Yes, he does get a letter occasionally. It is always from the same person, a man named Wilhelm Klein."

Schlosser grunted. Such an ordinary name was probably phony.

"Do you remember what city the letters come from?" Schlosser probed.

The landlady folded her fingers together. "I think the address was from Heidelberg."

The officers rose. "Thank you very much for your time," Schlosser said. On the way to the car, he said to Walter, "Are you thinking what I'm thinking?"

"That Wilhelm Klein is a fake name?" Walter offered.

"Exactly. Your American friends might be on to something here. Here's a man who has no family, no friends, and the only person who writes him uses a fake name."

Walter was relieved that his partner led the investigation. He had made enough decisions lately. "So, what do we do now?"

"Let's go to the barber shop and the *Gasthaus*."

The barber could not remember seeing a man who fit the description Schlosser gave. The landlord at the *Gasthaus* recalled serving a man with dark, pomaded hair.

"Very close-mouthed, that fellow," he said. "Couldn't get the time of day out of him if I tried."

"We're wasting our time here," Schlosser said after they stepped outside. "It is easy for a man to disappear if he has no family or friends to betray him. With all the strangers living in the towns around here nowadays, we're not going to find any useful information about him."

Chief Simmer came to the same conclusion after they returned to the station. "We'll write a report about the interview today and send a copy to the Air Police. Perhaps they can keep an eye on Falk while he works on base. And now, we've got to prepare for the secretary's visit. Tomorrow, Walter has to clean the car and the motorbike whenever they're not needed."

"What do I do?" Schlosser asked.

"You'll man the station while I have a meeting with the mayor."

Walter took a hose and rag and began to wash the Beetle. The water was cold and his hand soon lost feeling. Because his arm was still sore from the attack, he had to favor his left arm. He was wiping at the windshield to remove caked-on insects when Schlosser opened a wing of the window.

Schlosser ducked as Walter pretended to throw the rag at his partner.

"You'll never guess who just called," Schlosser said.

"Caterina Valente?" Walter knew that his partner was a big fan of the singer and liked to tease him about it.

Schlosser rolled his eyes. "No. But I admit she's a lot better looking than those men. The border police called. They've arrested a man who fits Müller's description. His real name is Horst Bukowski."

"No wonder he gave a false name. Such an unusual name stands out like a sore thumb around here." Walter approached the window. "How did he manage to get arrested?"

Schlosser chuckled. "Would you believe it, he was sitting on a commuter bus that takes coal miners to France. Had a suitcase full of loot on him. How dumb can you get?"

"Still, it took us a while to catch him," Walter said, feeling a weight drop off his shoulders. Now he felt confident that the other smugglers would get caught soon.

"Uh oh," Schlosser uttered and closed the window.

"Uh oh what?" Walter asked. He turned around slowly and stood face to face with Marianne. She wore a gray overcoat against the chill, but the drab color did not diminish her lovely face. Walter stood rooted on the spot, the rag still dripping in his hand.

"Good morning, Walter," she said. "I'm on my breakfast break right now and decided to come over real quick. I wanted to tell you that we heard from Benno yesterday."

"Yes?"

"He works on a barge on the Rhine River. He writes that he just had to get out of our village and see the world. He has already been to Basel and is on his way to Holland now. My mother was very relieved when she read the letter. She was worried that he might join the Foreign Legion or something like that. Perhaps now we can have a quieter life at home. Benno was fighting with my father all the time."

Walter threw the rag into the bucket and stepped a bit closer. "I have to admit that I thought for a while that he might be involved in a crime."

Marianne's eyes grew wide. "A crime? Surely, you didn't think he killed that woman?"

Walter bit his lip. He had probably said too much already. "No, I never thought he could kill anybody. There are other crimes besides murder."

Marianne ignored his last comment. Walter was relieved that she did not probe further. Her mind seemed otherwise occupied. "I saw Jeff last night. Walter, I'm so glad you helped me when I needed it most. I will never forget that."

"You don't have to thank me. I was just doing my job."

"Yes, but under the circumstances..." She paused. "I'm sorry if I hurt your feelings the other night."

"No need to apologize," Walter said curtly. "What's done is done. Now, excuse me. I've got some work to do."

"Sure, I've got to get back to the store myself," Marianne said, bidding goodbye.

Walter rubbed at the windshield with newfound vigor. If Schlosser was watching him, he would not give him the satisfaction of seeing his burning cheeks. How could he shake the crush he had on her? Perhaps if he didn't see her for a while, and a few months went by, he would be his old self again. He was glad that his work required his entire attention. If only he could get her out of his mind during his leisure hours.

"Where is Bukowski right now?" Walter asked when he reentered the station, carrying the bucket with his good arm.

"He's on his way to the jail in Kaiserslautern," Schlosser said. "I'm glad he's arrested and out of our hair now. We have enough to do without worrying about smugglers running loose."

Walter poured himself a glass of mineral water. "There are still two more suspects out there: Johnson and Mielke. And I sure would like to know who attacked me with a knife."

"Don't worry. We'll hear the results of the interview. How is your arm now?"

"Good enough to wash cars," Walter said with a grimace.

"You should have said that you weren't up to it," Schlosser suggested.

"No, it was all right. By the way, Marianne's parents got a letter from Benno, so he's accounted for. He works on a river barge now."

Schlosser snorted. "Is that all she said?"

"Yes," Walter said while he carried the bucket down the hall to the small kitchen. Sometimes Schlosser could probe a bit too much.

25

"Have you ever been on a duty like this before?" Walter asked Schlosser on their way to the base.

"Yes," Schlosser answered. "Our politicians all want to be in the spotlight and show they're good friends with America. But my most memorable day was parade duty after Germany won the World Cup in 1954."

"You were there?" Walter drew in his breath. "I wanted to see that, but I was in training and they wouldn't let us get away for a day. How was it?"

Schlosser smiled. "I took my wife and kid along because I didn't want them to miss it. They were standing close enough to me so they did not miss anything. The entire city of Kaiserslautern seemed to be out for the parade. I think only invalids and old people stayed home. I was posted at a traffic stop. When Horst Eckel's car stopped for a few moments, I managed to get his autograph—for my kid, mind you. I don't care much for these things, but I wanted to get it for my boy."

Walter remembered the euphoria over Germany's victory in overtime very well. And five of the soccer players were from Kaiserslautern, including the team captain! He had never been prouder of his home state than on that day, and thousands of others felt the same way.

They arrived at the flight line well before the appointed time of the official's visit. The German police officers filed into the hangar, where the NCO Club had delivered refreshments for them. They sank on the benches, reaching for the ham and cheese sandwiches and Cokes.

Walter chewed doggedly, but the white bread stuck to the roof of his mouth.

"I don't know about you," he said to his partner, "but I like German bread better than this stuff."

Schlosser nodded while he swallowed. "I agree. There's nothing like Baker Jung's rye bread."

Outside, the Air Force music band was tuning their instruments with a cacophony of sounds and the police officers had to shout at each other. After they finished their sandwiches, a kitchen aide produced ice cream for everyone. Walter was excited over the unusual treat of vanilla ice cream, but anxious he might drop some on his uniform. He was relieved when he wiped off his hands without an incident.

The officers took their places in a row next to a phalanx of airmen. Walter soon grew bored and began to think about the events of the past few weeks. His gaze wandered over the flight line with its F-86 fighter jets and the support buildings clustered around them. One of the structures looked strangely familiar and it occurred to him that it was the heating plant. You could see the flight line from there. Walter wondered why that fact had not occurred to anyone before. Did Falk perhaps record movements on the flight line? Was that why he worked there? If so, who could possibly be interested in such information?

In a low voice, Walter told his observations to Schlosser. His partner cocked his head. "We better run by the Air Police station after the visit is over."

At last, a convoy of cars drove onto the flight line where the troops and police officers were lined up in formation. Walter clicked his heels together and stood straight as a rod.

The Mercedes came to a halt and the Secretary of Defense exited the vehicle with his entourage. The Secretary, dressed in a dark overcoat, paraded along the formation and saluted each service member. He inclined his head slightly as he passed Walter and his fellow officers. Reporters from the *Rheinpfalz* newspaper, wearing their press passes on their lapels, hurried around taking photos of the important visitor. Walter recognized one of them. He worked at the office in Reichenbach and often called the station for news updates. After the entourage entered their cars to attend a meeting with the base commander, the reporter came over and stopped in front of Walter.

"Have you arrested anyone for the woman's murder yet?"

Walter breathed deeply. *Relax,* he told himself. *He's only doing his job.* "No, but when we do, you'll be the first to know."

The officers who overheard him laughed softly. The reporter hurried away to follow the cars to the headquarters.

"Well done," Schlosser commented.

Walter grinned. No one could say he was a slow learner. Schlosser was now talking to an officer from Kaiserslautern, and Walter joined them. But the city officer did not know anything about Roswitha's death investigation.

Schlosser and Walter drove to the Air Police station, where Jeff happened to be on desk duty. He motioned the Germans to take a seat while he finished a phone call.

"What can I do for you today?" he asked in his slow, accented German.

Walter told him of his observations at the flight line. Jeff tapped a pencil on the palm of his hand.

"Hm, we could go to the heating plant again and interview him," Jeff said. "Or we could stake him out at his home and hope he has something on his body that would implicate him."

Schlosser scratched his neck. "If we go to the plant again he might figure out we're onto him and lay low."

"Okay, we'll stake him out," Jeff said. "I need to talk to my supervisor, of course, and then we'll get back to you."

Schlosser nodded. "We'll also have to clear it with our chief. As if we didn't have enough to do already with this unsolved death case."

"Yes, the dead woman. How is that going?"

"Not good. We have made no progress at all," Walter said. "But we have some news. One of the smugglers just got arrested and we're now waiting for a confession report."

The phone rang again, giving the Germans an excuse to take their leave. By the time they arrived back at their station Chief Simmer had already had a call from the base.

"I'll send Adler from the mid-shift and an officer from Herrenhausen to watch Falk's residence. Tomorrow, Walter can watch the house by himself during the day—in civilian clothes. I need Schlosser to man the station because I have a meeting with Detective Junker about the progress of the Gregorius investigation."

Walter hoped to see the report. He felt a personal connection with the case because he was the one who had found the woman. For now, he was glad to be on a light duty, even though he had no idea how he would spend the time. On the way home, he passed a man pulling a handcart with a basket of apples in it. And then Walter had an idea.

26

Walter put on his late grandfather's corduroy pants, an equally old shirt, and a cap. The pants were much too short for him, but many people still wore hand-me-downs, more than a decade after the war ended. He hoped his disguise would suffice as a cover-up for a stakeout. Ingrid snorted with laughter when he entered the kitchen.

"Are you delivering potatoes today?" she asked between fits.

Walter grimaced. He was happy that Ingrid was laughing again, but did she have to do it at his expense?

"Something like that," he said cryptically. "How are you doing this morning?"

Ingrid yawned. "Pretty good. I slept like a rock last night."

Their mother stepped out to fetch something from the pantry. Walter said quickly, "I wish I could take you to Elvis, but my hands are tied…"

Ingrid shrugged. "Forget it. It's not the end of the world." It was a lie and he knew it. Just like he knew that he would never take her. Even if they could board a train to Friedberg, where Presley was stationed, who could say that the singer was actually in town? Perhaps he was in a maneuver or on vacation. Even soldiers had to get some time off. He hated to disappoint Ingrid, but what could he do about it?

Frau Reichert answered the door herself and Walter quickly explained his plan. She consented and they set off to the barn. As they passed the doghouse, a huge dog rose from the cobblestones, letting out a faint bark.

"Some watchdog," Walter remarked as the dog sniffed his old pants.

"Don't worry, he can tell whether a person is good or bad," Frau Reichert assured him.

"And what am I?"

"You're a good person. Otherwise he would have barked very loudly."

"Really, he's that good at detecting a person's character?"

"Uh huh."

"And what kind of man is your tenant? Does the dog bark at him?"

"Funny you should ask. Herr Falk never goes near the dog, so I don't know what Hasso thinks of him."

"What kind of dog is it?"

"He's part German shepherd, part ..." She shrugged.

They entered the barn. "We don't keep livestock or goats anymore, so we're just using it for storage," she said.

Walter chose a basket before they walked to the orchard together.

"When do you expect Herr Falk to come home from work?"

"Usually he comes home around ten o'clock, and then he wants his breakfast."

"Then you better go into the house," Walter said. "He could arrive at any moment."

"Do you have everything you need?" she asked, eager to please.

"Remember that I'm your nephew from Kaiserslautern who is picking apples for my family today, in case he asks."

"He won't," she said. "He keeps much to himself and has no friends in the village, as far as I know."

"Better to be safe than sorry," Walter said. "Do you mind if I cut some grass for my rabbits while I'm here?"

"I don't mind. The scythe is in the small storage room at the end of the barn. Help yourself."

She returned to the house after she stopped in the vegetable garden to inspect her lamb's lettuce.

Walter treaded around the orchard. The trees were picked over, but Herr Falk did not necessarily know that. He decided to cut his grass first and returned to the barn. Since the Reicherts did not farm anymore, he expected the tools to be in disarray. However, they were all in fine order, hung up on hooks or neatly placed in compartments on a wall shelf. Walter stepped closer to inspect the shelf and peeked into the bins. Nothing was out of place—hammers were in one bin, nuts in another, and screws in yet another—until Walter tilted a small container with chisels and other building tools. He whistled when he spotted a skinning knife.

"Well, well, what do we have here?" He pulled a handkerchief out of his pocket, wrapped it around the handle, and picked up the knife. It looked like it had been cleaned recently, which was strange since the family had no animals to slaughter and deer season had not yet begun.

Walter debated what to do. He wished Schlosser were here so he could ask him for advice. He could not take the knife with him without a warrant. He made a mental note of its location and vowed to ask the chief about it.

Walter grabbed the scythe from the wall and returned to the orchard with another basket. He began mowing the grass, making sure that he could keep an eye on the house and yard. After a few minutes, he felt eyes in his back.

Walter turned and saw an old man on the other side of the fence.

"Good morning," the man said. "I don't recall seeing you here before."

Walter stopped mowing and stepped closer to the fence while his mind raced for an excuse. "I'm Frau Reichert's nephew from the city. I'm here today to pick some apples."

"How odd that Ilse never mentioned you were coming." The man scratched the remains of his gray hair.

"She didn't know about my coming. It was a spur of the moment visit." That part, at least, was true.

"You're mighty late for that. The best ones have been picked."

Walter shrugged. "I'll just have to make do with what I can find."

Walter tried to remember Herr Reichert's first name but could not recall if he ever heard it. "Has my uncle slaughtered or hunted recently?"

The old man shook his head. "No one slaughters in the summer. And he hasn't had any livestock in years."

That was all Walter needed to know. If Herr Reichert had not used the knife, there was only one person who could have used it: Herr Falk. Suddenly, Walter's hands began shaking. He recalled the night when he was stabbed on his way home. Hot anger began to wash over him at the thought that Falk could be his attacker.

Let's not jump to conclusions. He repeated Schlosser's mantra to himself. But what if? In that case, it was best to have a battle plan. If Falk ever came home, then Walter had to have an excuse for entering the house. He decided he would ask whether he could use the lavatory, which was not far from the truth anyway. Yet, where was it? As a supposed relative of the family, he should know that.

After he had filled the basket with grass, he began inspecting the trees for ripe apples. The old man had been right. The lower branches were bare.

Finally, he heard the sputtering noise of a moped turning into the Reicherts' yard. Pretending to reach for an apple, Walter took a few steps so he could view the courtyard through the tree branches.

Falk put the bike on its stand and eyed the orchard suspiciously. He entered the house after scraping his shoes on the sisal mat.

Walter waited a few minutes and strolled toward the house. The kitchen door was ajar and he pushed it open. Frau Reichert had set the table with stoneware china and was pouring coffee in Herr Falk's cup. Falk had a small cutting board with a liverwurst sandwich in front of him. Walter entered the kitchen and asked, "Can I use your bathroom?"

For a second, Walter thought Falk eyed him with contempt, or at least with suspicion. Then a mask of indifference clouded his face. Had he recognized Walter from a previous encounter, perhaps before he attacked Walter with a knife? Walter had never seen the man before, but that didn't mean that Falk had never seen Walter. The boiler man was of less-than-average height and thin. He hardly seemed the type who would shovel coals for an entire shift. Perhaps that's why he seemed to be in a grim mood. He might not be used to physical labor.

"Herr Falk, this is my nephew from Kaiserslautern," Frau Reichert hastened to say. "He is picking apples in our orchard today."

The men exchanged the traditional *Guten Morgen* greetings before Walter took his leave. He had spotted the lavatory by the back door and entered it before heading back to his post in the garden. By noon, Walter had picked the apples and his stomach began to grumble. Would Frau Reichert invite him for lunch? He had not packed a sandwich. Walter had barely finished the thought when the kitchen window opened and Frau Reichert called, "Essen! Come and get lunch."

While Walter washed up, he heard Frau Reichert call Herr Falk to lunch.

"I'm not hungry yet," her tenant replied.

"But I've made something special because my nephew is here: yeast dumplings."

"All right, I'll be down."

Walter crossed the hallway and was almost run over by young Horst, who had just returned from school. The boy thrust the kitchen door open and flung his satchel on a chair. His mother promptly admonished him for treating his possessions in such a careless way. She motioned Walter to join her at the stove and whispered, "I thought if I invited him to eat with us, you might be able to learn something from him."

Walter thanked her for being so thoughtful. After all, Walter could not observe Falk if he remained in his room. He hoped that Herr Falk did not ask him any questions about the city. He knew from the newspaper what current events took place in Kaiserslautern, but had not actually been there in ages.

Walter asked, "What about Horst?" He pointed at the boy.

She stopped while ladling out the soup. "Horst, do you know what pretending is?"

A furrow formed on the boy's brow. "You mean, pretending I did my homework?"

She let out a short laugh. "Something like that." She lowered her voice to a whisper. "Today, you and I have to pretend Herr Hofmann is your cousin. Do you think you can do that?"

Horst nodded. "I'll give it a try."

"There's a good boy."

"I'll give you a chewing gum after lunch," Walter offered. He seemed destined to give away his gum to young boys.

Horst broke into a huge smile. "Can I have it right now?"

"No, silly, we're going to eat first," his mother chastised him. She put her finger over her mouth to warn Walter, but he had heard the footsteps on the stairs. Moments later, Herr Falk entered the kitchen. He looked less than enthused about the party gathered here. He grunted a *Guten Tag* before sitting down at his usual place.

What a nice fellow, Walter thought. Apparently, Falk had not yet grasped that people in the Palatinate were put off by anyone who did not bid a *Guten Tag* loud and clear. It was an unwritten law.

Walter pasted a friendly smile on his face. "Nice day for late October, isn't it?"

Falk averted his gaze, murmuring, "I suppose so."

Falk was about as personable as a lamppost. Walter concluded he either had a lot to learn or his colleagues would not have fared better under the circumstances. After all, if Falk really were a spy, he would have been trained to remain silent. Horst, on the other hand, dominated the table conversation by telling about a classmate who liked to pull a girl's braids.

"I think girls are silly," Horst said, slurping his soup.

Walter could not let that comment go unanswered. "Wait a few years and you'll think differently about them."

Horst shook his head violently. "Never."

Walter and Frau Reichert laughed, yet Falk did not move a muscle in his face. Frau Reichert rose to refill everybody's soup bowls.

"Are you working tonight?" she asked her tenant.

Falk barely looked up from his dumpling. "Yes, midnight to eight, as usual."

Walter wondered what in the world he would do all afternoon until he was relieved from duty. Were they staking out the right man? And yet, this man was suspiciously indifferent. Any normal person would have struck up a conversation with Walter about soccer or the latest news. Falk, on the other hand, remained completely inaccessible and monosyllabic.

What's your secret? Walter wondered. *Everybody has one.* Even though Walter had only a few years' duty under his belt, he had already grasped that truth. Or was it because a police officer dealt with mystery-mongers more than the general population? He decided to try a different tactic.

"I think I'll stay overnight," he said casually to the housewife. "I heard the girls in the village are pretty and I would like to check them out this evening." He winked at Horst, who contorted his face in disgust.

Frau Reichert picked up the bait. "You could sleep on the couch tonight, but what will you do all afternoon?"

"I think I'll give your barn a closer look. In the city, we don't have barns anymore, and it's been a long time since I've been in one."

Walter took a bite while trying to read Falk's expression. He did not succeed. If Falk was surprised that anyone would want to look at a barn, he did not show it. When Walter was sated, he asked for the newspaper out of sheer desperation. Soon Herr Falk excused himself, claiming he had to run some errands before going to bed.

DORIS DUMRAUF

Walter's mind raced. Now that Falk had seen him, he could not very well pursue the boilermaker. The man was already more than suspicious of Walter. Horst came to the rescue.

"I want to go play with my friends," he announced.

"Do you have any idea what kind of errands he'll run?" Walter asked Frau Reichert.

She shook her head.

"Horst," he addressed the boy, "would you do me a favor and watch where Herr Falk is going?"

Horst broke into a huge grin. "You mean I'll get to play a policeman?"

"Not quite. Be careful. Don't follow him. Just go to your friends' house and tell me later which direction he went."

Horst nodded and raced off. Walter sincerely hoped he had not just made a huge mistake. Yet, what other choice did he have, working by himself?

"Thank you for helping me out earlier," he said to Frau Reichert.

"Don't mention it. Are you looking for something in the barn?"

"As a matter of fact, I did want to ask you something: Does your husband hunt?"

Frau Reichert said, "No. Why do you ask?"

Walter told her about his find in the storeroom.

She replied slowly, "That knife is still around from when we used to have animals for slaughter. That was years ago."

"So your husband has not used that knife in years?"

She shook her head. "Not that I know of. Why would he?"

Walter rubbed his chin. "And yet I found it this morning in a bin where it didn't belong. Have you ever seen Herr Falk with a knife?"

270

"No, but you've just seen how he is. He would never carry a knife openly. And I'm not always in the house. In summer and fall, I'm often working in the garden or canning in the cellar."

"Yes, of course. If you think of anything else, I'll be in the barn, waiting for Falk's return."

"When I'm done with the dishes, I'll go to the cemetery to water the plants on our family graves," Frau Reichert said. "Will you be all right until I come back?"

Walter took a sip of mineral water and rose. "Just leave the back door open in case I need to come in."

He turned around at the door. "Can you tell me if there is a phone in the village?"

"There is a telephone at the post office. It's right next to the bakery, near the church. And the *Gasthaus* and the doctor also have one."

Walter thanked her and closed the back door behind him. He was tempted to go after Falk, but knew better than to act on his own. He could only hope Horst would not try to be brave and do more than Walter had asked him to do. He chided himself for asking the boy to help him.

Walter walked through the barn, carefully inspecting the windows. Most windows were so small and high, he would not be able to look out through them. The storage room was no different. He would just have to leave the heavy wooden door open to observe the courtyard and await Falk's return. Leaving the door ajar, he stepped into the room and looked around.

He wished he could enjoy his rare moments of idleness, but found he was on edge. Out of sheer boredom, he looked into the bins he had inspected earlier. He picked up the box that had contained the skinning knife and frowned. The knife was gone. Methodically, Walter inspected all the bins but could not locate the knife.

Walter was examining the last container when the door closed shut. He heard the bolt being pushed into the doorframe and shoes scraping the stone floor. He sprinted to the door and tried to push it open, but winced instead. His shoulder, still sore from the knife wound, did not take kindly to the abuse. Before hurting himself any further, he stepped back to review his options. Who would want to lock him in there?

"Horst, is that you?" he shouted. "This isn't funny!" As if Horst would pull a prank on a police officer… Nor would he have reason to lock Walter in.

The steps faded away, no louder than a mouse scurrying through a barn. Walter called for help, but who would hear him? Frau Reichert and Horst were both gone, and the old man next door was probably too deaf to hear him. And yet, he had to try. The window was too high and too small for him to reach, even if he had been able to climb up with his sore shoulder. The door was too heavy to pry open with any tools available to him.

Walter cursed himself for getting into a situation like this. He should have known better. Finally, he heard footsteps on the floor again. They seemed to be running.

"Are you in there?" a boy's voice cried out.

Thank God, Horst had returned!

"Yes, someone locked me in here. Open the door, quick."

The bolt was pushed back and Walter quickly stepped out. Horst and two other boys stood in the hallway. Their eyes sparkled with the curiosity of youth. They reminded Walter of the time when he was their age. He and his friends used to play cops and robbers. Somehow, he had always ended up playing a cop. Even then, the map of his life was already drawn.

Walter paused for a moment, eyeing the boys. Perhaps they could be of use to him.

"Horst, did you see where Herr Falk was going?"

"He walked in the direction of the post office. I did not see if he went inside because I stopped at my friends' house. And you said I shouldn't make it obvious that I followed him."

Good boy. He followed advice. "Yes, I told you that. I thought you were going to play at your friends' house."

"Yes, but their mother is cleaning floors today and told us to go somewhere else. So we decided to play in our barn instead. Aren't you glad we came back?"

Walter stroked Horst's dark hair. "I am very glad you came back. Did you see Herr Falk on your way over here or in the courtyard?"

The boys shook their heads. Walter motioned to them to come close so he could whisper to them.

"Listen to me carefully: Pretend you are going to play a game in the courtyard. You must have a soccer ball somewhere, don't you?"

Horst said, "Yes, I have a soccer ball in the house."

"Go get it, and then I want you boys to play a game and make as much noise as possible. If you happen to see Herr Falk, I want you to whistle at me with two fingers. Is that understood?"

The boys nodded, apparently eager to assist this stranger.

"Now, off with you—and don't forget to whistle!"

The boys took off, howling and hooting. Walter contemplated his options. If the boys had not seen Falk in the courtyard or street, it was quite possible he was still hiding somewhere in the barn. And Walter did not want any harm to come to the boys. That's why he had told them to play in the courtyard. They would be out of danger there, while still being able to observe the area. He would make sure the boys received a reward when all was over. Perhaps he could arrange for them to get a ride in a police car or fire truck. Boys loved that...

Walter turned serious as he scrutinized the center aisle that ran the length of the entire barn. His disadvantage was that Herr Falk probably had been in the barn on many occasions. Falk would know all the hiding places while Walter had to draw on his observations of other barns he had seen. Luckily, most barns seemed to be made from the same pattern: cloakroom and dairy were closest to the house while the pig and cow stalls were farther away, because of the smell and the flies.

Walter wished he had taken his pistol or at least his baton along, but since he was only supposed to be observing today, Simmer had told him to leave them behind at the station. After all, an apple picker had no use for a weapon. Stepping back into the storage room was not an option either, unless he wanted to risk getting locked in again. Careful not to make too much noise, he treaded back to the cloakroom, where he found a pitchfork hanging from a hook on the wall. He grabbed it and held it in front of him as if he were really going to muck the stalls. He seemed to be destined to work with pitchforks lately.

Thus armed, he walked through the center aisle, inspecting each stall for any recent activity. Suddenly, he heard a rush from behind. Before he could turn, something swooped over his head and all went black. Walter yelped in pain as the attacker yanked the pitchfork from his hands. His injured arm did not take kindly to the abuse. Walter flailed his arms around him, unable to hit a target. The assailant pushed him to the ground, where he dropped on his sore shoulder. Walter let out a loud groan. Steps hurried down the stall before Walter heard the opening of a bolt.

Walter struggled to get on his knees while pulling his weight on his good shoulder. He rose to his feet and groped at his head cover. It was an old blue work jacket. Walter slowly turned around to make sure he was alone. Wherever the interloper was, he was gone. Walter rubbed his shoulder and moved it gingerly in its socket.

Outside, the boys were hooting. The boys! He had to make sure that no harm would come to them. Walter hurried to the barn door, which was half-ajar. He pushed it open with his good arm and stopped in his tracks. Just a few steps away from him lay Lothar Falk on the cobblestones in front of the barn, clutching his knee and wincing in pain. Next to him was a soccer ball.

Walter pulled a pair of shackles out of his pant pocket and knelt down next to Falk. Falk moaned when Walter rolled him onto his back.

"Serves you right for hurting me," Walter said before putting on the shackles. Now that Falk was out of commission, the boys stepped closer to witness the proceedings.

"Boys, you did a fine job today," Walter said to the beaming children. "Now, I need one more favor from you. Can one of you run to the police station and tell them to call my station in Lauterbach? Tell them I caught a suspect." Technically, the boys had felled the suspect, and Walter intended to credit the youths in his written report.

Horst wanted to volunteer, but Walter declined. He needed the boy since he lived here. The eldest of the two brothers ran off to carry out the errand while his brother remained glued to the spot, apparently afraid to miss anything.

Frau Reichert returned from the cemetery, carrying an old metal watering can. Her free hand covered her mouth as she joined the onlookers. A few minutes later, a police car turned into the courtyard with a smiling boy in the passenger seat. The officer got out of the car and strode over to Walter. "What have we here?"

Walter introduced himself and quickly explained his disguise. "First of all, I have arrested this man for assaulting a police officer. But I suspect that was just the latest of his crimes."

"Your supervisor is on the way," the town police officer said. "I suggest we all go into the house now until reinforcements arrive." He turned to face the woman of the house. "Frau Reichert, may we intrude on you?"

She nodded as if the events of the day were nothing unusual. "Of course. I'll make coffee."

27

A quarter of an hour later, Chief Simmer pulled up in the police car. Walter and the local officer put Falk on the back seat of the Beetle and the acting chief thanked the officer for his assistance. They were ready to leave when Horst came running with a basket in his hand. "You forgot the grass for your rabbits," he said. Walter thanked him and put the grass next to Falk, who wrinkled his nose. Apparently, he was not a country boy.

"Can I have my gum now?" Horst piped out before the car could take off.

Walter chuckled. "Of course! I completely forgot about it."

He pulled a pack of chewing gum out of his pocket and handed Horst a stripe. "You've been a really good boy today."

Horst beamed while stepping back. The police car drove straight to the station in Reichenbach, which had a small jail.

"Detective Junker is on his way," Simmer informed Walter.

Walter raised his eyebrows. "Really? Can I attend the interview?"

"Of course. You're a crucial part of the investigation," Chief Simmer said in a softened tone.

They led their prisoner into an interrogation room. Chief Simmer had begun asking Falk his name, birthday, and occupation when Junker arrived. The detective looked as if he suffered from lack of sleep. He asked for a glass of mineral water and Walter went to the kitchen to fetch it himself. Junker nodded gratefully and raised the glass to his lips.

"Tell me exactly what happened today," he said.

Walter recounted the events of the day while Junker eyed Falk. The detective motioned Walter to jot down the information. "Name?"

Falk remained silent.

The detective raised his voice. "I'll ask you one more time: Name?"

"Lothar Falk," the prisoner barked.

"Date of birth?"

"November 16, 1919."

"Place of birth?"

Falk hesitated for a second. "Grimmenhalde."

Junker asked, "What state is it in?"

"Sachsen."

"Where did you live before you moved to Herrenhausen?"

Falk stared at the desk in front of him. "Why do you need to know that?"

"Just answer the question."

"I was in a refugee camp in Heiligenfeld, Bavaria. My family died in the war and I didn't know where else to go." Falk's voice was barely audible now. Had he finally lost his spunk?

The town's name sounded familiar to Walter but he could not recall where he had heard the name before.

"How long did you live in the camp?"

"From 1945 to 1955."

"You spent ten years in a refugee camp?" Junker asked. His voice sounded incredulous.

Falk shrugged. "I had nowhere else to go, so I began working at the warehouse and they let me stay on until the camp was dissolved."

Junker waited until Walter had finished his notes. "Did you know that Officer Hofmann was a police officer when you pulled the jacket over his eyes?"

Falk remained stoic. "Yes."

"And yet you attacked him? You have just made your case much worse. Why did you do it?"

"I heard Horst tell a friend that the police was at the door the other day. And then this stranger showed up today and I put two and two together."

"So, you have never seen Herr Hofmann before today?" Junker asked, enunciating every word.

Falk slowly shook his head. Walter was on the verge of asking him about the knife attack, but Junker was in charge now.

The detective continued. "I have a report from the Air Police that you were found searching through trash cans at Building 205 on base. What were you looking for?"

"I was looking for anything metal that I could sell to the scrap dealer who comes to the village every couple of weeks," Falk said.

Walter detected defiance in his voice, but could not figure out why.

"You were looking for metal in an office trash can?" Junker asked with raised eyebrows. "How much are they paying for typewriter ribbons these days?"

The officers chuckled. Walter turned around when he heard a commotion in the hallway. The door swung open and Chief Kleber entered. He looked thinner than Walter remembered and his cheeks were a shade paler than before his ordeal. Walter smiled at his supervisor.

"Good evening," Chief Kleber said to the assembled officers. "Please remain seated. I'm still on sick leave, but when I learned that an arrest has been made, I had to come by and have a look."

He pulled out an empty chair next to Walter and sank into it with a sigh of relief. "Please go on, Detective!"

"Where was I?" Junker asked, consulting his file again. "Oh, yes. Scrap metal. Are you sure you didn't take any documents out of the trash cans?"

Falk's face remained inscrutable. "I might have taken some pieces of paper to use as scratch paper," he said after a pause. "And what of it? They were in the trash can, so the soldiers didn't need them anymore."

"If they were in a trash can, perhaps. Are you sure they weren't lying on a desk or in a filing cabinet?" Junker asked.

Falk's chin jutted forth. "What exactly are you getting at?"

"That's what we're trying to find out, aren't we?"

Walter continued to stare at the vital information he had jotted on his pad. Finally, it occurred to him. He circled the town's name and wrote "Roswitha" next to it. Chief Kleber glanced at it and sat up straighter in his chair, emitting a moan of pain.

"May I interrupt for a moment, Willi?"

The detective agreed.

"Where were you on the afternoon of October fourth?" Chief Kleber asked.

For the first time, Walter recognized a change in Falk. Suddenly, the prisoner's face looked ashen.

"Answer the question," Junker snapped.

"That was over three weeks ago. How am I supposed to know what I did that day?" Falk said. "I probably worked."

"No, you didn't. We already checked that," Junker said. His voice betrayed the tension he must have experienced for the past few weeks. "I'll help your memory. On October fourth, the body of a young woman named Roswitha Gregorius was discovered in the moor near the base. Do you know anything about it?"

All eyes were now fixed on Falk. The boiler man stared at his hands without making a sound.

"All right," Junker said, "here is what I think happened: You live alone, have no wife, family, or friends to speak of. Women are not attracted to you. So when you had a work-free day, you drove your moped toward the base, hoping to find a woman at the club. You spotted Roswitha in the moor, walking in the same direction. When she wanted nothing to do with you, you got a little rough and whacked her over the head with a tree limb. Is that what happened?" Junker's voice had grown sharp during the last few words.

Falk shook his head so vehemently that Walter heard a crack in his neck.

Chief Kleber leaned forward toward the detective. "Can I say something to the prisoner?"

"Sure."

"You knew Roswitha from the camp in Bavaria, didn't you?"

Falk's mouth gaped enough for Walter to notice. *Here it comes,* Walter thought. *Here is your secret.*

"Did she reject you even there? And finally, when you met her again, you snapped. You couldn't take it anymore!"

"No," Falk said. "I never made advances at her."

Junker cleared his voice. "What was your business with Roswitha, then? We're very anxious to know."

Falk's index finger and thumb drew invisible circles on the table. Walter and another officer were busy taking notes.

281

At last, Falk slumped in his chair. "I did not collect metal for the rag man," he said through barely opened lips. "I was looking for documents to steal."

Junker sat up erectly. "What kind of documents?"

"Any documents I could lay my hands on."

"Why?"

Falk shifted in his chair. "To sell them."

"To whom did you sell them?" Junker asked.

Falk remained silent.

Junker asked, "What was in those documents that was worth money?"

Falk did not lift his gaze from the table. "I don't know. I can only read a few words of English," he said in a low voice.

Walter fought between the urge to laugh and admiring the brazenness of the prisoner. Had Falk lied to his employers about his command of English?

Junker also appeared to have caught the irony of Falk's statement. "You just rummaged through trash cans, hoping to find something good. For all we know, you could have just stolen someone's laundry list."

Falk looked up from the table. "Sometimes we had to burn documents at the heating plant. I told my contacts about it and they instructed me to snoop around for other papers."

Junker spoke again. "So you're a spy, aren't you?"

Walter looked up from his notepad. Falk had assumed a defiant composure, almost a smirk. "Yes, I guess you could call it that."

He's really proud of himself, Walter thought. The officers in the room began murmuring and moved their chairs closer, but Junker held up his hand to calm them. "Who were you spying for?"

282

"The East German government."

Junker pushed his chair back with a loud noise. "Excuse me for a moment. I have to make a phone call."

A few minutes later, Junker returned. "So you spied for the East German government. Where did you hand over the documents you stole?"

"Every six to eight weeks, I would take a train to Heidelberg, where I met a messenger at the castle. I handed him the papers and he gave me money."

Money. Of course.

"So, you spied for money?"

"Yes. Why else would I take the risk?"

Walter's pencil flew over the page.

Junker drank a sip of mineral water. "I fail to see where Fräulein Gregorius fits into this picture. Did you want to recruit her, perhaps?"

Falk's eyelids drooped over his shifty eyes as if a drawbridge had been lowered. "I did try to recruit her at the refugee camp. She wanted nothing of it. She said that she was hoping to marry an American soldier and move to the land of plenty with him. She laughed at my proposal, the little hussy!"

Junker rubbed his chin. "So you admitted to Roswitha that you were a spy. You moved here to do your dirty work and then, one day, you ran into Roswitha. That must have scared you quite a bit. Didn't it? After all, she could have gone to the authorities with the information she had. Is that what happened? You killed her to silence her?"

Falk shrugged. Junker jumped up and paced behind the chairs. Finally, he faced the prisoner. "Tell us from beginning to end how you encountered Roswitha Gregorius on the afternoon of October fourth."

A knock on the door interrupted the interview before the prisoner could answer. Tech Sergeant Shoemaker and Jeff entered the room. Junker requested two more chairs for the already crowded room.

"I called the Air Police because this concerns them too," Junker said. "Now, where was I? Oh yes, the day of the murder."

Falk jerked at the word *murder.* "I was headed to the base to rummage through some desks at the office buildings that are deserted on weekends. I used to pose as a janitor, but when this man caught me..." he turned his head in Jeff's direction, "I decided it was too dangerous to do that during the week."

Tech Sergeant Shoemaker interrupted him. "Did you ever keep any of the documents you found in trash cans?"

"Just once," Falk admitted. "That was before October."

"Did you ever steal anything from a desk?" Tech Sergeant Shoemaker continued.

"No. That was the first day I wanted to look on top of the desks," Falk said.

"Go on," Junker said. "You were headed to the base on October fourth..."

"Then I saw the woman in the moor, sitting on a fallen tree. I panicked because I had tried to recruit her. A young woman like that would probably not remember a man like me. But I could not take any chances. I parked my moped and walked up to her from behind. She didn't even recognize me." His voice sounded clipped now. "I grew angry because I had just made a big mistake. Had I ignored her, nothing would have happened. But it was too late. She now knew who I was and I feared she would report me to the police. I pretended to walk away, grabbed a tree limb, and hit her in the neck."

Walter resorted to shorthand to keep up with the confession.

"What did you do then?" Junker asked when the note takers had caught up.

"I touched her neck to make sure she was dead," Falk said, his voice betraying no emotion. "Then I dropped the limb, made sure that no one had seen me, and went back to my moped. That's all."

"That's all?" Junker asked, his voice dripping with sarcasm.

Falk shrugged again. Walter wondered what kind of a man Falk was to shrug off a killing. Was it all in a day's work for him? How could a man kill an innocent woman without any remorse?

Jeff stated for the record that Falk was the same man he had seen rummaging through a trash can in Building 205. For the next hour, the Air Policemen interviewed Falk about the document theft. When they were satisfied that Falk had never stolen any classified documents, Junker motioned at two German officers to put Falk in handcuffs. The wall clock showed almost midnight when the detective ended the interrogation. He asked a couple of officers on duty to escort the prisoner to the jail in Kaiserslautern.

Jeff rose and approached Walter. He grinned at the sight of Walter's clothes. "Are you working undercover again? Must have been quite a day."

Walter yawned. "Yes, it was quite a day. But it was all worth it in the end."

Walter was alone in the kitchen when the doorbell rang. He turned on the hallway light and opened the door.

Jeff stood outside, his shoulder leaning against the stone doorframe as if nothing had happened. He was dressed in khakis and a striped shirt. "Hello, Walter. May I come in?"

"Of course," Walter said, stepping back to let his guest in. "Come into the kitchen. I'm alone at home at the moment, so we can talk."

Walter pointed to a chair and Jeff sat down.

"I'll be right back," Walter said. He went to the cellar and returned with a couple bottles of Parkbräu. He put one bottle in front of Jeff and they both snapped off the ceramic stoppers.

"*Prost*," Walter said. They clicked their bottles together and drank.

Jeff's hands twirled the bottle around. "Marianne told me you had a crush on her. She didn't know about it. Honestly. And then I came and stole your girl."

Walter said quickly, "She was never my girl. I was waiting to impress her when I had a scooter. And now it's too late."

"I hope you don't have hard feelings against me about it," Jeff said, casting a sheepish look at his friend.

Walter cracked a half-hearted smile. "No hard feelings. It's my own fault. Who knows, she probably wouldn't want me even if you weren't around."

They broke into a laugh and Walter went downstairs to fetch another couple of beers.

"I'm sorry about your rabbit," Jeff said. "I had rabbits myself as a kid. Took them to 4H shows."

"What shows?"

"Never mind. It was probably something like the show you wanted to take Max to."

Walter swallowed. He still could not think about Max without getting a lump in his throat.

"Did you ever find out who killed him?" Jeff asked soberly.

"Yes. It was our friend Falk. He wanted to give me a warning."

"How did he find out where you live?"

Walter scratched his head. "He followed me one day when I went home for lunch. And then he scoped out the courtyard when I was sleeping in."

"Sounds like a monster to me," Jeff said. "Does the East German government have to rely on killers to do their spying?"

Walter wiped foam from his mouth with the back of his hand. He was glad that the conversation had moved away from his beloved pet. "Who knows what goes on in their heads? They seem to be puppets of the Soviet Union. Apparently, they stop at nothing to achieve their goals. But killing a young woman, a completely innocent woman?" He shook his head. "I will never understand that. What bothered me most was that Ingrid got kidnapped."

Jeff gaped at him. "Ingrid was kidnapped? By whom?"

"The smugglers, as we learned yesterday. I tried to warn her about those men, but she wouldn't listen. She thought I was a bore. And do you know why they were able to kidnap her?"

Jeff shook his head, leaning in closer.

"Because they promised to take her to Friedberg to see Elvis Presley. Can you believe that?"

Jeff rested his head on his hand. "Yes. I believe it. Even Marianne talks about him a lot. The girls go crazy over him."

"I like his music too," Walter said, "but why does he have to look so darn good? Why can't he look more like Buddy Holly or some of the other singers?"

Jeff burst out laughing and Walter joined in. When he had finished his beer, Jeff excused himself because he had to work early the next day. Before he left, Ingrid returned from a visit to her girlfriend. Her English was getting better every day since she worked at the BX. She joined the men at the kitchen table and tested out her English on Jeff.

"Where have you been?" she asked. "Are you okay?"

Jeff nodded and pointed at Walter.

"I'll tell you later what happened to him," Walter said.

Ingrid shot a look at her brother and he said, "Yes, he knows."

She blushed, but Jeff said quickly, "No problem. Don't be embarrassed about it. Marianne goes crazy over Elvis, too, even though she's dating me. I know it's hard to believe, isn't it?"

28
April 1959

Walter was feeding his rabbits after work. The long winter was finally over. It had brought not only Lothar Falk's trial, but also the trial of the smuggling ring. Falk had been sentenced to twenty years in prison while the smugglers had received rather mild sentences. During the trial, which the chief, Walter, and Schlosser alternately witnessed, they learned that Müller had attacked Walter with a knife. After seeing Walter dance with Ingrid, he had realized that they were related. The assault was his way of warning Walter to back off.

Fortunately, Ingrid had been able to give a statement behind closed doors. She, and her mother, would have been mortified to discuss her darkest secret in open court. Walter was glad that the episode was finally over for the family.

Ingrid had been rather subdued during the months since her kidnapping. She sought Walter's company and advice more often than before. She had even danced with him during the Fasching season when it was ladies' choice.

One thing had not changed, however: She was still obsessed with rock 'n' roll music and played her records every night she spent at home. Because the bedrooms were too cold to spend much time in, she had brought her record player into the living room. Mother Hofmann complained constantly about the noise.

Walter's mother interrupted his thoughts by calling from the kitchen window. "Jeff is here to see you."

"Send him out here," Walter said. "I can't come into the house with these clothes."

Jeff ambled into the courtyard.

Walter picked up his new favorite rabbit, Peter, and cradled it in his arm. "I would shake your hand, but mine is dirty."

"No problem," Jeff said, leaning against the rabbit cage. "Are you working next Friday?"

"Yes, I believe so."

"Could you get that day off?"

"I don't know. I would have to ask the chief first. Why should I take the day off?"

Jeff put on a poker face. "I can't tell you that, but I'm sure you won't regret it. Tell Ingrid to ask for a day's vacation, too."

Walter scrutinized his friend's face. It was not like Jeff to speak in riddles. "Can you at least give me a hint?"

"We're going for a ride. That's all I'm going to say."

"In your car?" Walter asked. "That's about all the invitation I need. You know I've long admired your car."

"Then it's settled. Meet me at my car at oh-seven-hundred next Friday."

"Why so early?"

Jeff grinned and swaggered away, his hands in his pockets. Walter stared after his friend. He had long given up trying to imitate the American's walk. He was too stiff to look anything but ridiculous. Yet he would gladly give up a week's pay to learn to imitate it.

At the appointed time, Walter and Ingrid waited by Jeff's car, which was parked on the street. Ingrid wore her favorite tight black pants and a short red sweater under her navy blue jacket. Marianne, who looked stunning in a tight skirt and a loose yellow sweater, soon joined them. Walter pretended a sudden interest in his shoes to hide his embarrassment. He had suspected Marianne would come along, yet his heart vibrated in his chest when he first saw her. After all these months and despite the assurances he gave Jeff, he still felt a pang of loss on occasion. Luckily, the girls' chatter drowned out his uneasiness.

Walter ambled around Jeff's Ford Fairlane. It was a shiny sensation in red and white and, the crowning touch, had white-rimmed tires. His friends would be green with envy when they heard about Walter's trip.

At last, Jeff appeared, wearing his favorite khakis and carrying his car keys in his hand like a trophy. Marianne turned her cheek and he planted a kiss on it.

"Who wants to sit on the passenger seat?" Jeff asked.

The girls waved their arms in the air, but Jeff pointed at Walter. "I think Walter would enjoy the passenger seat much more than you girls. You two can sit in the back and talk and giggle all you want to."

Jeff tilted the back of his seat forward, letting Ingrid climb in. She slid over to sit behind her brother. Marianne had to pull up her skirt before stepping inside the car.

"Now, why did you have to wear such a tight skirt for a car trip?" Jeff scolded her, half in jest.

Marianne tsked and wiggled her figure into the car, eliciting Jeff's whistle. Walter sank onto the red and white vinyl seat. Now it was his turn to whistle. The dashboard was just as shiny as the Ford's exterior.

"Go ahead," Jeff encouraged him. "You want to, don't you?"

Walter grinned senselessly while he let his fingers touch the dashboard as gingerly as if it were a Stradivari violin. It was a far cry from the vehicles he had to drive. Jeff inserted the key into the ignition switch and the engine purred to life.

Walter put his left arm on the top of the seats to face his friend. "Thank you. I've been dying to get a closer look at your car. This is nothing like the Volkswagens I drive at work."

Jeff drove around the block to turn the car around. "Believe it or not, a Volkswagen may be an advantage on these narrow roads. I sometimes have trouble maneuvering this car through the village."

He pulled onto the main road. They passed housewives and retirees headed to the bakery. Schoolchildren sidled on the sidewalk, pointing their fingers at the American car driving by. When Jeff passed Ingrid's bus stop, the girls craned their necks looking out the windows and waved at everyone they knew. Outside Lauterbach, Jeff turned onto the Autobahn heading east and accelerated the car.

"I bet we're going to Heidelberg," Marianne exclaimed. "I haven't been there in ages. It is sooo romantic!"

She leaned forward and blew air into Jeff's ear.

He said, "Stop it, my love, before I have an accident."

"I just want to know where we're going."

Jeff sighed with feigned exasperation. "I told you, it's a surprise."

Walter glanced at Jeff sideways. His friend seemed to enjoy his secretiveness immensely. Walter settled back in the seat and looked out of the windows. To his right, Holstein cows were scattered through the fenced-in pastures while on the left, fir trees and barren land hinted at the proximity of the air base. Finally, the Autobahn dropped from the hills to the valley of the Anterior Palatinate.

"There is Burg Altleiningen," Marianne cried. "I think there is nothing more beautiful than a castle surrounded by blooming trees."

Walter turned his head. "I don't know. I like the fall with its wine festivals better." He pointed at the vineyards left and right of the road where rows of grapevines formed symmetrical patterns. "Look, there is this year's crop."

Jeff inquired what they were talking about and Walter translated as best he could.

"I thought you were a beer drinker?" Jeff asked.

"I am, but I like to watch the wine queens and princesses," Walter said, grinning from ear to ear.

The novelty of the car ride had worn off a bit when Ingrid shrieked. Walter jerked around and noticed that his sister was pointing at Marianne's hand. A plain gold band glinted from Marianne's ring finger.

Oblivious to Walter's pain, his sister chattered, "Are you and Jeff engaged?"

Marianne nodded. Walter turned his head away from her and stared out the window. Jeff had not said a word about an engagement, but then, he was a man.

Ingrid continued, "So when are you getting married?"

"Not for a while yet. We have to get all the paperwork together," Marianne said. "You won't believe all the red tape involved when a soldier marries a German national. We have to go to the chaplain, the doctor, and my criminal record has to be checked out. It could be more than six months before we're all done with it."

Walter had himself under control again and decided to be a good sport about it. He punched his fist into Jeff's upper arm. "You sly one, you never mentioned anything about your engagement when I saw you the other day."

Jeff grimaced. "We would like to keep it quiet, at least until we have climbed the biggest hurdles of paperwork."

"Do your parents know yet?" Ingrid asked.

"Yes," Marianne replied in a sober tone. "You can imagine that they're not enthused about me marrying an American. But they must have been in love once and should be a little more understanding about these things. And I do love Jeff so much!"

"Of course you do," Jeff said.

The car was now rolling through the Rhine valley. All heads turned when Jeff approached the Rhine River between Ludwigshafen and Mannheim. A coal barge passed under the bridge as they crossed. Chemical factories belched billowing smoke into the pink sky as Walter gazed upriver. This part of the Rhine valley was the least interesting of all, he thought.

"The river here is much uglier than the area around Oberwesel," he said to no one in particular. "Two years ago, my police union organized a bus trip to a wine festival. We even took a ferry to the other side of the river. That was wonderful!"

Instead of heading to Heidelberg, Jeff took the Autobahn north at the crossing.

The girls were disappointed, but Walter had stopped guessing. He seldom ventured this far from home and enjoyed every minute of it. At the next rest stop, Jeff brought the car to a halt.

"I think we better get some refreshments before we reach our destination," he said.

"How much farther do we have to go?" Marianne asked as she exited the car and walked by his side.

Jeff looked at his watch. "About an hour or so."

"Then we must be going to Frankfurt, right?" Marianne said.

Jeff grinned and opened the door of the restaurant for her.

About an hour later, Jeff drove into a small town north of Frankfurt, much like a cowboy must have been riding into a Western frontier town. He seemed oblivious to the heads that turned at the sight of his car. Passing a farmer's wagon drawn by oxen, he neared the town center. He parked the Ford behind a plumber's van along the road and said, "Everybody out. We're here."

Walter opened his door and climbed out. The girls reluctantly clambered out of the backseat and stretched. "What is there to see here?" Marianne asked, not hiding her disappointment.

They headed toward a cluster of people gathered at the core of the village by the Raiffeisen feed store. A farmer's wagon, loaded with several sacks of feed, was parked in front of it.

The young visitors passed a woman dressed in an apron and headscarf. She was holding onto the handle of her bicycle to observe the happenings ahead. Walter's step grew a little faster because he wanted to get near the center of attention. His pace slowed down when he realized that he was looking at several Army trucks positioned around a World War I memorial.

"You brought us here to see a war memorial?" Marianne cried. "We could have seen those at home! Every village has one."

Jeff turned his mouth into a sly smile. "I know, but look who's on that truck."

On the bed of a truck stood a soldier in battle dress uniform, his back toward them. Jeff led his friends around businessmen in suits and shirt-sleeved tradesmen wearing caps. Several reporters pointed their cameras at the figure on the platform. Walter positioned himself behind a girl and two boys with school satchels on their backs. He looked up at the soldier on the truck and gaped.

"I don't believe this!" Marianne shrieked, her palms covering her face. "Ingrid, look who it is!"

Ingrid's eyes grew large. "It's Elvis, Marianne, it's really him!" she squealed.

"Girls, behave yourselves," Jeff said, beaming from ear to ear. "Otherwise, I'm going to be very jealous."

Walter shot Jeff a thankful look. His friend must have remembered that Ingrid was kidnapped because she wanted to see Elvis. Now Jeff had made good on her wish. Walter glanced at his sister and a weight lifted from his heart. The dark veil that had enveloped her since that fateful autumn day had floated away on an upwind of spring air. She stood transfixed to see her idol in person.

Walter turned his attention back to the action around the truck. Try as he might, Walter could not retain the jealousy he had felt toward the rock star for the past few years. If he was not above performing the ordinary duties of a soldier, then perhaps he was not as vain as Walter had imagined.

Presley held on to the edge of the memorial base while several soldiers on the ground hung on to the thick ropes that were looped over the crane. The men paused, giving the photographers an opportunity to take some photos. Grinning, the soldiers carefully lowered the memorial into place while Presley adjusted the top of the base. When everything was in place, several bystanders applauded.

Walter approached Jeff and took him aside. "I would like for Ingrid to get Elvis's autograph. Do you think that's possible? It would give Ingrid the thrill of a lifetime."

Jeff broke into a smile. "What a wonderful idea. I think we should all try to talk to him."

Walter looked around and spotted a German policeman at the edge of the proceedings. He wended his way around the onlookers and spoke with his colleague. The policeman pointed at a non-commissioned officer who was apparently in charge of the work detail. He gave a nod and told Walter to be ready any moment.

"What were you doing?" Ingrid asked when he returned to his friends.

Walter shrugged, pretending not to know. Ingrid's reply was a fist in his ribs.

"Look," Walter cried in an effort to divert the girls' attention. "He's getting off the truck."

After glancing at his superior, Presley clambered down from the truck and was soon surrounded by children. The older onlookers stepped back in confusion, making room for the younger people to proceed forward.

"Come on, let's get his autographs," Walter said.

Ingrid and Marianne whooped and searched through their purses.

"Are you looking for a piece of paper?" Jeff asked and pulled a small notepad and a fountain pen out of his pocket.

"You thought of everything, didn't you?" Walter said.

Jeff grinned. "I was a Boy Scout. Always be prepared, that's my motto. Come on, let's get in line."

The press photographers took some photos of Elvis with the village children and then backed off. Private Presley patiently began to sign autographs while his fellow soldiers started to place their gear back on the trucks. They were probably used to the attention their famous soldier friend drew.

Jeff pulled Marianne in front of him while Walter motioned Ingrid to stay near him. Their eyes glued to the star in his perfectly starched fatigue uniform, they made slow progress in the throng. Caught up in the frenzy, Walter did not mind waiting. Ingrid bobbed up and down for a better view.

"You're wearing out your shoes," he said, pushing down her shoulders.

"I can't help it. This is the most exciting thing that's ever happened to me in my whole life."

Finally, she stood in front of her idol, clutching the notepad and fountain pen Jeff had handed to her. His eyes shaded by his fatigue cap, Private Presley grasped the fountain pen and briefly touched her fingers. He poised the pen toward the paper and paused. "What's your name, honey?"

Ingrid hesitated. Walter came to her rescue and spelled, "I-N-G-R-I-D."

Presley wrote his autograph on the pad and handed it back to her. Ingrid stood rooted on the spot, oblivious to the commotion around her. Walter gently took the notebook out of her hand, turned a page and nudged her in the back. Reluctantly, she stepped aside to let her brother move ahead.

Walter felt thrilled and awkward at the same time. Awkward, because he had always believed it was a girl's mission in life to idolize a singer. Thrilled, because he would most likely never be this close to a celebrity again. He beamed at Elvis and handed him the notepad. If Elvis was disappointed at seeing a young man in front of him, he did not show it. He gave Walter a smile that would have lit up a cave before returning the pad to him.

"Thank you very much," Walter said and moved to the side where Ingrid was watching the proceedings.

"Oh, how I wish we had a camera," Ingrid exclaimed. "Wouldn't it be great to show such a photo to our children one day?"

Walter sighed. "Yes, it would be wonderful. Maybe we'll see today's photos in a magazine."

Ingrid's face brightened at once and she scanned the onlookers.

"No," Walter pleaded. "Please don't ask the reporters to take your photo."

Ingrid waved her hand at him. "I wasn't going to do that. I just wanted to see which magazine they work for so I can look for it at the newsstand."

One of the reporters approached Walter. "Would you like to have your picture taken with Elvis?"

Walter hesitated. Their mother would be mortified if their picture showed up in a magazine, but Ingrid would be ecstatic.

"I don't know," he said. "But it would be nice to have a photo of all of us. Could you mail us a print?"

"Of course."

The reporter positioned Elvis between Ingrid and Marianne while Walter and Jeff flanked them.

"All right, give me a big smile," the photographer said, clicking the shutter. "One more time and we're done."

Elvis gave the girls his infectious smile once again before bidding them goodbye to sign more autographs. Walter, who had stuffed the pad into his coat pocket during the photo shoot, took it out to jot down his address on a new page for the reporter.

The friends watched as the soldiers gathered all ropes and fastened them on the truck. At last, they mounted the truck bed and drove off. After the vehicles disappeared behind a corner, Jeff asked, "Anybody hungry?"

"I am," Walter said. "I could eat a horse." He glanced at his watch. "We better hurry before the *Gasthaus* closes."

The girls fought over the notepad while the foursome strolled around the town. Clusters of women stood together on one side of the road, chatting about the events that had just occurred while several schoolchildren milled around an advertising pillar, comparing their autographs. After inspecting the memorial, the town's men headed for the *Gasthaus,* and the travelers from Lauterbach followed them.

Walter ordered a *Schnitzel* with *Pommes frites*. Jeff followed suit while the girls ordered *Bratwurst*. After the waitress shuffled away with their orders, Marianne could not contain herself any longer.

"How did you find out that Elvis would be here today?" she asked, punching her fiancé on the arm.

Jeff gave a sly smile. "I don't want to talk about the tricks of my trade."

"Come on, we all want to know." She pointed at Walter. "Don't you want to know?"

Walter nodded. "Yes, how did you find out?"

The waitress brought their drinks and Jeff took a big sip of Coca-Cola. "When Walter told me that Ingrid wanted to see Elvis, I got an idea. I called up the military police at Ray Kaserne in Friedberg and asked them to let me know when their unit was ever on assignment off post. The other day, they called me and told me about this work detail. That's all there is to it."

"That's all, huh?" Marianne cried. "I had no idea that you were so sly to keep this to yourself."

Walter said, "Well, I think we should drink to the most exciting day of our lives."

They clicked their Fanta and Cola glasses together and compared their autographs until their meals arrived.

"Do you have any other surprises for us?" Walter asked Jeff.

"As a matter of fact, I do," Jeff said. "I just heard yesterday that the Crocodiles are playing at the Enlisted Club a week from Saturday. Would any of you like to go?"

Walter's face brightened. "I'll ask Fritz and Dieter, but I sure would like to get a ticket."

29

On Saturday evening, Walter and Fritz rode their bikes toward the base. They kept to the main road because they did not want to muddy their slacks on the field track.

"I hope you don't mind that I gave Dieter's ticket to my cousin Christa," Fritz said over his shoulder.

Walter suddenly felt hot. He gripped his handles tighter, hoping that his hands would not get too sweaty and betray his nervousness. "Why should I mind? And where is she?"

"She'll meet us at the entrance of the club. She just moved here to work as a maid for an officer's family."

"Ah, that's why I've never met her before," Walter said. "Where is she from?"

"She's from a village near Lauterecken. There are no jobs there, so she decided to come here. I guess she hopes to get an office job on base once her English is better."

"Sounds like she's ambitious. What is she like?"

Fritz said cryptically, "See for yourself. What am I, a matchmaker or something?"

Walter blushed. He did not want to be introduced to his friends' relatives. He was glad that Fritz began to talk about soccer. When they arrived at the club, they parked their bikes in a bike rack, locked them, and removed the clips from the bottom of their pants. Walter wiped a handkerchief over his dusty shoes and tipped his head toward a young woman standing by the entrance. "Is that her?"

Fritz waved at her. "Yes. Come on, let me introduce you."

They waited for a group of three soldiers to pass them. One of them whistled at the girl as she stood near the canopy. She averted her eyes from them and smiled at her cousin. Fritz and Walter shook hands with her. Walter did not want to let go of her hand. He suddenly felt giddy.

Why hadn't Fritz told him how charming his cousin was? Her brunette hair, curled outward at the bottom as fashion dictated, framed a rectangular face with a button nose and two inquisitive hazel eyes. She wore a white dress with a flower pattern and a flowing skirt that ended below her knees.

"I hear that you and your sister have seen Elvis Presley," she said to Walter, her eyes glittering.

Walter suppressed a twitch of jealousy. After all, he had been star-struck himself when meeting the singer. Yet he hoped she would not talk about rock stars all night.

"Yes, we have. At first, I didn't think I would enjoy it, but he seems to be a real nice man."

"Will you tell me all about it?"

"I will, if you sit next to me tonight." It was a long shot but what did he have to lose? He promised himself that he would not hesitate again when he met a girl he liked. And so far, he liked Christa. A lot.

To his surprise, Christa agreed. "I'll be happy to sit next to you. You're the only person I know who has actually seen him."

The small group approached the door to the club, awaiting their turn to enter. Walter hurried ahead and opened the door for Christa. Her face turned pink as she acknowledged the gesture.

"I'm so happy to be here tonight," she said. "Fritz told me about this club, but I've never been in one. Nothing ever happens in my village. I think I'm going to like it in Lauterbach."

Walter smiled. "I hope you will."

They entered the foyer behind a group of rowdy soldiers. One of them looked Christa up and down, whistling softly. Walter shot him a frosty look and the soldier turned away. At least for this evening, Christa was his date. A date! He was excited beyond words. Was this what falling in love was like? In the past, he had always struggled for the right words when he was interested in a girl. He vowed not be tongue-tied all evening.

Across from the bar, a jukebox abutted the wall, glistening under the foyer lights. Elvis Presley belted "Hound Dog" from the record that rotated on the turntable. Walter faced the jukebox, kicked his heels together, and saluted.

Thank you, Private Presley. I think it's going to be a wonderful evening.

About the Author

Doris Dumrauf grew up in the West German state of Rheinland-Pfalz during the Cold War. By the time she was born, numerous U.S. Army and Air Force installations dotted the landscape. After high school and an apprenticeship, she worked as an administrative clerk on a U.S. air base. Now living in the U.S., she regularly visits Germany. During one of her trips, she bought the book *Air Base Ramstein: Bilder, Geschichten, Erinnerungen*. She was intrigued by the history of the air base, and the idea for *Oktober Heat* was born.

She has published numerous articles in magazines and newspapers, and is also an award-winning nature photographer and public speaker.

Made in the USA
Columbia, SC
05 May 2018